A NOOSE OF LIGHT

£3
UT

Seamus Cullen

A NOOSE OF LIGHT

Futura

An Orbit Book

First published in Great Britain in 1986
by Futura Publications, a Division of
Macdonald & Co (Publishers) Ltd
London & Sydney

ISBN 0 7088 8178 5

Printed and bound in Great Britain by
William Collins, Glasgow

Futura Publications
A Division of
Macdonald & Co (Publishers) Ltd
Greater London House
Hampstead Road
London NW1 7QX

A BPCC plc Company

For Nellie and Annie and Harry and John

With deep thanks for the kindness
help, encouragement and faith of
Gerry Hanley, Herbie Brennan and
Earl and Norma Dorfman

Awake! for Morn in the Bowl of Night
Has flung the Stone that puts the Stars to flight:
And lo! the Hunter of the East has caught
The Sultan's Turret in a Noose of Light.

Rubayyat of Omar Khayyam

I

FROM THE HILLOCK THAT STOOD above the desert like a sentinel before the mountains and pinnacles to the southwest of the gleaming city, Bashtahal seemed like a great ship of white walls and minarets contained within the fortified outer walls; from the eternal east, the sun broke past the earth's rim and bathed the glittering city in a cascade of brilliant rosy hues, turning it into a sparkling mount of jewels that twinkled and flashed before the rising sun. Eerily, Bashtahal appeared to rise taller in response.

Opening his eyes partially, Anwar gazed at the storybook fantasy unfolding before him. Seated atop the hillock, his legs crossed and hands resting on his calves, he breathed deeply, slowly exhaling a soundless prayer of gratitude for the new day. Lips parted slightly, he was at once totally immobile and completely aware. The slight dawn breeze played with his pure white hair and the beard which fell nearly to his waist, giving a sense of movement to his entire face; but the long, somewhat aquiline nose, the high, broad brow and the deepset eyes were stationary, as though every feature had been chiseled by sun and wind over a very long time. Delicate as parchment, deeply lined, the skin was like dark mahogany etched by countless years of airborne sand. No one in the city could say with certainty just how long Anwar had been there, keeping his silent vigil atop the low hillock. It could not have mattered less to him. Yet, he was keenly aware that this very day, two hundred years earlier, The Prophet had started his Hijra from Mecca. Anwar's father had been five when he stood with his own father as the silent throngs gathered. When his father was fifty-five and Anwar five, the old man told the boy how Mohammed had reached down and touched his head.

1

The once white woollen robe that covered his body was frayed and tattered, patched in many places with bits of green cloth. He owned very little else. A water gourd, a small leather pouch which hung from a leather thong about his neck, concealed beneath the ancient robe. A few layers of unsightly carpet donated by townspeople upon which he sat. Passing caravans left food for him; women from the city brought what they could spare. It wasn't much, but there was not that much left of Anwar; his needs were very modest.

He knew when the two men left a well-concealed ravine in the foothills behind him, as they had done every dawn and every sunset since arriving five days earlier. They climbed to a ledge protected by an overhang and watched the road – if a trail across the desert could be so glorified – that meandered through the hills on its way from Bagdad, past Bashtahal and then on to Mecca and Medina. They also watched Anwar. He never watched them. But he knew they were waiting for their leader; the one who had found the ravine and left the other two to guard it. Four asses and three camels. Each ass had been burdened with two heavy jars which nearly touched the road. Hakim and Mirza – the two men – had protested; the leader, Najmuddin, was not interested. He had walked to Bashtahal. Why does a man with two followers, three camels and four asses approach a city on foot?

Near the main gate inside the city, Maryam kneeled by the well and drew water, pouring it carefully into the large gourd held steady on the ground between her knees. When she looked up, instinctively aware of some disturbing scrutiny, she saw a tall man leaning against the open gate, staring at her. His robe was dusty, skin and beard dark and unwashed. He had the look of a thief or worse. Suddenly, she remembered hearing about a stranger in the city, a mysterious man named Najmuddin. He had been talking to groups of townspeople about religion. He looked more like a bandit than a holy man; even as she thought this, she was aware that Najmuddin's stare had intensified.

2

She looked up again and the arrogant face told her, with looks alone, how ripe she was, how much he desired her.

Maryam lifted the gourd to her shoulder and gathered up the drawstring bag filled with as many dates and brown meal cakes as she had been able to slip from under her mother's watchful eyes. With an annoyed swing of the shoulder, she passed the man with her head high in the air. They're all alike, she confided to herself. The lords of earth, the masters of poor inferior women. She drew her cowl more closely about her head, raised her veil higher as she stepped out onto the road, trudging purposefully toward the distant hillock to the west.

Well before she neared the hillock, she saw a movement on the ledge some distance behind it. Narrowing her eyes, she made out the forms of two men. She slowed her pace and pondered. Why would two men want to stand up there? To watch the road, Anwar…or her? Then she thought about the tall man she had seen in town, the one called Najmuddin who looked like a cut-throat. A sudden premonition suggested all three were connected. She slowed her pace again and tried to remember what the neighbours had been chatting to her mother about. Yes, something to do with a prophet. A new prophet…but how could that be? Had not The Prophet been the last prophet? Yes, one of the women had said this, that there would be trouble if the stranger continued with this heresy. There had been threats, but somehow this Najmuddin had overcome it all. The women said he possessed a silver tongue. Some confusion about saints and prophets.

Maryam saw the men climbing down what seemed a perilous path from the ledge and, in a few moments, they disappeared from view. When she arrived at the base of the hillock, she looked up at the white hair and beard which were picking up golden glints from the sun. For more than a minute, she stood with her eyes wide and lips parted: it seemed like a whirling ring of golden fire surrounded Anwar's head. He held out a welcoming hand toward her and she began the ascent, feeling serenity and excitement fighting in her breast.

3

She watched him moisten his lips with the water – the small spring behind the hillock was so erratic; at times a mere trickle under which the natural rock basin would retain hardly enough evil-looking water for stray animals to drink. And what a terrible sulphurous taste! She wanted to fill him to overflowing with the crystal-clear water of Bashtahal's well. He moistened his lips again, then swallowed enough water to satisfy a small bird. Breaking one of the rough brown cakes in half, he placed one piece in his mouth and munched very slowly and carefully. When this was consumed, he allowed himself a date. She knew he would keep the stone in his mouth for the balance of the long day.

Her mind wandered back to the scene at the well, pondering on the significance of the man who had eyed her with such self-assurance. His gaze had so disturbed her, she had noticed little else. Certainly not the rich merchant standing in the door of the silversmith's shop. Tall, lean and exuding an almost palpable strength of body, will and mind, he had watched the girl fill her gourd and return the stare of the stranger. The stranger had not interested him: the roads these days were filled with dubious characters who covered themselves in dust and anonymity. But the girl, the girl. Such grace and breathtaking beauty in the mere movements of her hands. As she rose to depart, the renowned merchant pulled his burnous more closely about his face and turned away. And it is said, he mused with a pang, that she is promised to the silversmith's apprentice.

Maryam knew only of the other man, the lanky stranger. For reasons she could not yet decipher, her intuition told her he augured trouble. And those other two men she had seen on the ledge…would they not be part of this ineffable scheme too? She watched Anwar take another small sip of water before placing the other half of the meagre cake in his mouth. He stretched forth his hand and she inched forward on her knees until, sitting on her heels, her head bowed forward, she felt his touch on her brow. Like the cool waters of a stream, the touch calmed her, bringing a moment's delightful peace to her troubled heart. The hand did not move away and, before she understood what was happening, her mind seemed to float back to a darkened and deserted garden. She actuallly smelled the cloying, rank vegetation, the soured sweetness of untended flowers. She saw the night sky, recognizing the moon as it had been the night before. After her mother had gone to bed, she had slipped from the house to meet Ali in this secret garden, Ali her intended. Maryam shuddered. His whispered endearments quickened her blood, as did the touch of his hand on hers. Walking in the dark, his arm encircling her waist, she remembered how her eyes had misted over until the pale moon itself was a misty blur. He had turned her toward him, with sudden violence pressing her body to his and she had felt it, that dreadful, frightening thing poking at her through his robe, seeking her out, pushing with rude and unbridled passion. When she had pulled away, trying to break free of his grasp, his wounded sob accused her. The hissing still sounded in her ears: his passion was natural, her ridiculous revulsion was not. How could any man marry a woman who thought his body was repulsive…but she had not heard the rest; hands over her ears to blot out the male indignation, she had fled the rank garden.

Anwar drew his hand back quickly. He did not have to look over his shoulder to ascertain a new presence come to upset the tranquil morning. Looking into Maryam's mind in order to understand the shadows of dread and uncertainty playing havoc with her, he had been unwary. An invisible presence stood on the highest pinnacle and dwarfed the mountain with his ethereal immensity. Had this entity read her mind through his own? Withdrawing to those inner reaches of his mind no mystical entity could reach, Anwar said to himself: you are a careless old fool…and getting more senile every day.

No other ear but his would have heard the quick puff of air atop the pinnacle, but Anwar knew that they were no longer under that fell scrutiny.

'You are worried, Maryam,' Anwar announced

5

softly, his voice rasping from lack of use. 'So much bedevils you. If you do not truly love Ali...*all* of Ali,' he added significantly, 'then you must not blindly honour your mother's wishes. Nor the promise Ali's father *says* he received from your father before he died.'

She found it difficult to discuss such a sensitive subject. Hemming and hawing, she approached her apparently unreasonable dread from many angles, but the subject defeated her. How can one say a given part of the human anatomy creates the same mindless terror that is usually reserved for spiders, snakes or scorpions – even mice – in other women?

'One woman's beloved kitten is another woman's scorpion,' he chided her gently. 'Who is to say why these symbols haunt us so? You alone can resolve this, but it must be in your good time and on your terms. Bravely swallowing a scorpion does not dislodge the secret loathing.'

Maryam reached forward and pulled the cowl up over Anwar's head to protect him from the sun's increasing ferocity. He caught her hands between his gnarled and nut-brown fingers as she drew back. Again she felt the blissful transmission of peace and power; her mind soared and she became aware that what seemed a frail shell which could be blown away by any wayward wind was actually stronger than the mountains surrounding them. She smiled. How many times had she been aware of that? Once more, she had been making mountains of ant hills.

'You are worried too about the man named Najmuddin, the tall and silver-tongued stranger with hind legs like a camel...the one who wanders about your city whispering about the coming of a new prophet. You noticed the men behind me on the ledge as you walked here?'

She nodded rapidly, giving voice to her fears: 'Is it not heresy to talk about a new prophet when it has been clearly written in the Qur'an and the Traditions that the last and greatest prophet was Mohammed? And then there is the confusion about saints and prophets...'

'Maryam, there is no confusion. A prophet speaks with the voice of the Lord, a saint listens to the voice of the

6

Lord. Sometimes it is the same voice, then again, sometimes it isn't. Yet again, which of us is qualified to authenticate the voice of the Lord?'

He watched confusion and despair spread across her face like ripples chased across a pond by a capricious wind. With love, he tried to make her understand. The true believer knows in his heart that God appoints his prophets. Another, who is just as true a believer in his heart, can also realize that the mind must exercise scepticism in all things. Initially, is it not possible for an inspired man to appoint himself? His inspiration might well be divine. In some cases, divine madness. The divine resides in every being; some ignore and bury it, others bring it to full fruition. Many become intoxicated with God. A few – but very few – evolve until they are truly united with God. Does that make them saints...or prophets? Before Mohammed wove the cloth of a precise theology and his followers cut and sewed the garment of religious practice, the brotherhood of the poor, those known as dervishes, had taught the Unity. Many were revered as saints. A man who devotes his life to becoming a whole man, a purified man, becomes that and nothing more. Other men proclaim him a saint.

'But what are these men doing?' she cried out.

'Doing?' he asked, smiling. 'They will entertain the simple and the gullible. They will offer them a miraculous holy man who will perform wonders for them. For this, Najmuddin and his helpers will relieve the people of Bashtahal of as much silver as they can. When the silver runs out and the novelty wears thin, then they will move on. If they are lucky, before the caliph's vengeance overtakes them.'

'They are criminals then,' she declared. 'Can you not stop them?'

'Why should I do that?' His eyes twinkled with mild amusement.

'My heart tells me *you* are the holy man they have in mind. If not, why do they camp here, why do they keep watch over you?'

'For the very reason you have given. I am to be their wonder-worker.'

'Anwar...please?' she begged, 'don't say this. How can you help these villains to steal from the people...you, of all people?'

'Now, now, Maryam, you cannot put two and seven together and hope to have four. They are looking for a performer; not a genuine fakir, but a trickster of the bazaars. However, as a great philosopher once said, a dog who bites off more than he can chew inevitably chokes on his own greed. Stop your worrying and leave this problem to me; have faith that, with the help of God, I can solve it.'

'But the money...' her protest continued.

'Who knows, but one of the miracles could be the conversion of Najmuddin and his helpers, Mirza and Hakim? Would you not be pleased if the people gladly paid for miracles and the silver was distributed among the poor?'

'You can do this, Anwar?' Maryam's eyes brightened and a smile made the surface of her thin veil twitch.

'If it is *nearly* impossible to create the wonders we term miracles, my child, think how much harder to turn them off, once started.'

'You are trying to ease my mind,' she objected, 'but it is not a light-hearted game. If you help these men, what will happen to you? Will the caliph's soldiers not punish you too?'

'I have no asses, no camels, Maryam. If these men have stolen things from the treasury in Bagdad, they did it with no help from me. Before you ask, when I know more about it, I will tell you. What is more important right now is *you*. You have come to a crossroad in your life...'

'But you have taught me almost all I know about life,' she protested. 'Will you not help me now?'

'There comes a time in each life when that person must begin to design his or her own destiny. The Prophet's directive about total submission to the will of God does not relieve you of all responsibility. God is the architect of the universe. Maryam is the architect of Maryam. What will you do now?'

8

'Oh, Anwar, I do not know. I am torn apart. I ask myself: can I truly love Ali if I have this…this…'

'This terrible revulsion?' he finished for her. 'The cure for that may be stranger than you could ever imagine. Seventeen is not a great age…'

'I should have been married years ago,' she whimpered.

'What others do is not necessarily what you should do. Can you tell me what love actually means?' He stopped talking and watched her head shake in hopeless dilemma. 'Think about it, dear child. You have learned to meditate…so do it. I have asked you a question most men or women can never answer. I fear this Najmuddin fellow will be returning here shortly. The winds will sigh, the birds will hide, the heavens themselves will be disturbed. Go now, lest you be made unhappier still.'

'May I come again tomorrow? Please?'

'Yes, of course. But look into your heart deeply. The longer you stand undecided at a crossroad, the harder it is to move on. But come early, before the dawn. Before Najmuddin and his rascals are about.'

II

NAJMUDDIN WAS LONGER ON HIS journey than expected;
Hakim and Mirza strained on their ledge, anxious eyes
scanning the road for any telltale sign of rising dust.
Anwar smiled. The air was charged with their tension and,
in the distance, their muttered comments had the harsh,
dry quality of a hornet's charge. Adjusting his cowl to
shade his eyes more thoroughly, Anwar judged the exact
position of the sun setting behind him. When the rim was
barely above the highest pinnacle, he folded his arms
across his chest and breathed deeply, closing his eyes to
mere slits.

In a few minutes, his body began to shimmer, as
though a fine vibration coursed through him. He might
have been sitting on the hub of a wheel, one controlled by
slowly moving gears and cogs beneath the hillock; with no
apparent effort, his body, legs still crossed and arms folded
across his chest, began to rotate clockwise. When he faced
the pinnacle to the west, which a few moments earlier had
been behind him, he came to rest. The pinnacle was now
in a direct line between his own face and Mecca.

He did not see the sun so much as experience it in his
body, mind and soul. With profound humility, he paid
homage to God's most awesome daily manifestation. Nor
did he see the two men as they might ordinarily impress
themselves upon one's sight. He was focussing before
them and behind them, above and below them and at the
same time through them. What his special vision beheld
was a complex arrangement of brilliant fibres, so fine and
so closely interlocked as to make a spider's web as coarse as
hempen ropes. These luminous forms told him about
strengths and weaknesses, about the spans of life already
past and what still was left. Emanating from them were the

excited waves of anticipation...reflecting the exact progress of Najmuddin as his long strides brought him closer to the hillock and mountains. Night would arrive before Najmuddin of the purposeful strides.

The pinnacle pierced the upper rim of the fiery red ball and transformed it into a jagged crescent. With an inaudible sign, the glory of heaven disappeared, but not before sending long fingers of magenta up to caress the peaks; thousands of vermilion arrows stabbed the darkening vault overhead. As they raced across the sky, Anwar, his heart bursting with wonder, rotated once more, as though on an invisible wheel, to face the east. The vermilion arrows fell, and in falling created a shower of stars. Day became night in one cooling sough of the wind. The secret creakings of the earth's crust changed tune and timbre, waiting for the fresh night to be filled with new sounds unknown to day. For a brief moment, the stars seemed to descend upon Bashtahal as tiny pinpoints of light; the city's lamps rose to greet them. Stealthily, Najmuddin skirted the hillock as the men on the ledge scrambled down to meet him.

Anwar heard the soft shuffle of footsteps at the base of the hillock behind him; at the back of the mound which faced the mountains, the muted clunk! of a pick dug into the relatively soft earth.

With fastidious reserve, Anwar wondered about their reactions when they finally explored the hollow cavern below him. It was not likely they would discover the modest hole and tunnel that was hidden below the tattered rugs upon which he sat. True, he had trained his body so thoroughly that for most of the night and day, his digestion, respiration and heartbeat functioned at such a minimum level it could be compared to the hibernation of an animal. He consumed so little food and only the water necessary to keep such low metabolism balanced. Yet, once a week he did have to relieve his intestines. It was not often nor much, but how many years did it cover? He sighed. In the arid desert what would it amount to now? A small heap of desiccated dust.

As that thought went through his relaxed mind, he upbraided himself for carelessly wandering. It was too late! High above the pinnacle at his back, he heard the telltale Pop! A moment later, a voice inaudible to all but Anwar, an insinuating, cajoling voice, began tempting his inner ear.

'The little girl didn't bring you much to eat, did she?' The dust and sand to Anwar's right stirred, rose up in a tight spiral much like a miniature tornado, levelled suddenly to drift across the area in front of Anwar's folded legs. The whirling dust settled and in its place a gorgeous golden platter appeared, heaped high with sliced pomegranates, ripe figs, dates and cakes made with honey and sesame. To the right of these delicacies a tall silver ewer encrusted with precious stones sparkled in the first rays of the rising moon. It was filled with a pale, aromatic liquid.

Djinni and their childish tricks, Anwar speculated. Yes, the apport was quite real. The cakes delicious and the liquor refreshing and no doubt intoxicating; not because of alcohol, naturally. Probably liberally laced with haoma. Anwar smiled and shook his head inwardly, not visibly. Poor, simple children...total materialists.

'Our noble holy man has lost his appetite?' the disembodied voice asked with an attempt at sincere concern. Anwar concentrated on the glorious yellow moon, near-gibbous and rising splendidly over the towers and minarets of Bashtahal, strewing sheets of silver across the sands. The golden tray and all it contained disappeared soundlessly.

Why does he waste his time with me? Anwar wondered.

'Why does who waste his time with you, Anwar?' the voice asked, coaxing. 'Who wastes his time, tell me who?'

'If you keep reading my mind,' Anwar countered aloud, 'you will dissipate all your energy. You might not have the strength to get back...there.' He paused to listen to the furious crackling of the sand where his tormentor sat, invisibly imitating his victim's posture. Anwar's eyes could mark his outline if he so chose. He did not choose.

12

'Please don't bother yourself with my problems, Anwar. I am here to help you resolve your own. You know who I am, don't you?'

'Why do you take us for such fools?' All he had to do was say the Djinn's name. It was all he needed to manifest himself physically in the reality of this world.

'Anwar, you are the wisest human alive, who takes you for a fool? I want to help you get rid of these men...before they discover your rather vast collection of...you know what.'

'Precisely. No thank you, I'll keep my soul if you don't mind.'

'Now you *are* being a fool!' The Djinn's fury could not contain itself.

'At least we agree upon that. It takes a human lifetime to become wise and only a second to become a fool.'

'That's not what I meant,' the Djinn pleaded, changing his tone tactfully. 'Those men are magicians. They have stolen a terrible form of magic from the caliph's treasury. Do you know what they can do to you when they find your...droppings, shall we say?'

'Sweep them aside to make room for the coffers of silver they hope to collect from all those lovely, superstitious sheep, sleeping innocently beneath yonder moon.' Anwar's gentle voice belied the acerbic words.

'You are misunderstanding me on purpose,' the Djinn accused. 'Those men can enslave you with their magic. They can make you do whatever they wish. Do you want to be a cheap performer, a marketplace mountebank...a charletan?'

'You do weary me, indeed.' Anwar groaned with mock frustration. 'They are not magicians, they are simple, straightforward rogues. Not common thieves and cut-purses, mind you, but clever men who can make the multitudes part with silver cheerfully, voluntarily.'

'And you...holy Anwar...will help them?' There was genuine shock in the Djinn's voice. Anwar held his stomach to suppress the surge of laughter straining to break free. Only a rogue could be so shocked by such roguishness.

13

'Indeed I shall,' Anwar assured him firmly. 'Now, I must warn you. Najmuddin, the creator of this splended scheme, will soon be here. He is a notorious Djinn-hunter. Somewhere on his person he always conceals a small brass urn with a tight stopper…'

A nasty growl near his ear cut off the speech. Below and behind them, the sound of heavy tools flung to the ground heralded the end of the evening's excavation. Anwar felt the movement of the Djinn's presence; he knew his tempter was looking down the side of the hillock. Anwar raised one hand slowly and placed it inside his robe, closing his fingers over the leather pouch he wore around his neck.

'I am not joking,' Anwar called out softly. 'Najmuddin has strange powers…powers that can make you so weak you will spend the rest of eternity in a prison no larger…'

Before he finished speaking, he squeezed the object inside the pouch. The Djinn's breath exploded in the night as though he had been struck a terrible blow in the diaphragm. A snapping sound sent eddies of dust whirling about the small plateau; Anwar divined the Djinn was now standing atop the highest pinnacle, glowering down at him and rubbing his painful stomach.

Hawwaz, the Djinn whose name Anwar refused to say or think, blew his ephemeral self up with wind until he towered so high he dwarfed the mountain itself. Petulantly, he thought about blowing Anwar across the desert. No, that was self-defeating. You must not let him get under your skin like that, he admonished himself. Slyly, slyly captures the fox. He watched Najmuddin crawl out of the hole his men had made at the western base of the hillock. His fury mounted as he realized once more it would take thousands of souls like those to equal the power potential of Anwar's. Djinn-catcher, indeed, he huffed. Yet he rubbed his stomach carefully.

Hakim crawled out after Najmuddin and held his palm upward toward the sky.

'What can it be, Najmuddin? Look how it sparkles in the moonlight. I have never seen such a fine powder, could it be powdered gold?' he asked hopefully.

'You are such a stupid fool,' Najmuddin snapped back. 'It is our lucky day, I tell you. We have found a magical substance…almost as though it had been buried there just for us…waiting for us to discover it.'

Crouching low, Mirza eased himself out into the fresh air. 'Our lucky day,' he mimicked Najmuddin. 'What kind of magic can you make with that dust?' Dust he had disturbed clogged his nostrils and he had a violent fit of sneezing.

Hakim echoed the question as he flung the handful of dust skyward. Sneezing and wiping the tears away with the back of his hand, Mirza saw nothing. Najmuddin and Hakim watched a shower of tiny stars disappear as they floated toward the earth.

'With the power locked in those jars, with fine strands of copper…'

'What's copper?' Mirza asked stupidly. Hakim laughed and Mirza jumped at him with his fist raised. Najmuddin pushed the irate man so hard he tumbled backward and landed on his back, his heels in the air. Hakim controlled his laugh this time.

'Copper is the red metal we took with the jars,' Najmuddin intoned pedantically. 'It is mixed with iron to make bronze…'

'We have to make bronze now?' Mirza whined, bending over to beat the dust from his robe.

'Stupid, will you shut your mouth and listen?' Najmuddin looked at Mirza for a moment before continuing. 'On second thought, why should I waste the breath? You stay here and finish the digging. We want an aperture just big enough to squeeze through, no bigger, understand? Then we have to conceal it. A frame of scrubwood from the ravine should be just right. We will make a daub here near the pool to cover the frame. When it is finished, it must be able to fool the eye of any simpleton from Bashtahal. Stay here and keep working, Mirza. Hakim and

15

I will see to the technical part...oh, yes, remember the entrance has to be large enough to get the jars through...understand?'

'That's unfair!' Mirza yelped. 'I want to know about the bronze and the jars and...'

Najmuddin reached out and caught Mirza's nose between his powerful thumb and forefinger, forcing him down until he knelt at the feet of his tall chief.

'Copper, fool, not bronze. In the jars, there is a magic force, a great secret known only to the caliph and his chief alchemist. It is a force which resembles lightning. Don't ask me how these apprentices of the devil manage to capture lightning in a jar. But if we create a large and intricate tangle of the copper strands, tying them all together and then attaching them to the jars...and each jar to the next...we will make the night glow over...' he lowered his voice and pointed to the top of the hillock where Anwar sat, beyond their line of vision... 'over *his* head. It will look like the stars came down to crown his saintly head.'

'Then why do we need that dust?' Mirza yanked his nose free and sprang to his feet, challenging Najmuddin to answer that puzzle.

'Idiot, if you could think as well as talk, you wouldn't have to ask.' He turned to Hakim. 'Can you answer this fool?'

Hakim scratched first his beard, then his chest, pondering. 'Well,' he tried with tentative caution, 'if the moon makes it sparkle, then what Najmuddin told us is in the jars, that will make it sparkle like the stars...just as he says.'

'How will you keep it up in the air...' Before Mirza could finish the question, Hakim kicked his backside resoundingly.

'With water, just like daub,' Hakim sneered with superiority.

'With spittle, actually,' Najmuddin corrected, 'but it's the same general idea. Now, get to work, Mirza. Everything must be finished – if we have to work all night to do it.'

Standing like a lordly collosus atop the pinnacle, knuckles pressed into his naked hips, Hawwaz stretched

16

one enormous foot out and placed it carefully in the ravine where the men had tethered the animals and made their camp. With an inaudible Pop! Hawwaz shrank to his normal eight foot height and stood near the tethered camels and asses, regarding the jars which had been secreted behind a dense clump of scrubwood. He squatted over one of them and sniffed. His vision cleaved through the thick earthenware and he studied the suspended plates of metal he could not identify. Native cunning told him something was missing and he suspected that something must be a liquid of sorts. If he was correct in that assumption, he reasoned, then Najmuddin's merry men were in for a disappointing surprise. They had risked their lives for a useless treasure.

Hawwaz stood erect and looked about, his ears vaguely attuned to the approach of the men. Hutti, his companion and mentor, had always said a little bit of ignorance was a dangerous thing...or was it knowledge? He shrugged. If those things do not work, Anwar will not be in great jeopardy. If Anwar is not in great jeopardy...say, his life hanging in the balance, a razor-sharp scimitar about to swish down at his scrawny old neck...yes, let's see how dry his humour is when that moment comes. There is work to be done!

He pounded an invisible fist into an immaterial palm. Hutti! He would have to enlist his aid. There was always a price for that and the price was always galling. What would the old slyboots exact this time? Something horrific, no doubt.

Najmuddin's voice echoed hollowly off the ravine walls; there was a puff, an eddy of swirling sand and Hawwaz was gone.

III

With long, powerful, purposeful strides, Hawwaz walked across the limitless expanse of a dazzling plane. It resembled the earth plane he had just left in some ways. Were an ordinary human capable of visiting there in physical form, he would be blinded by the sparkling, perfect beauty, seeing a deep, aquamarine vault overhead shedding soft light everywhere, yet apparently without sun, moon or stars. Beneath his feet, the ground would appear as a luxuriant carpet of deep purple, springy and soft, a form of vegetation unknown to him. The abundant trees would sparkle with diamonds and rubies, gems of every description; everywhere his eye cast itself, there would be yet another magnificent fountain, again made of gems and gushing skyward a geyser of twinkling crystals. Were he keeping pace with the mighty Djinn, all of this would appear to be flying past at an incredible speed. To Hawwaz, whose proper dimension this was, trees were trees, fountains were fountains. The fruit of the trees did vary, some more tempting than others. And there were minor differences in the fountains: his eye roved now and then, finally spotting the one fountain that was his.

When he located his particular fountain, he altered course and drew up to it with evident delight. Standing in its descending, glittering shower, he drank in its life-giving beauty with every atom of his fantastic being. The fruits of this infinite garden nourished him and satisfied his hungers. Immortality was renewed at the breasts of female Djinni. Only the fountain that was his could replenish his superhuman powers.

In the mythologies of man, Djinni are normally depicted as burly creatures in baggy trousers and upturned slippers, either naked from the waist up or wearing

18

small, open waistcoats. Above their coarse and leering features, there is usually a large turban with an enormous diamond in front; at the waistband of the trousers, two wicked daggers and a large scimitar.

Standing under the fountain's spray, Hawwaz was naked and more breathtakingly beautiful than anything in the fabulous landscape. More than anything else, he resembled an eight-foot tall statue of Apollo lovingly cut from the finest marble by an ancient Greek master, a living marble of the palest emerald hue. This magnificent body was laced with a network of fine golden lines which bore no relation to the normal paths of the human bloodstream. Along every section of the intricate pattern of golden veins, tiny pinpoints of silver began to appear as the fountain's mist coated his body. The longer he stood there, the brighter the silver points became, creating an aura that surrounded Hawwaz from head to toe. The powerful inundation made his stature increase and the muscles in his body flash electric charges. An ancient Chinese doctor, could he visualize this scene, would be amazed to note how precisely the golden lines matched the charts of the life energy or pranha flow. Of course, the silver pinpoints were what the old doctor would immediately recognize as the acupuncture points. At this time, in the ninth century, Chinese doctors had been charting such things for centuries.

Reluctantly, Hawwaz left the cascade and flexed his muscles. With his burnished, dark red hair falling in ringlets to his shoulders and the two small horns of gold at either side of his brow, he resembled a youthful, beardless version of Michaelangelo's Moses. There was no hair on his body either and, once out of the fountain's spray, the most outstanding feature became awesomely evident. From his naked abdomen hung a penis that would have done credit to a stallion. The same deep ruddy gold as his hair, it terminated in an exposed tip the colour and transparency of a huge, polished ruby. Where the scrotum of a human would be suspended, Hawwaz had one magnificent globe the lustre of a pearl. Held in place by an invisible energy force, it would have seemed detached if it did not

19

move so precisely with the Djinn. As he moved, his body flashing in the subdued light, the opalescence of this great sphere became fiery. Hawwaz took up his league-consuming stride once more and headed for a tree just visible on the far horizon.

Stretched out full length under the tree, Hutti looked up toward the branches laden with fruit: to him they appeared as large mangoes rather than gemstones. Suspended beneath the lowest branch, the misty form of a beautiful woman floated in the air. Her long, jet-black hair hung down her back, falling just short of splendid, alabaster buttocks. Legs folded under her, shoulders thrust back and arms extended at each side as though to maintain her balance, her flat abdomen and firm, up-tilted breasts were engagingly youthful. Even in the soft twilight of this alternative world, her wraithlike presence, her near transparency, made her appear unreal.

With a deep frown that made his small, golden horns point forward, Hawwaz drew up to the tree and planted his feet wide apart, his clenched fists pressing into his narrow hips. He glared at his friend, the older Djinn, with deep disapproval.

'Hutti, what do you think you're doing?' he demanded.

'Oh…little brother! Didn't see you, I've been concentrating on this delicious morsel. How was your trip?'

'Never mind about my trip,' Hawwaz retorted, 'what are you doing with her…whoever she is?'

'Oh…her?' Hutti asked, feigning total innocence as he pointed up to the girl questioningly. 'Medina. Stopping off on her way to Mecca, I think…I can never get earth time and our time straight…she might have been going on a pilgrimage. She collapsed with a fever. You know how most humans are, they sometimes leave their bodies at times like that…'

'With a little help from you?' Hawwaz asked sarcastically.

'What are you so upset about? I'm returning her shortly.'

20

'Yes, and what if her physical body dies while her spirit is up here? Do you know what our women would do to you for interfering with a female mortal spirit?'

'Oh, pish-tush. She's not going to die, she's too young and healthy.' Hutti turned his gaze toward the young Djinn. 'Considering that I practically brought you up, that I've taught you everything you know, just as a real big brother would, I don't take kindly to all this moraliz–ing, Hawwaz. You're much too stuffy for your age.'

Hawwaz caught his tongue just in time, remembering he had a great favour to ask. It wouldn't do to put Hutti in a bad humour now. He stretched out on the soft ground next to Hutti and cushioned his cheek on a large, lavender mushroom.

'I'm not moralizing, I'm worried about you. Why do you take such chances? It is one thing to gain a human soul through that human's consent. You can't be punished for that. That wraith up there is useless to you, it's only an ast-ral body. What kind of a thrill can you get?'

As though to demonstrate, Hutti drew in a long breath of air. The suction drew the weightless apparition down until she rested on his groin. His penis contracted under her, curved upwards until the ruby tip pressed into the ethereal navel. The girl was pushed up and back until she rested above the Djinn's toes. The penis shot out, gently moved her legs out and down, then settled between her open thighs. Hutti inhaled again and she slid down the long length of the shaft like a child on a bannister until she was arrested soundlessly against his groin.

'Of all the stupid, childish games I've ever seen,' Hawwaz muttered to himself. 'Look,' he drew his face closer to Hutti's, 'she can't feel it down there…' he pointed down, then vaguely from side to side…'on the earth plane…wherever it is, Medina I mean. *You* certainly can't feel it, so why do you waste your time?'

'You've never tried it,' Hutti huffed defensively, 'so how do you know? Try it just once and then tell me you can't feel anything.'

'Nonsense! Do I have to eat sand to find out it isn't

nourishing?' Hawwaz looked at the girl, then stared at Hutti. 'Wouldn't it be just my good fortune that her body in Medina died at the moment I touched her. No thanks!'

Hutti reached out, folded the girl's legs under her and then set her, like a weightless toy, on the soft purple carpet between them. Affectionately, he put his arm around Hawwaz's shoulders.

'If you insist on being such a timorous prig, how will you ever enjoy life? You've never had a human woman…in the flesh. It is so delicious, so rewarding, so…good for the ego, you have no idea, little brother.'

'I'm not in the market for a demon son, thank you. Can't see it's made *you* any happier.'

'I'm not talking about that,' Hutti countered irritably. The mention of his ill-tempered demon son, Musa, was usually enough to put him in a bad mood.

'No, you're not,' Hawwaz pressed his advantage, 'nor are you talking about the egomaniacal delights of human girls in the flesh…how many times did you try to make one call out for you, to give you the substance in their world to consummate the act?' Hawwaz flashed gleeful teeth, sparkling brighter than polished crystal; Hutti scowled and turned away. 'You're talking about this shadow men call an astral body…*body*? Hmmph!' He pushed Hutti's shoulder to force his attention back to the diatribe. 'Is *this* giving you the ego thrill of your life?'

'She feels it,' Hutti sniffed. 'She'll never know why, she'll never remember anything, but somehow, the caresses of men – for the rest of her life – will leave her…well, if not cold, certainly not touched to the very core…'

'Owwww!' Hawwaz yowled in desperation. 'You are the greatest egomaniac…'

'Shhh!' Hutti held a long, tapering, elegantly shaped forefinger to his lips. 'Her body could be aware of a frightening or threatening vibration. Do me a small favour…do I often ask you for favours?…*do* one for me. Just extend your ranji and wrap it around her…pull her toward you…drink in the loveliness…she truly is lovely, isn't she? That's all. Do that and let her slide up and down

22

as I did. You will see her sleeping lips part, her delicate, luxuriant black lashes flutter. Don't be so selfish, give her that pleasure.'

All the time Hutti had been talking, the word 'favour' had held the forefront of Hawwaz's attention. He reprimanded himself inwardly; if he didn't stop talking down his nose, Hutti would never do *him* the favour he needed so badly.

Shrugging with consummate boredom, Hawwaz flashed an internal order to his penis – his ranji, as they referred to it – and there was no response. His eyes became wide as moons. He had just ordered his ranji to coil itself about the girl's waist and settle her atop his groin. The ranji shot straight out and buried its tip under his foot.

Hutti turned to regard the pained and shocked expression on his friend's face. Then he looked down at the rebellious ranji. He fell back and began laughing uncontrollably.

'Very funny,' Hawwaz mumbled, trying to contain his fury. He glared at his disobedient penis until fire literally poured from his eyes. The penis cringed but would not encircle the girl.

'Don't you remember what I told you about the hanging gardens of Babylon?' Hutti asked, breathlessly fighting for control of his rampant laughter.

'Hutti, I don't think this is funny!' Hawwaz's ranji was now vibrating wildly under the fiery stare.

'Two of the Chosen Persons were watching an elephant Nebuchadnezzar had brought from India.' Hutti was enjoying himself so much it didn't matter whether his friend was listening or not. 'The Indian atop and the men on the ground couldn't get the elephant to wrap his trunk about a heavy log. A crowd of Egyptian slaves stood about staring. One of the Hebrew captives shouted over, asking the men if they had never heard the law of Hammurabi which pertained to the situation.'

'So?' Hawwaz finally stopped beaming heat at the stricken but still disobedient ranji. He raised his right eyebrow and waited.

'The captive waited a moment or two,' Hutti continued in a serious and rather pedantic voice, one that Hawwaz particularly could not abide, 'and then said: "A watched putz never coils."'

'A watched what?' Hawwaz's incomprehension was total.

'Putz,' Hutti repeated. He shook his head sadly a few times. 'You have the same trouble as the Babylonians. They never bothered to study Aramaic either.'

'What?' Hawwaz sounded as though he would explode. Hutti fell back and began laughing again. Just before Hawwaz drew back his hand to smash his friend's face in, he recalled the favour. Instead, he extended the menacing hand and began shaking Hutti's shoulder, trying to recapture his attention.

Very stealthily, Hawwaz's ranji lifted itself and swayed, much like a snake. The girl really was lovely. Turning his ruby tip to check on his master, he noticed that Hawwaz was fully occupied trying to control Hutti. Very gently, the ranji eased further toward the girl until he was nuzzling his ruby tip against her left nipple. One by one, her arms came down from their extended position; the left one stroked the bright ruby nestling at her breast. A moment later, Hutti's ranji raised itself; with a wriggle of delight, it slithered over to the free nipple and soon the other hand was stroking his head.

'Hutti, listen to me please, this is important.' Hawwaz shook the quaking shoulder more vigorously. Hutti stopped laughing and cocked his head. 'That alchemist you told me about in Bagdad, the one you thought might trade his soul for gold…'

'I never said that,' Hutti denied, suddenly quite serious. He knew very well from the vague, oblique approach that Hawwaz was fishing for something. While waiting for Hawwaz and dallying with the girl's astral body, he had been wondering how he could wrest a favour from his young friend. He smiled inwardly, savouring the opportunity which seemed about to drop in his lap, so to speak.

'You mean…it was not Bagdad?' Hawwaz didn't try to cover up his disappointment.

'No, it was Bagdad…I meant your *literal* interpretation. He is *not* worried about gold.'

'Then how can you…' Hawwaz began, dumbfounded.

'Literal, did I say? Crass materialist! Transmuting base metal is merely symbolic for these so-called wise men. It is his mind and soul he is trying to purify…and he is quite old. He's afraid he'll die before he can transcend his common animal state.'

'A very learned dissertation, I am sure. Just what are you talking about?' Listening to Hawwaz, Hutti probed for hidden guile. Could his friend really be so naïve?

'Simply stated, he doesn't want to be hurled into the nameless, wailing void without sails or rudder. He wants to be free to travel this and other planes beyond human existence…and from time to time, in another guise, return to that world they all hate to leave.'

'You mean,' Hawwaz laughed for the first time since he arrived, 'he doesn't know what will happen to that precious soul of his when *you* get your hands on it?'

'Oh, don't be so dramatic. It would be a gentle captivity. After all, if he completes his life work, he will bring me almost as much power as that Anwar you are so anxious to capture…Say! Does this pussy-foot line of yours have anything to do with Anwar?'

'You've often told me Anwar is much too wily for the likes of me,' Hawwaz answered evasively.

'That's not a direct answer to a direct question,' Hutti smiled, sensing his young friend was in a corner. 'Though it is true enough… Anwar will no doubt slip between your over-eager fingers.'

'While you capture your alchemist and have the laugh on me, is that it? Hawwaz sounded genuinely hurt.

'Do you think the alchemist doesn't think he'll do the same to me? Get what he needs, the cunning old codger, then leave me whistling into my empty hands? He knows the gamble and so do I. My chances are no better than yours.'

'But surely if…'

'Surely "if" nothing. Now, come to the point. You want something from "Uncle" Hutti, don't you?'

'Well…' Hawwaz hesitated, wanting to put the request straightforwardly, yet dreading the price. 'What would you ask in return?'

'Hawwaz, don't play games with me. Don't ask me how much I would pay for a pomegranate until you show me the fruit.'

'There are a number of jars in the caliph's treasury. Eight of them were stolen. They contain a form of magic, they are supposedly filled with captive lightning. I want to know how they work. I want to make sure they *do* work.'

'No, you don't. The whole story, please.' Hutti folded his arms across his chest with an air of finality that told his friend wheedling and crafty omissions would get him nowhere. Deflated, Hawwaz told him about Najmuddin and the plans he and his villanous helpers had for fleecing the citizens of Bashtahal. Elaborating his story to convince Hutti he was not holding back, he even mentioned Maryam and her visits to Anwar. To gain interested compliance, he even praised her beauty.

'You *want* these men to succeed?' Hutti asked, his features ablaze with astonishment.

'Certainly…don't you see? I suspect the caliph has already discovered the missing jars…I mean, that eight are missing. I would not be surprised if each one is not marked with a secret cipher. When the caliph's soldiers have the knife to old Anwar's throat, that's where I step in and save him.'

'You honestly believe he will call out, call you by name and invoke your aid?' Hawwaz nodded eagerly. 'Little brother, how stupid can you be? Compared to a mere alchemist, Anwar is beyond caring about life or death. Do you not realize who and what he is? You really think such a dervish, the wisest of the wise, will call out for you when he is offered his freedom from life?'

'Oh, stop romanticizing, a man is a man. When his throat is about to be cut, he will not be filled with noble thoughts.' Hawwaz sounded sure of himself, but the wiser Hutti could see his bravado crumbling.

'If you had the sense you were born with, you would approach this strategy with singleness of purpose. Let Anwar see it in everything you do...and do it most clumsily. Make him think it is the only thing you can think about.'

'Then what? Have him slip through my fingers so your prophesy comes true?'

'Would I do that to you?' Hutti shook his head with pained disbelief. 'How could you? No, you ninny, that would be a smoke-screen only. Anwar would not raise a hand to save himself. Now, think for once. What would make him call out, for what would he sacrifice *anything*?' Hutti paused, searching his friend's face for a sign of dawning insight. 'Silly, for that girl...that's who!'

'You've lost me again.' Hawwaz yawned with vexation.

'She comes to visit him? Is he not always slipping off in his meditations, leaving his body? How many times have we been aware of his presence here? Pick your moment, then get to that girl. You know how to create an irresistible heat in human women...'

'You mean, I should plant a demon in her?' Hawwaz was deeply shocked.

'You want Anwar and you want to keep your scruples too?' Hutti roared with laughter. 'You are not to be believed.'

'You don't understand,' Hawwaz protested. 'It's not my scruples. I don't understand why he should call out afterwards...it would be too late.'

'Not if you're just a little smarter. Don't you see? You have to control yourself, make it seem like it's happening...but hold back!'

'I think you are trying to pull the wool over my eyes. Why should he care so much? So the girl has a demon, so what? So, he will bite her nipples and neighbours will shun her, he'd be a terror to all other children. Then, suddenly he will be gone. Why should that upset Anwar.'

'It has to do with a certain history, one I don't feel like telling anyone about. Just believe me, Anwar is one human being who would sacrifice anything to save that girl. Think about it. You'll have a much better chance than with those silly magical jars of yours…I mean, the caliph's.'

'Will you find out for me in Bagdad?' Hawwaz coaxed.

'I have to get this girl back,' Hutti turned his head, but the two ranjis anticipated the move and each was nestled next to his master's leg. 'I wonder why she's holding her hands in front of her breasts like that?' Hawwaz shrugged. 'Two trips like that would be dangerous without replenishing myself at the fountain.'

'When you get back from Bagdad, you could stop there…then take this girl back. Or, tell me where she is…I mean her body…and I'll take her.'

Hutti stole a sidelong glance at his young friend. Trust him to bungle it. 'Let's discuss that when I get back.'

'Before you go, what price are you going to demand?'

'I have a plan, a plan to get the woman of my desires…'

'Oh, no you don't. We tried that once before.' Hawwaz sat bolt upright, an unconcealed look of fear on his face. 'We're no match for them, they'll tear us to pieces again. How long did it take us to put ourselves together then? Our women will be hunting us very soon…if I get torn apart, it's goodbye Anwar.'

Hutti was just as terrified as his friend, but he concealed it well. The Djinn women were much stronger than the men, it was true. And they did not give themselves to love-making; they pursued and overpowered the men, ravishing them with vehement lust, sapping their strength with incredibly insatiable lasciviousness. Just once in his life, Hutti wanted to surprise and overpower the woman he adored. To have her *his* way. The only way an impregnating consummation could occur. Hutti longed for a son and was desperate enough to risk certain torture to achieve it…especially with Aysha. But his plan would never work without an accomplice.

He described his imaginative scheme, an architectural inspiration. Each time the women invaded their realm, only the men knew where the Fountain of Forgetfulness was located. When Hawwaz saw the way Hutti planned to disguise this fountain, he would understand how fool-proof the scheme was. And Hawwaz wasn't taking chances, only Hutti. All his friend had to do was hide under the camouflaged sculpture. All he had to do was grab Aysha's heels or ankles at the right moment. He might get splashed with the fountain, so what? He would dream for a few hours, nothing more. He did want the information from Bagdad, did he not?

'I think you're crazy,' Hawwaz said at last. 'The minute I touch her, her friends will come to her rescue. We'll be torn to bits…but not before we're so badly raped and drained and bruised it will take days…'

'Little brother, trust me this once. Stop worrying. Just wait here and keep an eye on her until I get back from Bagdad, agreed? When you see my plan worked out, you'll stop worrying.'

Hawwaz looked up as Hutti levitated to his feet in one vaulting motion. He leaped into the air, a soft Pop! echoed over the plane and he was gone. Hawwaz picked up a large diamond lying near the tree trunk and hurled it at the ruby tip of his ranji. It ducked deftly and Hawwaz yawned, stretching out flat. In a moment he was fast asleep.

IV

Mirza worked on through the night, quietly if venomously, only the occasional muffled curse reaching Anwar; with a perfectionist's zeal, the man laboured to create an undetectable concealment for the entrance to the cavern beneath the hillock. Pricking his finger on a thorn in the dark, Mirza voiced a louder obscenity. Wincing, Anwar decided to leave for more peaceful fields.

In his mind, he created a tunnel that started at a point of nothingness where it touched his skull and zoomed upward toward the star-filled heavens, to lose itself in the vast vault above. His inner eye perceived the tunnel as lined with deep, velvety pile that was constantly changing hues from the deepest black to the softest silver. When it no longer seemed to extend upward, but in all directions at once, he contracted all of his consciousness until his total existence was a dot in the centre of his spinal column. He willed this concentration upwards into the tunnel entrance. For a fraction of time too small to measure, everything ceased: awareness, memory, even Anwar himself. Then, as a pale but luminous essence, he moved across a shadowy land of subdued light. Here and there, subtle flashes of colour reached him: blues, greens, yellows, deep reds. Vague shapes formed silhouettes here and there, some resembling trees, others much like tall fountains. In a sense, it was the same plane Hawwaz had traversed earlier; Anwar didn't see it as the Djinn had, nor would the Djinn easily recognize Anwar's visualization. To Anwar, or his astral body, it was one part of the astral plane with which he was very familiar. To Hawwaz, of course, this was the real and solid world of his rightful dimension. And there would have been no mutual frame of reference if the wraith of the girl sitting near the sleeping Djinn had not

30

cried out softly, somehow recognizing a compassionate presence. Hawwaz heard nothing. Anwar heard a sound not unlike the tinkling of a camel bell rising from the depths of the sea. He harkened to the plea and guided his passage toward the dim sound.

To Anwar, the girl became clearly visible while the sleeping Djinn remained a faint shadow form. The old man lifted her gently and set her upon her feet. She placed her hand inside his extended one and followed him unquestioningly as he led her back in the direction from which he'd come. At one point, he stopped and studied her passive face and closed eyes. After a few moments, he had a clear image of her physical body and its exact location on the earth plane. He then turned his inner eye toward the hillock and looked down the tunnel stretching up from his own physical body. The solid Anwar sat there like a graven image. The heartbeat was almost non-existent. Expanding his vision, he watched the tired Mirza, his night's work done at last, trudging wearily toward the hidden ravine. Across the broad desert plain, the night stretched untroubled and undisturbed between the mountains and the ghostly, moonlit city of Bashtahal.

Pulling the girl close to him and enfolding her in his arms tightly, Anwar concentrated on a vision of one of the narrow alleys in the city of Medina. Slowly at first, then with blinding acceleration, the two figures vanished, to appear simultaneously in that very alley. Anwar released the girl and took her hand. Gazing at her navel, he made out the near indistinguishable silver cord stretching toward a closed door. He put a guiding arm around the somnambulistic essence of the girl and led her to the door; both figures moved easily through the thick wood.

In a small chamber at the back of the house, Anwar found the fevered body of the girl stretched out on a pallet of straw. In a corner of the room, an old woman sat on the floor, her legs sprawled out, her head bent over her bosom as she snored loudly. With a gentle touch on the back of the spiritual girl, he pressed her forward and watched the one blend into the other as the silver cord disappeared. Kneeling

31

next to the pallet, he touched the fevered brow with one hand and pressed the other down over her solar plexus. He remained immobile for many minutes, attuned to the inner pulsations of a dangerously ill young woman... hardly more than a child, she seemed. She stirred as his healing hands fought with the fever, her eyelashes fluttering. Then she sighed and the heat seemed to leave her tortured body and rise to the ceiling. With a nod of satisfaction, the shadowy presence of Anwar disappeared. For an instant before his consciousness left the house, he was aware of a familiar and furious presence; a very real threat hung in the air as Anwar vanished. Many leagues away, across the vast desert to the east, the old man slid down the tunnel and into his own body.

Outwardly serene, Anwar needed time to shake off the unpleasant sensations and the fatigue the last moment out of his body had encountered. That it had been Hutti, that unseen presence, there was no doubt. Arrogant, wilful children to the last. All he would have cared about was to get his astral plaything off his hands before the actual girl had died. Her death would mean nothing as long as the Djinn's hands were clean. Anwar knew that she had been only a whisker away from death. Careless, thoughtless, every one of them...but why could *Hutti* not have been a little more caring?

Muscles flabby, stature reduced considerably and his face pinched and seething with anger, the weakened Hutti stood under the showering forces of his own fountain for a long time. He wanted to tear Hawwaz limb from limb. He had planned to replenish himself before venturing back to earth once more, but when he returned from Bagdad and found Hawwaz asleep and the girl gone, he hadn't dared to pause for another instant. For the first time in his long career, he had nearly become lost on the return voyage from Medina. That meddling old Anwar! How had he known about the girl? Anwar would never forgive him, never! He nearly had his vengeance this time.

When he towered over the sleeping Hawwaz, Hutti

once more resembled man's imagined vision of the sun god of antiquity. Firm and radiant, he gazed down at his friend like the lord avenger.

'Wake up, you stupid fool!'

Hawwaz bounced off the purple veldt and stood, blinking vacantly. His sleepy eyes focused and he smiled at Hutti. He blinked again. The girl was gone.

'You've taken her back already…'

'I've taken no one back, thanks to you. You want a favour and I can't even trust you that far…'

'Hutti, what are you talking about?' Hawwaz was startled, his eyes darting everywhere at once.

'She isn't here, if that's what you're looking about for. Your old friend Anwar has been here. Just came and took her away while you slept on and on and on.'

'Anwar?' Hawwaz's breath whistled through his teeth. 'Are you sure? How could he…'

'How many times have I told you not to underestimate him? Because of you, I nearly disappeared forever…you and your precious old holy man.'

'I don't understand…'

'You don't understand,' Hutti mocked. 'When I got back here from Bagdad, she was gone. When I got to Medina – without replenishing myself, may I add – the last essence of Anwar just escaped me. I didn't even have strength enough left to reach out and sunder his silver cord…'

'You wouldn't!' Hawwaz was visibly trembling. 'You couldn't do a thing like that…could you?'

'That's neither here nor there. Do you realize I nearly got lost on the way back, I was that weak and upset?'

'I am sorry. Oh Hutti, I am, I am.' Hawwaz sank down to the ground and buried his face in his hands.

Hutti gazed down, the abject apology dissipating his anger. Finally he sat down next to his friend and began telling him about his trip to Bagdad.

Many rumours about the famous jars had spread through the city. The superstitious believed they each contained a Djinn who would do the caliph's bidding each time he rubbed a jar. Of course, no one could answer a simple question: if the caliph had one such jar, why would he need more? But the alchemist knew they were designed by a wizard in the caliph's employ. Somehow, this inspired genius had developed a system for accumulating small amounts of lightning in the jars. Plates of metal were suspended in an acid solution and a reaction was thus created. By attaching a copper strand to one side of the contraption, another strand to the opposite side, one could bring the two strands within close proximity of each other and a spark would leap across the gap. A fascinating toy, to be sure. Link two or more jars together and a rather large spark would leap across a wider gap. Fascinating as the jars were, the genius who had invented the system still could not come up with a practical use for them, but that did not mean the theft would go undetected or unpunished.

'Hutti,' Hawwaz confided, 'there is no solution in those jars; they will not work.'

'Of course not…you told me that already.' Hutti was bored with the whole ridiculous business.

'What will I do…the scheme will fail?' Hawwaz sounded deflated.

'Anwar doesn't need those silly jars, he has the brightest aura I've ever seen.'

'Yes…you've seen, I've seen…but *humans* can't see that!'

'Well then, when those thieves rig the whole thing up, you make the copper glow. That's not so hard.'

'Easy for you to say,' Hawwaz answered testily, 'but that will take a lot of energy…from me.'

'Then stop dashing back and forth…you and your obsession with Anwar! Besides, I want you here when the women come. With your head screwed on tightly and your attention on *my* project.'

'If it's as foolproof as you say, what are you worried about?' Hawwaz couldn't hide his nervous foreboding.

'For one thing, all our brethren will be gathering shortly. I don't trust many of them. They'd enjoy watching me torn limb from limb again. It will take time to disguise the Fountain of Forgetfulness and I'll need your help. It has to be finished before *any*one gets here.'

'Then let's get some sleep,' Hawwaz suggested, 'I don't want to be tired for *that* ordeal.'

'Don't you try to slip away,' Hutti warned. 'You mess this one up and *I'll* tear you limb from limb.'

V

MANY STARS STILL STUDDED THE sky, but the moon had set and the pre-dawn darkness was deeper now than it had been in the middle of the night. Stepping cautiously from behind an outcropping of rock where she had hidden to listen carefully for any signs of activity from Najmuddin and his men, Maryam gazed up at the barely visible outline of Anwar above on the hillock. Nothing stirred; it was too early even for the first breeze that heralded a new day. All seemed quiet and peaceful, as it had that first early morning when her father brought her to meet the holy man.

Worrying that she had been too intent on arriving before dawn, she hesitated, holding the gourd of fresh well water pressed to her body; the kerchief full of cakes and dates dangled listlessly from her other hand. Once more, she concentrated her thoughts, her unusually keen inner awareness sweeping the area. She could detect nothing amiss, yet she agonized about disturbing Anwar. Don't disturb, she commanded herself, join him. When he is ready, he will let you know.

In another realm of being, as Maryam carefully and quietly stole up the hillside, Hawwaz watched Hutti stride across the purple landscape in search of more precious building materials. Stupid! Sit here and watch this pile of stones while he brings back more. This mad scheme of his will never work. The young Djinn tried to focus on Hutti's project, but his mind wandered back to Anwar with a will of its own. When Hutti disappeared over the horizon, Hawwaz gritted his teeth and concentrated his forces. A moment later, he towered above his favourite pinnacle, behind and just west of Anwar's hillock. Stretching his neck, he picked out the details of Najmuddin's camp hidden in the deep ravine. All was calm; broken

36

snores drifted up on the still air. Anwar was there, but the preterhuman abilities of the Djinn established immediately that he – the real Anwar – was not in his body. Then he became aware of a new presence approaching the hilltop. His body began to tremble with anticipation.

Placing her meagre offerings on the ground, Maryam folded her robes about her and sat facing Anwar, her legs crossed and feet tucked under her. Although as a disciple she had progressed in many ways, she was not yet so advanced as to detect the looming, invisible entity grinning down at her from the high pinnacle. As she had been taught, she folded in on herself until she had stilled everything save her awareness of her own mind which she filled with the vision of Anwar, as clear to her as though her eyes were open and the sun shining brightly.

Soon, the still and perfect image of Anwar she had created internally began to shimmer; as she observed carefully, the years seemed to drop from his shoulders and face. The young Anwar was fair and unwrinkled, his eyes opened and bright. A curling beard of burnished bronze moved as his smile broadened, everything about him beaming love and tenderness to her alone. His eyes invited her to come closer. He knew about her terrible dreams, how tormented she was. With such terrible dreams, it was no wonder she had developed such a fear of male sexuality. A terrible, frightening ramrod, like the mast of a ship, being pushed at her furiously. But it did not have to be like that. It could be gentle and loving, tender and concerned, caring and compassionate. It could waken in her the will to love and breach the dam holding back her own limitless warmth, a love great enough to encompass all of mankind.

Maryam experienced something she had never known. A liquid flame took hold of her, bathing her body in a light so splendid her limbs weakened and giddy fires raced through her, penetrating every atom of her being. The heavens filled with a music unlike any sounds she had ever heard. Her head moved, being called irresistibly by a cosmic force beaming a message to her. Her eyes closed, in a trance only partially of her own making, she faced the west, raising her head until her closed eyelids were centred on the unseen image rising above the high pinnacle. She felt Anwar's arms reach out for her, to lift her and place her on his crossed legs. There was something more, something there so fascinating, so awe-inspiring that it should have terrified her but didn't. Vague though it was, it was the most important thing in the world, a thing she could not live without. Call out, she seemed to urge herself, call out and it shall be yours. All you have to do is say yes, say it with all your heart. If you accept, if you declare your want, it shall be yours.

In the upper floor of a small house in a narrow alley near the great mosque in Mecca, an almost fully material Anwar sat beside an old woman dressed entirely in black. She held his hand between hers, pressed to her trembling lips. Before them on the floor, a shallow bowl filled with a milky substance shimmered in the deep gloom. The surface of the liquid revealed two disparate pictures. On the left, very indistinctly, the watchers could see Hutti striding across the astral plane, his arms loaded with bright jewels. On the other side of the bowl, Maryam's enraptured face shone clearly, her head uplifted, her lips parting to utter a call. The next second, Anwar disappeared, the milky surface turned dark and the old woman in black began beating against her thigh with her fist, emitting a strange ululation unlike any sound issuing from human lips.

As Maryam called out, Hawwaz's gigantic form condensed, shifted and became material at her side. In one swift motion of his arm, he bowled the mesmerized girl over on her back, lifting the hem of her robe with the other hand, falling on her all in one flowing sequence. The ruby tip of his ranji touched her open, inviting vulva as the heart-stricken Anwar dropped back into his body. And as an arm, a huge and extremely muscular arm, reached from nowhere and extended a hand between Hawwaz's legs. Clutching the pearl invisibly suspended from Hawwaz's groin, the hand yanked mightily. With a muffled howl of pain that echoed thunderingly off the mountains, the frustrated Djinn was gone.

Anwar shuddered and forced his stiffened body into action. Leaning forward, he examined Maryam carefully. Her vulva was swollen and slightly purple from the contact. The old man searched carefully along the ground between her sprawled legs. Crystals of sand had been scorched and blackened, but nothing more. He sighed audibly and offered up a silent prayer of thanksgiving. Then, with the dedicated skill of a physician, he drew pouches of leather from beneath the folds of his tattered carpets. In a small bowl, he made a paste from different powders and unguents and applied it to the girl's swollen parts, covering the sensitive area with a cloth which he knotted at her hips. Lifting her as though she weighed no more than a baby, he laid her across the carpets and arranged her robes decorously. Settling himself further back, he mixed a new potion from a different selection of mysterious ingredients and filled two small squares of clean cloth with what was now a substance like putty. He rolled the squares between his palms until he had two spherical pills. When satisfied with his handiwork, he placed the small spheres in a tiny leather pouch with a drawstring closure. When all the unused powders, unguents and compounds were stored away under his carpets once more, the old man picked up the water gourd and began the ritual cleansing of hands, mouth, face and feet before the sun broke free of the earth's rim.

He kept his vigil over the girl as he prayed for her well-being. Hawwaz had found the channel, had reached her mind. And the first time is the hardest, as it is with so many things. Next time, she would be more vulnerable still. Djinni did this to women for no apparent purpose…well, there was egotism. Look what it did to the poor victims. They gave birth to what seemed a normal child at first. As it grew, snarling and fighting, demanding and surly, its strangeness became ever more apparent. At about the age of ten, the hair began to take on that deep, telltale rufescence and the skin developed a greenish undertone. One day he was there, the next day gone. One day he awakens to the discovery of his awful powers. At the same moment, he encounters the ultimate terror: he has no soul. A demon, belonging to no world, he amasses power and treasure and torments mankind in any way he can. Not the least by capturing beautiful women and turning them into helpless wantons. Nothing helps, nothing can ever satisfy the howling fury of the children of limbo. They live in a darkened world, vulnerable to the Djinni to the ends of their lives. Unless, he added wistfully, they have that extraordinary strength of character granted to few. And the will to learn the arts which can protect them.

Maryam stirred and whimpered in what was now a normal sleep. Anwar placed his palm on her brow and spoke softly, telling her that she would remember nothing of the experience, that gratefully her mind would blank out the near fatal event. She could not live with that memory, he assured himself, stroking the fair brow softly. Knowing that would not just harm her, it would defeat her forever at this stage of her life. Later, when she had the strength and acquired the wisdom, nothing would or could defeat her.

'Maryam!' He raised his hands and clapped the palms together. Her eyes flew open, she gasped and tried to struggle to a sitting position. With a kindly smile, the old man helped her. She was shocked to find herself on his carpeted roost and edged away; his hand restrained her, assuring her she had not trespassed.

'Master, what happened?' Her face was haunted, but he knew she could not identify the reason behind her anxiety.

'You came very early, child. And you fell asleep. I put you there so you would not be bruised when you awoke.' As he spoke, the word bruise drew her attention to a tenderness in a place that made her blush profusely.

'You will not think of that, Maryam, not now. Accept from me on pure faith that all is well. When the time comes for you to know, it will be there.' He picked up the little pouch he had prepared for her. She watched him place it in the palm of her hand.

'When was your time of the moon?' he asked, blushing

40

slightly himself. 'Were it not important,' he added, 'I would not ask.'

'It was over three days ago. I am now purified,' she answered simply.

'Good.' He rose to his feet with a great deal more agility than might be expected for his outer wizened frailness. 'For reasons of delicacy, I must go off for a few moments. While I am gone, you are to take one of the small objects from the pouch. Insert it inside yourself as deeply as you can. It is to remain there until the next time of your moon. When you remove it, you are to rinse it sparingly in warm, pure water and keep it on a dish, well covered and protected until it is time to re-insert it once more. You will find, to your surprise no doubt, a cloth covering that part of your body. When you have done what I have prescribed, replace the cloth and keep it there for the balance of the day. Believe me when I say that it is better not to ask questions.'

With a sprightly step and unbelievable strength and vigour for one so ancient, Anwar bounded down the far side of the hillock. He was amused rather than annoyed that he had to find a new place for the calls of nature. True, he had reduced the need to a level few physicians would credit, but it would not be diplomatic to use the cavern beneath his carpet any longer. Why disillusion poor Najmuddin?

Maryam was sitting where he left her, a new blush suffusing her puzzled face. She held up the pouch enquiringly. He smiled and inclined his head to one side as he arranged himself on his carpeted dais.

'Questions, questions,' he murmered indulgently. 'Listen, and you will learn what you need to know, not what your curiosity dictates. If there are questions I do not answer, remember what I told you. When answers are needed, answers are there.'

For the time being, she must consider the first phase of her life was over. Using the term 'for the time being,' he assured her, indicated no more than the need for a complete break with her past. To follow a path, one must be prepared to change, even if the idea of drastic change appeared painful and frightening. For those who followed such a path, searching for complete unity, the very personality may have to be destroyed and recreated...many times. If she perceived love as the great moving force between human and God, then there could be no barriers to complete acceptance...of everything.

Thus, Maryam must be ready to move on. For the time being – once again – her life as the young daughter of a widow in the city of Bashtahal was over. Her role as a disciple would continue, but under entirely different conditions. As soon as possible, she was to leave for Medina. Asking how she was to do this, what she would tell her mother...all of this was beside the point. Move her steps westward. The next oasis was not far. The next caravan would leave there soon, it always did. A young girl on her own, attached to a caravan, would be in great danger. She would know how to keep the bond between them alive; if danger became too overwhelming, he would know and come to her. However, each obstacle she conquered for herself would enhance her own life force. The time had come to put her teacher's teachings into practice.

'What will I do in Medina...or must I divine that for myself?' she asked without umbrage.

'No. You will find the street of the goldsmiths and there, in the house of Ahmed, the gem-setter, seek a young woman of your own age who is called Fatima. She is convalescing from a terrible fever which nearly took her life. She needs you. Your love, your devotion and your caring. When she is well and ready, then you will proceed to Mecca. Very near the great mosque which houses the Kaaba, in a small dwelling in a smaller alley, you will find an old woman entirely clothed in black. She will seem hard and fierce to you at first, but she is considered a saint in her community. Her name is Farah, and she gathers medicinal roots and herbs. Many of the most wretched and hopeless in Mecca owed their lives to her great skill and kindness. The ground floor of her house is ideal for your new career – yours and Fatima's.'

A small panic seized the girl and she blanched. Without realizing it, her hands covered her womb protectively; yet she could give no name to the sudden premonition.

'Yes, Maryam, in Mecca you two will begin new lives...as prostitutes.'

The girl's head dropped and her chin touched her chest. The agony in her body, the terror in her mind and the tears streaming down her face continued unabated for minutes on end. Finally, as though she had resolved a great problem in her soul, she raised her head once more. The faint glimmering of a new knowledge reached out to her.

In a sublime and detached way, Anwar began a discourse on the dissolving of personality, the art of freeing oneself from the conditioning which blocks true perception. In their new lives, they were to learn a humility of spirit. It would be degrading only if they perceived it as such. Rather, they should be learning about human weakness and frailty. Behind every swaggering, self-important male lord of the universe hid a frightened boy, a child beset with the demons and devils of his own devising. In giving themselves, they would become the nurses of men's souls, chalices that were being purified by selfless acts of devotion, not debased and degraded.

They were to deny no man and they were to ask nothing. Whatever was offered was to be accepted gratefully. They were to keep nothing save what was essential to feed them. The rest would be for the poor and wretched, to be given freely and unstintingly. Those hours not needed for sleep or for their new occupation they would devote to Farah and her mission.

Once more the tremulous young head bowed. 'We are to reject no man?'

'If you were to reject even one – for no matter what reason – your ego would conquer you. If you are ever approached by an entity that is not of this world, no matter how well disguised, you will know. He who is not human is to be rejected and refused at any cost. As you go through the flames, as you burn away that which is the mere dross of this life, you will know...and you will know why. And in knowing, you will find you share something of this nature with Fatima. However, all that is part of your road of discovery. When that phase of your life comes to an end, you will know that too. Also, in which direction to place your footsteps.'

Maryam nodded, a new look of resignation on her face. She twirled the pouch by its drawstring, then looked up at Anwar.

'The other one is for Fatima?' she asked. Anwar nodded assent. 'These will protect us like amulets?'

'They will protect you for much sounder reasons than market place magic,' he corrected.

He watched her as she stored the pouch in the bosom of her robes. The strong determination she had displayed, the resolve based on resignation began to flee as she prepared to leave. The frightened face assumed a beseeching look.

'Maryam,' Anwar intoned, rather sternly for him, 'think about the aches and hardships of others. About how much needless misery there is in the world. It is filled with poor, lost souls who may never attain what you have attained so far. Throw away your fearful pity for yourself and give completely of all the compassion you can garner.'

Maryam blushed, but this time in shame. She tried to find words of answer, but there were none. She bent forward and kissed the old man's hand.

He watched her march with new resolve across the plain toward the distant city and his heart went out to her. Closing his eyes, he prayed fervently for her safe-keeping.

VI

THE MOST MAGNIFICENT HOUSE IN Bashtahal stands by itself, aloof from its neighbours, pure white and sparkling in the sun near the southern wall of the city. Although surrounded by elegant gardens on three sides, the most exquisite garden by far forms the central court. Fruit trees, palm trees and shady eucalyptus are set off by numerous fountains and delicately designed tableaux of flowers and rocks, all combined to create a fairyland of serenity and coolness even the mid-day sun is powerless to subvert.

Ibrahim ben Yussef emerged from his vaults and counting rooms at the rear of the gardens and locked the strong door. Deep in thought, he strolled through the garden to a space reserved for him between a shade tree and a small fountain; thick Persian carpets covered the fine grass and in turn were heaped with cushions. The man, his mind seemingly light years away, settled himself on the carpet and folded his legs under him. Placing a small cushion over his knees, he placed his hands, palms up, on the cushion to stare at them fixedly. They were clean and white in the etiolated light. For the third time in the last few weeks, he had been stricken with a strange sickness in the counting rooms. His stomach turned over, his brow broke out in drenching perspiration and his hands – even in the interior gloom – had turned deep red, so crimson they looked as though they had been soaked in blood.

His gorge rose and he was forced to spit a bilious mouthful at the base of a young date palm. He wrinkled his nose in disgust; Ibrahim ben Yussef was a fastidious man and found such bodily discharges obnoxious. It was no hallucination, he warned himself, flipping his hands over to search the backs. It really happened!

'Each time a caravan has returned,' he whispered to

himself, 'each time I have counted the profits, the sickness comes over me. It is so bad I can hardly contain myself, the urge to vomit is so strong. As though silver and gold coins had become putrid meat. And the hands...the hands.'

He reached out to a small silver tray near the edge of the fountain and lifted the fine gauze netting to choose a date and pop it into his mouth; savouring it, he selected a small sweetmeat before letting the netting drop back in place. As he chewed slowly and reflectively, he tossed his head back and the cowl of his fine, light and pure white woollen robe fell to his shoulders, disclosing a freshly shaven and deeply tanned, well-formed head. The soft light revealed effectively the first silver strands in his squared and luxurious black beard. His face was a fine one, more Persian than Arabic, the nose thin and straight, the eyebrows highly arched over large, sensitive, soft brown eyes. A handsome man, Ibrahim had not lost his youthful, athletic grace through self-indulgence. Over six foot in height, his large frame was extremely well-muscled and trim. For the richest man south of Bagdad and east of Mecca, he had always been abstemious and rather ascetic, regarding the friends of his youth with sorrow when he saw their thick jowls, fat bellies and dissipated faces. The sorrow was genuine and not laced with self-righteousness.

Ibrahim forced his mind to review the sequences of this new phenomenon which so unnerved him. He easily recalled the first day. On his way to the mosque, the exhausted messenger had nearly collapsed at his feet. Three rich caravans at great risk – in fact, almost given up for lost – had straggled into Bactria. Reassembled, the first was well on its way to Bagdad. Sending one of his household attendants home with the messenger, orders were given to provide food and rest for the weary traveller. Ibrahim had lingered on the steps of the mosque, deep in thought. Just then, she had walked by. It was the first time he saw her. A simple girl, of no consequence, promised to a silversmith's apprentice, she had passed with the regal elegance of a queen. It was as though his mind had been frozen in a block of ice. The very movement of her delicate hand throwing back the sleeve of her garment had excited him beyond the bounds of reality. And then her head had turned, her eyes grazing him. Had she looked at him? Not really. Those unworldly eyes had pierced his mind and soul, looking past him into other worlds beyond his ken. Even after she had passed and turned a corner to be lost from sight, his heart had pounded, cutting short his breath. Fixed in that spot, he had struggled against the force of her no-longer-there presence.

Boldly and improperly, she had passed unveiled and uncovered. The luminous eyes, slate gray with undertones of green, had burned themselves into his conscience. And the hair, full and thick, tossed by her stride and the channelled wind of the roadway, had its own unique quality. The flank of a thoroughbred bay mare, he remembered telling himself. What is this? he demanded of himself. A mere girl, a child passing through the town and you create ecstatic poetry to put the Persian masters to shame? A mudpie! A nothing! If you are so enamoured, buy her! Ten pieces of gold and two healthy camel mares and she is yours…with the mother's quivering blessings.

Buy? a sterner Ibrahim demanded of his wayward self. He struck his thigh with a clenched fist, bearing down with great force. Did you not buy those four cows who waddle and loll endlessly in the harem? Filling themselves with sweetmeats from dawn to dusk? What pleasure is there in that?

His mind roamed over images of the four fat ones. Useless. Barren. He could not bear to touch any of them now. To be trusted, a merchant must have substance and he must conform. Ibrahim keeps an empty harem? His wife died how many years ago? One wife only? Who would ally his fortunes with such an odd fellow? Yes, a harem is for wives. One must conform.

All those many years ago, she had said: Know of my love. It endures as the stars endure. Know, no matter where you are, no matter what you do, I am here. And as long as Allah permits me to draw breath, I want you, I love you, I need you, I desire you. There is no diamond in the world large enough, no mound of gold high enough to force my eyes away from you. Marry as many as you wish, but please, never deny me you.

For all those years, there had been only her. There was room for no other. Three wonderful sons she had borne, blissfully and courageously. The fourth came into the world dead, taking his mother with him. Too many bitter tears spent, Ibrahim, he advised himself, God will know you pity yourself excessively.

She was an angel among women, his Maryam. Strange, that girl of no consequence, the one who had moved him so deeply that first time before the mosque, had also been named Maryam. Stranger still, on that very same day, my stomach turned over and, in the counting rooms, my hands turned blood-red.

A young boy opened the door at the far, front side of the garden and ran rapidly down the twisting, intricate path, leaping gingerly to miss contact with any of the profusely growing flowers. The son of Ibrahim's most trusted cameleer, the unusually bright young Abdullah was learning to read, write and do sums under the willing tutelage of Ibrahim's clerks. The boy knelt in front of the great merchant and touched his forehead to the ground.

'What brings you here, Abdullah?' Ibrahim asked softly. The lively and intelligent boy had filled a place in the man's heart, a place left vacant by his sons who commanded the caravans from the western sea to far Cathay.

'Master, Hassan ibn Mohammed has arrived and begs audience with your grace.'

'Hassan?' Ibrahim muttered to himself. 'Surely, he is still in Bagdad.'

'No Master, he has just arrived in Bashtahal…with forty-three camels, seventeen horses, fifty asses full-laden and more than one hundred raggle-taggle pilgrims bound for Mecca.' Abdullah touched his forehead to the earth with emphatic certainty.

Ibrahim laughed, leaned forward to pat the boy's head and order him to rise.

'Abdullah, you are fast becoming the ears and eyes of

my household. Tell me, do you count everything that moves, stands or sits still?' The boy stammered, his upturned eyes filled with adoration. 'Never mind, tell our worthy guest he is most welcome. Then, run to the kitchen and bid them do honour to our guest and our house.'

As the boy trotted back to the main door, Ibrahim's lips tightened over his teeth. 'Do honour to our guest,' he repeated softly to himself. 'What will he have concealed up his sleeve this time?'

Hassan's caravans travelled the most dangerous routes to India and beyond. His ships plied the Mediterranean to the western shores of North Africa as well as to Spain. He took many risks, did our Hassan, and lost many fortunes. Enough to keep many princes in idle luxury for a lifetime. The fortunes he made far outnumbered the ones he lost...yet it was never enough. The world did not contain an adequate amount of gold and silver to satisfy Hassan. Ibrahim upbraided himself for the uncharitable thoughts. Many would say his own riches would satisfy any number of less greedy men.

After many eloquent formalities and even more elaborate delicacies served by a number of bowing servants, ewers of water and clean cloths were brought. Both men made the ritual ablutions and prayed together when the muezzin's call sounded over the rooftops. The air was then serene; each man infinitely patient. It would be bad manners indeed to press a guest to reveal the true reason for a visit.

'Revered companion of my youth, did you see my sons when you passed through Bagdad?' Ibrahim asked casually as he polished his already spotless nails with a cloth.

'I did indeed, honoured friend,' the portly man answered unctuously. There was nothing about Hassan which did not satisfy him immensely; he preened as he wiped delicately at the short, pointed black beard and closely trimmed moustache. 'I can report that they are well and prospering. The youngest had just arrived from Bactria

49

where he had gone to meet one of your caravans from Cathay. The two eldest will be taking the lion's share on to Byzantium, but the youngest will go to Mecca with the balance. He begs me to inform his father that he looks forward to stopping here on his way back. To pay proper homage and tribute to his worthy father,' Hassan added; from his own glib stock, Ibrahim was quite sure. All is silver, including his tongue.

'I am pleased,' Ibrahim assured his guest, 'and may Allah bless your kindness.' Hassan bowed his head and Ibrahim repayed the formal gesture. 'Tell me bearer of good tidings, how did you find the – uh – climate in Bagdad?'

Hassan placed the cloth on a tray and looked shrewdly at his host. 'Since the death of our beloved caliph, Harun al-Rashid – May Allah grant him every happiness – such a short time ago, the city deteriorates, my friend.'

For a long while, Hassan vented his spleen about the devious politics, schemes and counter-schemes, power struggles and all the ills that could befall the inheritors of Islam's leadership. Then he lapsed into a strange story. Some treasure had been stolen. Was it gold, jewels, silver? Men whispered like women, or the eunuchs in a harem. Rumours slithered through the corridors of power. A captain and his watch of guards had been put to death. One of Hassan's most trusted cameleers remembered a strange sequence of events at the time. Three men buying camels and asses in the middle of the night. Who buys animals in the middle of the night? You'd need your eyes and wits about you in the daytime in a Bagdad market. Before dawn the following night, did the same three men not pass Hassan's driver, mounted on their camels, four asses in tow? The asses were so heavily burdened, they stumbled along. Each bore two enormous jars which practically touched the ground as they shuffled by. What could those jars contain? Possibly the stolen treasure?

Ibrahim smiled indulgently. 'It is only a rumour

that treasure was stolen – or so I inferred before. Maybe it was some of that ghastly oil the Greeks are so fond of.'

'Would you chance leaving the city at that hour...with eight jars of...olive oil? Hassan demanded, looking perturbed. Ibrahim shook his head in negation and laughed softly. 'Allah alone knows how they got past the guards at the gates.'

'Silver, dear Hassan. That is a secret we *all* share with Allah. The bigger the gate, the larger the purse.'

'One has not heard of throats cut among the guardians of the gates,' Hassan huffed pedantically.

'Has *one* heard of the three strange men who arrived here not long ago? My drivers report that two of them lurk about the ravines in the hills to the west. They did not report three camels and four asses, however. But one of the men has been roaming the city, predicting the imminent advent of a new prophet.'

'This man was pointed out to me today...Najmuddin, I believe he is called. A ruffian and cut-throat if ever I saw one.'

'That was my feeling the one time I saw him,' Ibrahim agreed.

'If the authorities hear about him, he'd better watch out for the head on his shoulders. When it comes to heresy, they don't play games.'

'Heresy?' Ibrahim smiled broadly. 'You take them too seriously. They are merely confidence tricksters. They will beat drums, make a lot of noise, produce someone who will foam at the mouth and speak gibberish. And they will interpret the gibberish into fortune-telling. The gullible will produce silver, the rogues will produce nonsensical dreams. The most Najmuddin can lose is a hand.'

'Is this Najmuddin the prophet, or is it one of his henchmen, Ibrahim?' Hassan asked with evident interest. Interest in the mythical treasure, Ibrahim was sure. Dear, dear Hassan...with a fortune perhaps as large as that of the Abassid Caliphate, he would risk his neck for eight huge jars...which could contain olive oil.

51

'As they seem to be camping behind the hillock where the old holy man sits, perhaps they have chosen him. The eternal guardian of the hills.' Ibrahim hoped Hassan would not see through his gentle spoofing.

'Old Anwar? Are you serious?' Hassan's voice choked up. He seemed genuinely shocked.

'Well, if I were Najmuddin, I would certainly want someone who looked like the real article. Who better than a man who reminds one of the descriptions of the ancient Hebrew prophets? Among those strange dervish orders, the man who wears the patched robe is quite often gifted with superhuman powers...or so they say.'

'Supernatural powers?' Hassan scoffed. 'To do what? Get "intoxicated" as they call it? Sing and dance and fall down in a trance? My dear Ibrahim,' he admonished gently.

'Chide me as naïve if you will,' Ibrahim answered humbly. 'There are many things in this world I do not pretend to understand. Strange things, the sort of things a man can see and feel and an unnamed terror sends chills up his spine...yet no matter how he may try, there is no explanation.' Ibrahim paused to measure his guest. The nervous tic in Hassan's cheek and the restlessness of his eyes confirmed the depth of his superstition. 'A man who has been sitting up there for more years than many townspeople can remember...he must have learned some awesome things, Hassan,' Ibrahim continued, lowering his voice to an ominous and mysterious pitch. 'Have you ever encountered him?

Hassan spread his hands out over his knees and concentrated on a small, pink flower near the fountain. His lips parted hesitantly, yet he found it difficult to disgorge the words struggling for freedom. Never had he told anyone about his experience, fearful of verbalizing what must sound like a bad dream, perhaps the invention of a fevered mind. Yet, it was such a burden, one he so desired to share. Was there anyone more likely to understand than his wealthy peer?

Many times Hassan had seen this inscrutable girl:

walking through the streets of Bashtahal, her eyes seldom finding yours but when it seemed they did, you knew they were looking through you. He had seen her leave the city at the first light of dawn more than once. Carrying a gourd of water and a kerchief tied at the corners, she walked with the air of a princess from some other world, never seeming to hear the ribald suggestions of caravan guards and drivers. Once he had seen her standing mutely before the hillock where the old holy man sat.

On his last journey from Bagdad, he had pressed on through the final night, fearful that the beasts were overly tired and could not endure one more day. At the end of the caravan, Hassan did not pass the hillock until the first pink glimmers began to illuminate the eastern sky. Dimly limned above, was the figure of a woman kneeling before the immobile Anwar. Her veil was cast aside and her cowl thrown back. Even in that sparse light, he would have known her anywhere. Hair like the flank of a fine bay mare.

The description, echoing his own earlier thoughts word for word, made Ibrahim stiffen involuntarily. The muscles of his abdomen tightened painfully. A nobody? The intended of an apprentice no one had noticed but himself? His teeth grated at the sound of ill-suppressed lust in Hassan's voice.

The thirsty, exhausted camel balked and complained, but Hassan held him steady, unable to leave the scene on the western skyline. As he squinted, the holy man's head turned slowly. Hassan knew he was being scrutinized mercilessly. Even though the eyes were too far away to be seen at all, he felt them bore into his very soul. He lost track of time; the sounds of the camel bells were lost; in truth, time stood still. He was suspended in a free-standing moment which attached itself to eternity. How, he did not know, but he was aware of being addressed. Did the soft sounds themselves cover that distance – surely a gusty shout would be needed?

'Will you drive all those camels through the eye of a needle, worthy Hassan?' The whispered words were so clear the old man's mouth would have to be right next to his ear to effect it. Hassan felt so giddy, he nearly slipped from the saddle.

'Jesus, the saint and prophet of the Christians – he whom we call Isa ben Maryam – said it would be easier to drive a camel through the eye of a needle than for a rich man to gain the kingdom of heaven. What about you, Hassan? Will you drive all those camels, laden with your riches, through the eye of a needle?'

There was no detectable malice in the question, rather a concerned pity; yet Hassan was so startled he imagined himself struck dumb. The old man knew his name...in the half-dark...from that distance! Anwar gently directed him to look at his hands.

Even before the last words were spoken, a lightning premonition caused Ibrahim to bury his own hands under his thighs. No sooner had he done so, he saw a telltale red-dening tinging his guest's fingers. Ibrahim's wayward stomach began to betray him.

'Would you believe,' whispered the agonized Hassan, 'when I did look, they had turned bright scarlet? I swore blood was dripping from them, down the side of my camel to splash upon the thirsty sand. Never before or since have I been gripped by such a singular terror.'

With a slow resigned gesture, Hassan held out his hands to inspect them. They were the normal, deeply tan-ned hands of a traveller. Feeling faint, Ibrahim spread his own hidden hands to help steady himself.

'He told me I was seeing the blood of countless camels I had driven to death by exhaustion and greed,' Hassan continued, his voice reflective and philosophical. 'The blood of guards and drivers who had battled brigands to protect my precious goods. The blood of the poor, meticulously exacted to fill my coffers.'

'You are over-reacting, honoured friend,' Ibrahim placated with less than the conviction required. 'After all, think of the conditions. In that light, at that time of day, nearly falling from your saddle with weariness...?'

'Ibrahim, I too have said all those words to myself. I

saw what I saw and I *know* I saw what I saw. I cannot explain it away. When I could no longer hear his voice, I finally found the strength to look at him once more. That girl was on her feet, one hand covering her mouth. She was staring at me and suddenly I could see her clearly, as though standing in front of me. She was staring at my hands! Staring at them with a look of loathing unlike anything I have ever seen.'

'Has it...' Ibrahim paused, pressing his thighs down on his hands...'have your hands ever looked that way again?'

Hassan folded his hands complacently across his expansive paunch. Ibrahim predicted the lie before the words were spoken: 'No, only that one time.'

Although the uneasy feeling would not leave him, as a good host, Ibrahim knew he should start leading the conversation away from the depressing subject. Hassan had not come to him to discuss old Anwar.

'Well, then, what will you do?' he asked with a teasing smile, 'give your riches to the poor and take up the begging bowl? Become a devout fakir yourself?'

With a pained expression, Hassan looked skyward as though asking Allah's guidance.

In less than an hour, Hassan arrived, verbally, at the purpose of his visit. A marvellous opportunity had presented itself. A chance to make more profits in less time than anyone would believe. Unfortunately, he didn't have the time to buy the one hundred extra camels he would need...and need them by the end of the week he would, or the deal would escape his clutches. One hundred of the finest camels available. Where would he find them – all of them – save right here, in the herds of his best and truest friend?

Any and every beast lost on the hazardous journey would be replaced. Ibrahim would enjoy five percent of the profits, no questions asked. And there would be a bonus of twenty-five young camels to boot. Five months was all Hassan needed.

His nerves still on edge about his own hands and

Hassan's, Ibrahim dearly wished he could agree then and there and end the visit. Just say yes and have done with it. That would be like having an empty harem. An affront of the worst kind. No, the time-honoured bargaining must proceed. Thirty camels would but cover the future losses of use; a camel safely returned could be a spent camel. And what about the huge losses in profit he would suffer through five whole months when one hundred of his best camels were far away? Ten percent of the profits was the absolute minimum that a man could accept. Of course, both men knew that seven and one-half percent would be the ritually preordained figure. And twenty-five camels. Just as surely, as a special token of his esteem, Hassan would insist that his friend accept a truly wondrous stallion of exceptionally fine breeding.

VII

ANWAR LISTENED TO THE WIND soughing across the sandy plain below and coursing up the hills behind him: trying to catch the sun and cool it before it dropped below the highest peaks. It will cool soon enough, he reminded the nervous wind. Opening his eyes to greet the evening, he absorbed the deepening blue over the city, its first fires beginning to twinkle. In his mind, he retained still the vision of the two men seated in the cool garden. Two rich and powerful men, so alike and yet so totally different.

Ibrahim, he mused, has great strength and is not tied to his fortune. Hassan lives for nothing else. The tall man is shamed by what he sees in his hands, the short, fat one entertains with his story. He is unabashed, but not without fury and hatred. Everything for Hassan is external...and linear. He would not come back here to ask why. Ibrahim? He might be here before the night ends, and he will demand an answer. Will he be ready to accept the answer? He broods about his life and questions much. Fifty years on this earth have given him wealth and little else, save memories. How differently each views the world. Hassan sees Maryam and only lust possesses him. There is that which is pure and noble in Ibrahim.

'Anwar!' A harsh and rasping voice challenged the evening's stillness. The old man's head turned slowly; with innocent and unperturbed eyes, he took in the long, slender, knock-kneed shape of Najmuddin. Giving no sign of recognition, he simply waited.

With four long strides, Najmuddin closed the space between them. At the very edge of Anwar's carpets, he collapsed like a wooden-jointed toy, his ankles crossed and his chin resting on his bony knees. His friendly smile reminded Anwar of a grinning crocodile.

'Anwar, it is time we had a serious chat…oh, by the way, I am called Najmuddin.' The twisted smile still playing indolently with his lips, the tall man waited. Anwar did not respond. Clearing his throat, Najmuddin continued: 'Tomorrow night you will be famous. It will mark the greatest triumph in your long and worthy life. Tomorrow night, you will become a great prophet…what do you think of that?'

'There is but one prophet,' Anwar answered disinterestedly, 'and he was the last prophet. I have no intention of becoming a heretic, thank you.'

'We do not intend to claim you are a prophet, we are not so foolish. Hint at it, yes. You will be merely the great saint and sage of this era. An oracle, a man of miracles.'

'And who will make me all these wondrous things, you?' Anwar closed his eyes.

'*We* will, that's who,' Najmuddin hissed, a little less pleasantly, 'Najmuddin and his helpers, Mirza and Hakim. Very soon now, my helpers will be boring a small hole behind you and passing up some copper strands from the cavern below. When we have arranged everything, you will be surrounded by magical lights. The glow surrounding you will baffle the people, create terror and wonder in their hearts. They will offer up their questions and problems. Your name means light, and what light they will see! Surrounded by that heavenly glow, you will tell them what they wish to know.'

'Why should I do that?' the old man asked blandly.

'Because they will pay so much silver just to hear you, Anwar, that is why.' Najmuddin's teeth glistened in the dark. 'Everyone will pay gladly, and lots will be drawn. Only a few lucky ones will be chosen each evening. Yes,' he savoured the thought, 'they will pay over and over. Silver will flow like water from a fountain.'

'It is apparent that you love silver,' Anwar explained patiently. 'What may not be so apparent is: *I* have no use for it.'

'Of course not, we know that,' Najmuddin edged closer. 'It would be crass of us to think otherwise. Just the

58

same, we will set a small amount aside for you. The important thing is, you will become *famous*. Soon, people from as far away as India and Spain will be travelling to consult *you*. You will be honoured and respected as the *greatest* holy man of the age.'

'Thank you very much for the offer,' Anwar replied graciously, 'but I don't want that either.' He shifted his gaze to the evening star twinkling over the city.

'I have been very patient with you, you cantankerous old fool, and patience is not my strongest virtue. Try me no further.' Najmuddin slid his right hand inside the folds of his robe and withdrew a small dagger in a leather sheath. With a flick of his wrist, the sheath flew off to reveal the slightly curved blade.

'Look, Anwar,' Najmuddin muttered, pulling a hair from his beard. Holding it between thumb and forefinger, he raised the hand and held it near the old man's face. With a deft movement, he drew the blade across the hair just above his thumbnail. It sheared the hair neatly.

'An excellent dagger, there is no doubt,' Anwar admitted. 'Unfortunately, I have no use for it, but thank you just the same.'

'I came here tonight to address a great seer, not a silly old fool, so stop playing games with me!' Najmuddin placed the needle-sharp point of the dagger against Anwar's knee joint and pressed down. The knee did not yield and Anwar seemed totally uninterested. Najmuddin shifted his weight and kneeled in front of the old man, pressing the handle with both hands.

Without turning his head to look, Anwar slid a hand along his leg and touched the blade lightly with his finger. As though struck by lightning, Najmuddin's body was lifted and thrown backwards, his arms and legs flailing the air helplessly. He landed a few paces away, sprawled on his back, the thud knocking the breath from his body.

Najmuddin gasped, the breath whistling in his throat as he scrambled to his feet, crouching low to regard Anwar with frightened eyes, his mouth agape. Anwar was watching the dagger with total fascination as it sank down until the hilt touched his knee. The old man's hands were resting in his lap. He shrugged and reached down to lift the knife. Holding it between thumb and forefinger, as Najmuddin had held the hair from his beard, Anwar gazed at the steel of the blade. It had rolled up into a tight coil under the hilt. Anwar threw the useless instrument on the ground at Najmuddin's feet.

'You are very persuasive, Najmuddin,' Anwar noted without guile. 'Obviously, your scheme could not succeed without me. Keep that in mind should you get carried away again. For that reason – namely that I will have to do almost all the work – you and your two assistants will receive fifteen percent of the proceeds...'

'What!' Najmuddin's mouth worked recklessly, trying to form more words, but Anwar's quiet, determined voice cut him off.

'Yes, that seems reasonable enough...you realize, I could pay you normal wages, so do not complain about your share. Yes, and each night, the money will be counted in front of me. My share will be stored in a spot I shall designate below – against the cavern wall farthest from your new entrance. Any questions?'

Outrage, mayhem and terror fought for possession of the dumbstruck man. His mouth worked, but no sounds issued forth.

'You may be wondering why I seem so naïve as to believe you could be trusted to follow my instructions ...or not to steal the silver when the amount became too tempting to resist. The answer to that is quite simple.' Anwar leaned forward, tilting his head to one side and pressing the palms of his hands against the ground in front of his legs.

'The answer to what?' Najmuddin asked stupidly, his dazed mind finding his thickened tongue at last.

'Mirza and Hakim will give you that answer...any moment now,' Anwar informed him in a voice that sounded most strange to the still quaking man.

A moment later, first one scream, followed by another and louder one, reached the hilltop. The two men working in the cavern ran out into the night, screaming at the tops of their lungs.

'Help, help, Allah protect us,' Mirza's terrified voice filled the night.

Najmuddin ran to the edge of the hillock and stared down. His two companions were running toward the ravine as though the devil himself was on their heels. He shouted imperiously, but they kept running.

'What did you do to them?' he cried, turning on Anwar. As he did a sound rose from below that was so distinct he could not confuse it with any other on earth.

'I?' Anwar asked. 'I did nothing. I presume you can identify that sound, Najmuddin.'

'Snakes!' Najmuddin wheezed. His knees could be heard clashing together.

'Yes, serpents to be sure. Rather large vipers...formidable asps, to be exact. It is really their cavern. However, if they are not disturbed or...annoyed, they will not harm you. Are you afraid of them, Najmuddin?' Anwar knew very well that snakes terrified the tall man beyond reason.

'It's a trick, an illusion, some form of black magic, you old devil,' Najmuddin spluttered. The hissing became louder.

'If you really think so, please go down and look. But do be careful. Something has upset them. Normally, I have no problem with them.'

'No, thank you.' Najmuddin drew closer, his footsteps uncertain and hesitating. 'Anwar...can you control them?' he whimpered.

'No, but you can. Just be honest and straightforward. They always seem to know when some evil thought invades the peace. Now, you had better go after your companions...' Anwar held up a hand to draw Najmuddin's attention. The hissing could no longer be heard. 'It is safe now, they can continue their work without fear. Oh, yes, tell them they have to bore no holes... there is one already.'

'A hole? One from below to here? One we can push the copper strands through?'

'Of course,' Anwar smiled benignly. 'Your coming was foretold a long time ago. Go, catch up with your companions, Najmuddin.'

The old man turned his head to watch the rattled man scramble down the side of the hill with all the grace of an intoxicated crab. Shaking his head, he reflected on the jars. They will be distressed indeed when they find them useless. Anwar had made an astral voyage to Bagdad. The ancient alchemist had greeted the projected holy man with great warmth. Yes, he had admitted, a Djinn had visited him, one he recognized as Hutti, by name. He was also interested in the jars and if they would function. No, he had been told, they lacked ingredients of a very involved nature. A rather deep knowledge of chemical actions and reactions was needed. Before Anwar left, he had been able to help the alchemist. Not that he had solved his final problem…the alchemist had already done that; it was merely that he had not seen the solution in its true light. The man's transcendental joy had warmed Anwar's heart.

A small whorl of dust began forming to the old man's side, creating a minute spout of rising sand. With a look of long-suffering resignation, he waited for the almost indiscernable Pop! his ears were attuned to. Even if one of their days is roughly equivalent to one of our years, he thought, they certainly do waste their time like children.

'Well, old friend,' the soft, insinuating voice whispered in his ear, 'I hear you are about to become the new prophet. Are you good at making world-shaking prophesies?'

'If not,' Anwar answered dully, 'I am sure you are. And you *are* here just to offer me your fantastic services. Perhaps you are also an alchemical genius?'

Hawwaz didn't answer the provocative question; his mind was intent on the key word. What had the old man up his sleeve concerning alchemists? The meddling old fool seemed to know everything.

'If you are,' Anwar continued with no enthusiasm, 'you might be of great use to that man Najmuddin, the one who dreamed up this prophet business.'

'Why is that?' Hawwaz asked guardedly.

'A very good friend of mine assures me his magic jars are useless. They have no lightning stored in them. On the other hand, you are something of an expert with lightning...'

'Who told you that? About the jars, I mean?' Hawwaz demanded testily.

'Oh, a friend in Bagdad...'

'So, you've been flitting over there too, have you? Our psychic traveller has been meddling again...'

'I wouldn't say that,' Anwar rebuked him mildly. 'After all, I was invited in a sense...which is more than I can say for a certain friend of yours who was interested in the mystery of the jars.'

'Ah-ha! One day, that inquisitive nose of yours will get you into very deep trouble. Hutti had a good reason for going. Your "friend" needs him very badly.'

'On the contrary, my friend needs no one now. He has completed his life work. If I'm not mistaken, like all good alchemists, he has simply vanished. Your colleague will never find him.'

'That's a lie! He is committed to Hutti, his soul is no longer his own.' Hawwaz was furious and gusts of wind blew sand all over the hillock.

'His soul is purified and belongs to no one,' Anwar pronounced with conviction. 'Your conniving partner may have promised him something, but that's as far as it went. No, there is no bond there.'

'Because of *you*! You meddled and stole him away,' Hawwaz accused.

'Your clan is hardly in a position to call others meddlers. And I don't know why you should be so furious...after all, your good friend would be insufferable once he had his hands on a soul like that. He could make you do anything. Which reminds me, what did you have to promise him in return for his fact-finding visit to Bagdad?'

Anwar felt the air vibrate as the Djinn bent every effort to control his temper. When the air currents stopped humming and the sand settled, the old man chuckled softly.

'Knowing your elder conspirator,' Anwar continued with good humour, 'I am sure he has a new scheme to capture one of your females. And that will terminate in the usual fiasco. With both of you torn limb from limb, it will be quite peaceful for a while.'

'You think you know everything, don't you?' Hawwaz snarled.

'Knowing the obvious is no knowledge at all,' the old man reckoned serenely.

'Where's your little friend, Maryam, Anwar? She hasn't been here lately,' Hawwaz insinuated.

'You know very well she was here this morning. You thought you were very clever with that disgusting performance of yours. Not that clever, however.'

'Perhaps next time I will be. And when I am, I'll have you just where I want you.'

Anwar didn't answer. In the stillness, they both heard the scraping of sandals and the sound of metal being bounced off the ground.

'What's that?' Hawwaz's neck extended like a giraffe's and he swept the ground behind the hillock with his eyes.

'Najmuddin and his helpers. They are bringing the copper strands to erect their magical light display…which won't work,' Anwar added with a small cough. 'Perhaps you can help them. They would be delighted.'

'Help them what? Fill those jars with lightning?'

'Either that or keep the serpents at bay,' Anwar offered.

'Snakes? Snakes?' Hawwaz squeaked.

'You *are* repetitious…yes, snakes.' As the old man said the word, a hissing from below reached them.

The wind buffeted Anwar, then all was calm again; Hawwaz was gone.

'I wonder why so many people deplore snakes?' he asked himself. Shrugging his shoulders, he began folding himself inwardly. It was time to leave again; he calculated quickly how long it would take Najmuddin and company to prepare their structure, then slipped out through the tunnel he had projected.

VIII

Maryam shivered and drew even closer to the two old women with whom she shared a sleeping rug. All day long they had trudged after the caravan, in the midst of a mob of ill-tempered pilgrims. Cowl drawn down over her head and veils tightly wound about nose and mouth, the girl had tried to make herself identical with the two old widows. Yet, each time she looked up, the two rear guard camel-drivers had leered at her. Somehow they detected she was not one more old woman.

Satisfied that she was part of one large and misshapen lump of humanity, she began to relax. With her face resting on her forearm, she felt the waves of exhaustion passing over her, her bones throbbing in response. Two brief stops during the day and then on into the night to find these few scrubby trees and a pool of sulphurous water. The march to Medina stretched out endlessly before her bleary eyes.

A soft, sliding sound whispered over the sand, then another. The tired girl was alert immediately, fighting off sleep. Turning very slowly and inconspicuously, she edged to one side, her legs drawn up under her, arms braced to spring to her feet. It must be those camel-drivers, she told herself, sniffing her out like two hungry wolves.

Another slithering sound was cut off abruptly, followed by a loud thud and the pained wheezing of violently exhaled breath. More thuds followed, then all was quiet again. Maryam had rolled over and over, away from the sound, before bounding up to crouch low over her knees, arms extended to ward off an attacker. Nothing materialized. Two frightened camels struggled to rise, then sank back as though pressed to the ground by a giant, invisible hand. The soft Arrgghh! of a fretting camel reached her. Then, from behind her, someone called her name. Maryam whirled. Anwar stood there, looking extraordinarily luminous in the night, his hand extended toward her. An aura of many colours pulsated from his form.

Maryam ran to him, her arms extended. She knew he had caught her in powerful arms, yet the arms seemed insubstantial. Her feet left the ground and her vision blurred; no, it wasn't that, Anwar had covered her eyes. But the wind screeched unmercifully and she felt herself pounded by it so hard that she buried her face in Anwar's shoulder. But was there a shoulder? She wondered, terrified by the horrific noises and the eerie sense of flying…yes, actually flying at blinding speed.

It all stopped as abruptly as it had started. When she opened her eyes and raised her head, she saw she was standing in the middle of a narrow street, in a town or city…but where? Anwar answered her question, but she didn't hear actual words. They were in Medina. For many reasons, it would not have been safe to allow her to continue with the caravan. Time was contracting, dangers increasing.

She felt her hand being drawn forward and she followed Anwar's none-too-distinct shape; he pushed open a door and they entered a small house. At the end of a corridor, he once more pushed a door open and they entered a sleeping chamber. Two low couches stood side by side. In one of them, a girl with long raven hair slept. A light coverlet had been kicked away partially and one leg hung over the side of the couch. The black hair covered the girl's shoulders and chest, but one breast was exposed. Anwar bent over, settled the disturbed leg on the couch and covered the girl.

'This is Fatima,' she heard Anwar's voice in her mind. 'She is expecting you and your place has been prepared,' he pointed to the empty couch with its folded coverlet. 'Together, you will be equal to the next stage of your voyage. Love her with all your heart, Maryam.'

'But…but…' she began to whisper in panic. Before she could utter another sound, Anwar was no longer there.

By the time Maryam's words ceased, Anwar was pressed into the flank of a camel near the spot where he had found the girl. Two camel-drivers were bent double, sitting on the sand and holding their assaulted midriffs. As much as he hated violence, Anwar knew had he not confused the men and caused them to attack each other unwittingly, they would have pounced on Maryam and dragged her away.

The premonition which had brought him back to the caravanserai so speedily suddenly became more apparent. Drawing himself into the deep shadow of the unaware camel, he peered intently at the hollow in the sand where Maryam had been lying. A tiny eddy bubbled in one spot, then began criss-crossing the area with some obvious intent. Anwar heard a soft snuffling. The beam of a star filled the hollow and Anwar made out a vague, tiny figure, no taller than the first two joints of a man's finger.

The old man bent over and placed one hand over the nearest, semi-conscious cameleer's mouth, the other squarely on his solar plexus and lifted the man to his feet with a powerful jerk. The startled man felt the pain leave his midriff; he was standing with no effort. But he could neither move nor utter a sound. Vaguely, he knew there was someone there, but did not see Anwar bend over and pick up a small urn which had been turned over in the scuffle. Made of brass, it contained a tight lead stopper. Anwar placed this in the cameleer's hand and extended his arm, the finger pointing to the tiny form searching the sand in the hollow.

Directed by the old man's thought, the driver inched forward on his hands and knees, the stopper of the urn caught in his teeth. With the cunning of a fox and the speed of a mongoose, he sprang forward and clamped the urn down. Forcing his free hand under the sand, he plugged the stopper into the container's neck and leapt to his feet. He turned and held the urn toward Anwar's approaching figure. The urn vibrated wildly, nearly tearing itself free of the restraining hands. Anwar reached into the pouch around his neck and withdrew a ring, a heavy silver one

67

with a design cut into the flat, upper surface. Anwar pressed this down on top of the stopper and held it there for a few seconds while smoke curled up around his hand. When he removed the ring, a six-pointed star was burned into the stopper. When the ring of Solomon was safely back in its pouch, Anwar beamed more information into the driver's mind. His eyes became so large with delight, Anwar had to press a calming hand down on his shoulder to keep him from shouting and jumping about. Dumbstruck, the driver's companion watched the shadow play with no comprehension, his mouth agape as Anwar disappeared. The first driver ran to his friend and held out the urn, whispering the secret of its contents. The second driver became jubilant with unrestrained greed.

Back in his body, Anwar's face became animate again, filled with a sad, sweet smile. Poor, foolish Hawwaz. How obvious that he would trail Maryam. When he blew himself up to the size of a mountain, no light on earth would easily detect him. But in the minute size he chose to search the sands where Maryam had been, he was vulnerable to a beam of starlight. Since the earliest times, children had been told stories about Djinni captured in jars and oil lamps, vessels and urns, their great powers locked in with them. Had any one of them been caught as easily as Hawwaz...by two slow-witted drivers? King Solomon, yes. One of the truly great magicians, the master of his age, he was reputed to be a peerless Djinn-catcher. Anwar touched the pouch containing Solomon's ring with reverence and deep respect.

Anwar sighed and bowed his head. Nights like this took a lot out of him. Projecting himself was no great effort, but having to transport physical bodies was debilitating. He hoped Maryam and Fatima would reach Mecca with no further intervention on his part. The holy city of Islam seemed to have a dampening effect on even the powers of Djinni. Yes, soon Hutti would be searching for his friend. God grant he did not find him too rapidly. Then there was Ibrahim. He might easily arrive before the new day. Stay here and sleep, you old fool, he told himself.

Fatima woke to find a girl sitting on the pallet next to hers; her legs were drawn up and her face rested on her knees, arms wrapped about her shins. The raven-haired girl blinked, assuring herself she was awake. Through the fever and after, so many times dreams were like reality and the daily routine of the household like a vague dream. Particularly the visits of her guardian angel, the saintly personification of a grandfather who cured her illness and told her many things. Including the name of this new dream with auburn hair sitting on the next couch.

A shudder passed over the bent shoulders and a soft sigh broke the stillness. No dream, Fatima corrected herself. She reached over and touched the other girl's arm. A startled rush of breath cut off the sigh and Maryam bolted halfway to her feet, only to fall backward, nearly losing her balance. Fatima tightened her grip on the arm, helping Maryam to right herself. They looked into each other's eyes for a few moments, then each was overcome with a fit of laughter.

In less than an hour, Maryam had told Fatima about her journey. She watched the dark-haired girl's amazed eyes when she got to the part about Anwar spiriting her from the caravanserai to the room in which they sat. Fatima gazed intently at the haggard face and then touched Maryam's bruised and swollen feet. Without a word, she rose and took two light woollen robes from pegs fixed to the wall. Silencing Maryam's protests, she removed the girl's heavy travelling garment and the lighter one she wore underneath. When they had both donned the thin, white robes, Fatima took Maryam's hand and led her silently throught the dark house.

At the far end of the expansive garden, a corner of the wall was hidden behind trellises which were covered in flowering vines. Behind the trellises, a large stone cistern rested on a high, wooden platform. A low bench with ewers, basins and a large water dipper was fixed to the wooden platform. Fatima took off her robe and threw it across the vine-laden trellis behind the bench; she whispered to Maryam to do the same, then helped the girl step up onto the bench. Dipping water into the largest basin, Fatima found a fresh cloth among the vines and began lathering Maryam's body, scooping water from the basin to rinse her down. Putting a smaller basin on the ground, she sat Maryam on the bench and made her lean forward. Soon, over Maryam's protests, her feet were soaking in the water still warm from the day's sunshine and Fatima was vigorously washing the thick, curly auburn hair. When she was satisfied, Fatima ducked around the trellises and returned with two large sheets of thick cotton cloth. One she wrapped about Maryam's head like a turban, and with the other began drying her body. She rubbed and rubbed with the care of a master smith burnishing gold. And the skin was golden, she thought, an almond-gold with rosy blushes here and there.

When Maryam was dry and wrapped in the sheet, Fatima mounted the bench and began dousing her own body with cascades of water. When she stepped down, Maryam removed the sheet from her own body and began drying her friend's. As she did, Fatima unbound the other large cloth and rubbed the wet, curly hair.

With a warning finger pressed to her lips, Fatima gathered up the two robes in one hand and took Maryam's arm with the other. Leading the startled girl naked across the garden, Fatima giggled and whispered about the uproar if her family saw the pair of them walking so outrageously through the moonlight. When they arrived back in Fatima's room, neither could suppress the fits of silent laughter. They pushed the two couches together and collapsed, side by side.

When Maryam's laughter finally subsided in a long sigh, Fatima covered them both with one of the coverlets and put her arm around Maryam's neck, settling the girl's head on her own shoulder. Holding her new-found friend close to her, Fatima listened to the soft words pouring into her ear. Bashtahal sounded rather primitive, but the girl's hesitant account of the young man named Ali was stranger still. Although she had no direct experience of men herself, it seemed so odd that Maryam should be that terrified about their bodies. Could that *thing* really seem like a battering ram, an instrument of such horrifying dimensions, more frightful than a snake? Being very sensitive, Fatima found she could put herself in Maryam's place.

What disturbed Maryam more than anything was her last visit to Anwar. Her dream of Ali attacking her with a ramrod the size of a ship's mast was bad enough. She remembered she had been close to Anwar, her heart appealing for his help and the next thing...she was stretched out in front of him. She had been unconscious. But something had happened. A presentiment that something very real had attacked her, something possibly more frightening than any of her ludicrous dreams. Then there was the other side; Maryam buried her face in Fatima's neck and shuddered. Deftly, Fatima coaxed, telling her that unless they told each other everything, they would not be able to forge mutual defences. Maryam said it was a sensation of such deliciousness, such overwhelming bliss almost realized, she could think of no way to describe it since she had nothing with which it could be compared.

Fatima asked simply and straightforwardly where this sensation had been felt. She raised herself, freeing her arm to lean on the elbow and look down at the blushing face next to her. Smiling, she shook her head and leaned forward to kiss the closed eyelids and the bridge of the small, delicate nose. Again, she asked: where? Shyly Maryam's hand moved down until it hovered just over her neatly shaved mons veneris. It throbbed inside and out, it had lasted all the day, following her like an independent presence, a sensation with a life of its own.

Had she examined herself, Fatima wondered? Perhaps there was something there. Maryam sat bolt upright, reaching for the heavy robe Fatima had dumped at the end of the other couch. She took out the pouch and handed it to Fatima. Shyly, she described the contents and its use. Anwar said they were to be absolutely scrupulous, never

71

to alter the routine. Fatima agreed that they must place implicit trust in their mentor. But she could not define why Maryam's story had touched such a responsive chord in herself. She told Maryam about her own vague dream of being in another world where she experienced…or thought she did…sensations of just such an overpowering intensity. Then suddenly, she was standing in the alley with Anwar…just as Maryam had a bit earlier. She remembered coming into the house with him and finding her own body on the bed. The next thing she knew, Anwar was taking the fever away from her.

They talked on about Anwar's teachings; Maryam would have to transmit so much over a short period of time. Each knew the other was avoiding the one topic they could not yet face. Yet, when they arrived at Mecca, face it they must. Although unspoken, the dread passed from one to the other, communicating itself with as much force as words could create. Impulsively, they threw their arms about each other, pressing themselves close together to keep the world at bay for as long as possible. Lips pressed to ears, they murmered and whispered, trying to comfort each other. Neither was aware of how their bodies had become entwined, legs circling and dividing legs, arms squeezing backs, hands fretfully stroking. Not till each realized with a sense of shock that bodies were becoming drenched in a headlong release of passion did each draw back, self-consciously. Maryam sobbed with a sudden sense of abandonment and Fatima reached out, pulling her close again.

Thighs and bodies swimming in love, breaths coming ever faster, they could no longer control the haunted sounds of longing and pleasure. When the dizzying moment came, at exactly the same second for each, their mouths devoured each other, tongues fiercely probing to cut off the screams of delight they felt.

With motherly devotion, Fatima dried Maryam's body with her light robe. Maryam tried to return the favour, but Fatima said she would dry in the night air soon enough, that poor Maryam must be exhausted. They argued about which was worse, marching across a desert, or suffering the enervation of a terrible fever. Voices stilled and arms and legs entwined once more, they began to drift toward sleep when Fatima remembered the pouch.

Maryam sat up abruptly. 'Would you prefer me to leave while you do it?' she asked.

'Are you serious?' Fatima moved closer, resting on her elbow. She reached up and cupped Maryam's breast in her hand, guiding it toward her. Gently, she took the nipple between her lips and ran her tongue over it. Maryam gasped and clutched the back of her friend's head pressing her closer. She could not control her moans. Fatima lifted herself higher and kissed Maryam's mouth, then settled back on the couch.

'I want you to do it for me,' Fatima said, holding the pouch up. Maryam gasped. 'You've done it before, Maryam, you know how. Please?' The plea was so strong, so vibrant and passionate, Maryam began to tremble visibly.

With nervous fingers and quaking heart, Maryam undid the pouch and rolled the cloth ball out on her palm. With her lip caught between her teeth, she watched Fatima's thighs part, her knees move upward.

'Don't be afraid, beloved sister,' Fatima whispered. 'As a pledge of love and friendship, each month we will do this for each other.'

Maryam drew her knees under her and moved down on the couch. Trembling, she parted the smooth lips and found the entrance. It is so soft and wet, she thought absently, wondering at how easily the small sphere moved up the passage. She smelled the heady warmth of Fatima as she withdrew her fingers. In a delirium that surrounded her and controlled her actions suddenly, she leaned forward and pressed her lips against the raised knee. She no longer argued, she no longer pondered. Her lips wanted the knee, her tongue wanted everything. Slowly her head sank down, gathering the skin of the thigh in her mouth, feeling the dampness against her cheek, then her nose. It was so soft and tender, so sweet and musky, strong and animal and blended with attar of roses; delicate to the lips, sweet to the tongue. Gathering it willingly to her, she exulted: it is not frightening, but gentle and loving, kissing me in return. She hardly heard the choked gasps, the groans and fluttering cries of ecstasy above her. Reaching under her friend, she clasped the buttocks in both hands, endeavouring to keep Fatima from flying off the bed. She felt strong hands grasp her face, lovingly pressing it closer still.

Far across the desert to the east, a camel bleated its rude *Arrggh!* into the night. The sleeping driver, holding a brass urn closely clasped to his bosom, stirred at the sound. Inside the urn, Hawwaz beat furiously and impotently against the walls of his prison.

IX

IN THE WEEKS SINCE HIS meeting with Anwar, Ibrahim had indeed changed in many ways. His flight into poverty now seemed the least of them. He remembered with amusement how that in itself had been the major stumbling block. How could one give away everything he owned? The sheer physical impossibility of it had overwhelmed him. Yet, now it was all gone as though it had happened overnight.

The tall, gaunt man leaned forward and stirred the small fire, adding a few spare sticks to the embers. The empty oasis, its fringe of palms and scrub growth surrounding the water hole, was quiet and peaceful. Obviously, from all the signs, no caravan had passed in days. Stars filled the sky and he could still make out the glow of the moon sinking into the desert beyond the trees. Anwar said such solitude was good for the soul...a man could hardly avoid looking inside himself. He leaned back against the trunk of a huge palm tree and closed his eyes.

Visions of his servants, retainers, guards and drivers flickered through his mind like ghosts who had all but lost both names and features. Poor Abdullah had shed so many tears; at one moment of sorrow and abandonment, the next a furious blend of frustration and incomprehension. All the rest had gladly accepted their good fortune without question. If the great merchant chose to give away all he possessed for the life of a wandering fakir, surely that was a good thing in the sight of God. So many fine beasts and so much money! Why complain about the master's decision? Not Abdullah. The boy had calculated everything. What had he said? One hundred talents, nearly one million golden dinars...yes, Abdullah, expressed in silver, an impossible sum. The boy had stared for hours at his own huge pouch of silver and gold coins. He seemed torn in half; in unburdening himself, had he put an unfair burden on the young lad? He was different than all the rest. He felt the burden immediately…and feeling it, had pondered for days on end why his revered master had done what he had done.

Realizing the disturbing train of thoughts he had inadvertantly put into motion, Ibrahim had taken the boy into his confidence. He described the warning he had read in his own hands. How he had gone to confront Anwar after hearing Hassan's story. Anwar was right: Ibrahim's life was an empty one and it had not been warmed by gold. When the meeting ended Ibrahim had much to think about. Even stranger, he began to realize that everything Anwar said had already been said without words in his own heart. He had even asked Anwar if finding his own soul would make him happy. Anwar smiled before answering. At least, he said, you won't be able to upbraid yourself for never having tried. Really, what could be worse, what could make him more unhappy than that? To reach an end without ever having found the beginning.

The boy wanted to come with him, for Ibrahim had expressed what he himself had never been able to. It took great patience and gentle explanation to convince Abdullah that his former master was in no position to undertake a disciple. Until we know what perfection is, how can we transmit it to others? At last, he had convinced Abdullah to visit Anwar. All proper paths in life are the same, yet they diverge. Anwar could tell him what Ibrahim never could.

It took even longer to persuade Abdullah that it was indeed possible to approach Anwar. True, Najmuddin was always there and hundreds of people arrived daily to consult the sage. But in the hour before dawn, Najmuddin and his men slept. If Abdullah approached the old man, he would speak to him. To put the boy's mind at ease and break some of the tension, he had told him a story Anwar had related. It was an object lesson about the dangers of greed; perhaps one day it would become an important teaching story.

It seemed there was a Djinn who recently had been furious with Anwar. The Djinn's friend had been captured – with some help from Anwar – and the volatile Djinn suspected as much. For his own reasons – which had to do with two girls arriving safely in Mecca – Anwar took his time in telling the Djinn where his friend could be found. The Djinn threatened everything imaginable, he shook the hilltop and rattled the mountains. He frightened Najmuddin and his cohorts out of their wits. When the old man was finally sure that the girls were safely arrived, he informed the Djinn about the camel drivers who had captured his friend. It is a well-known fact that the holy city of Mecca, the home of the sacred black stone of Abraham, has an inhibiting effect on such as Djinni. Or so it is believed by the faithful.

The Djinn located the caravan with little trouble. Of course, when he arrived in the dead of night, his captured companion was even easier to find. Creating a phantasmagoria only the two stunned camel drivers could see, he lured them away from the camp and out into the open desert. There, he told them they could have any three wishes they wanted. If they would surrender the urn and its prisoner, he would fulfill their hearts' desires.

The driver who had the urn clasped tightly to his breast responded immediately. Bring me, he said, a mountain of gold so large it could not be housed even in the great mosque in Mecca. There was a blinding flash and a great cloud of red smoke so dense it filled the night air. Slowly, it drifted off and there, in its place – a mere two hundred yards from the astonished drivers – was an enormous block of gold. Delirious, they ran to it, ran around it a number of times, patting, digging their nails into it, gasping for joy.

Suddenly, the second driver had a paralyzing thought: When the morning came, the whole caravan would see it. They would be robbed, raped of their incredible treasure. Without thought, he called out to the Djinn: 'You must create a place to hide it so only we shall know where it is.' Before the words were fully spoken, a huge hole appeared in the sand, again about two hundred yards to one side of the golden mountain. 'That's no good,' the first driver said, 'it has to be inside the hole.' Too late he realized the third wish had been expressed. With a terrible grinding roar, the huge block lurched across the sand and fell into the hole, to be covered immediately by sand. The coveted urn flew from the driver's nerveless fingers and exploded in the sky. An eerie screech reached the ears of the desolate men and once more the desert night was calm and serene.

Abdullah heard the story with fear and wonder. After many minutes of deep thought, he asked what happened to the hapless men. One, it seemed, raced to the spot and began digging like a wild animal. When the day broke, he was never found. The other had been struck dumb; he went into a complete shock from which he never recovered. It is said he became a beggar and now sits near the great mosque, mutely holding up his cup for alms from the pilgrims.

Ibrahim stirred the fire again, feeling the night chill penetrate his now tattered robe. I must sleep, for soon I must be on my way, he warned himself. If I don't find a community where I can beg my bread soon, I will never reach Mecca. And that is important. The early hours and the late are the only ones good for travel on foot. And I must bathe this weary body.

Even as he endeavoured to sleep, his mind returned to Abdullah. He missed him, knowing the lad had taken a place in his heart, a place usually reserved for his own sons he now hardly ever saw. God grant him peace. And that his footsteps may be guided toward the wisdom he seeks.

X

Maryam stood just inside the garden door, drying herself and listening to the sounds of approaching night. In the garden, wrapped in a light robe, Fatima hung the washing on lines with competent, industrious hands. With hardly any discussion, soon after they arrived here many months ago, they had agreed to reserve the first and last hour of the day for silent meditation. They bathed, prepared their frugal meals, cleaned house and washed their clothing with no words spoken. In so doing, they had sharpened their senses, but especially the inner, psychic ones that perceived the world and its beauty with an expanded and somewhat different tone of reality.

Anwar had said that during these two periods of the day, there was a separation between the day and night, like a tiny chink between two quite different worlds. It took a special sort of seeing to appreciate more than the five physical senses observed. Not so much seeing the day blend into night, or night into day; with practice and deep concentration, each one could be seen, separately and distinctly. And each could be held like that, apart, as one looked into that chink between them. In time, one would realize that this separation was symbolic of the chink that existed between different worlds, like the fabric of space and time dividing, offering new dimensions to eyes which could really see.

Eyes which could really see, she repeated in her mind. As our minds have begun to perceive so much that was hidden to us only a short while ago. No longer did they quake with fear when the knocks sounded at their doors. In performing their services for all callers, a new dimension had indeed been found. They serviced bodies but looked into souls. And in so doing, things had been put in their correct perspective. Today, they could laugh. And spend many hours learning from these strange, exotic experiences.

Hanging the large cotton sheet on one peg, Maryam took the light robe from another and wrapped it about her. They were the same two robes they wore that first night in Fatima's home in Medina. Wryly, she examined the sleeve. Soon, they would fall apart from sheer exhaustion. Thinner and hardier than they had been at the start, she and Fatima seemed to gain in stature as the poor robes fell into rags. She turned again to watch Fatima. Smiling, she felt tears struggling to leave her eyes. How beloved she is, how loving and caring and good. How can I ever imagine life without her?

Bent under a large sack balanced on her head, Farah the old herbalist moved down the narrow alley. She paused for a moment to look at the two small doors at the front of the house. Each with an initial painted on it. M for Maryam. The mother of the Christian prophet was called Maryam. And F for Fatima. The Prophet's daughter was called Fatima, the one who married Ali, The Good. Why did he do it to them? Why did he send them here to be whores? They never say more than it is their destiny. And they say it cheerfully…as though to say, we are just lucky. They give nearly everything away, they work tirelessly for the poor, they have become so learned in my own arts I hardly know what I would do without them now. Why did he do it to them? Admit it, you old cow, they are like daughters to you. Like the…the decent children you could never have.

One of Farah's many arts was that of moving impeccably. In her black robes, save in the glare of the mid-day sun, she seemed more a shadow that a three-dimensional person. She would arrive and leave without stirring the air, her steps inaudible. Even in her own two small rooms above the girls, it would be impossible for most to know if she were home or not. She disturbed nothing, created no untoward vibrations. She entered the side door and mounted her ladder with the lightness of a zephyr.

Maryam touched the doorpost lightly and Fatima turned, her brows raised quizzically. Maryam pressed a finger to her lips, then pointed upward. Fatima shook her head in amazement. Maryam could sense everything. Particularly at these two special hours of the day. Fatima was convinced that Maryam had developed a form of clairvoyance. How else would she be able to say, 'The coppersmith will be here in a few minutes. Don't be surprised if he brings you dates soaked in honey and sesame.' How would she know that if her 'other eyes' were not out in the market watching the man?

Fatima walked through the low doorway and entered the clean, orderly room where they cooked, ate and slept. Below a small window next to the door, a charcoal fire glowed. An oil lamp burned on the little table where they shared their meals and, above the low bed they also shared, a votive lamp threw its light down on the shelf supporting it. Next to the lamp was a shallow dish covered with gauze. On the far wall, heavy draped coverings hung over the two doorways leading to the cubicles where they worked. Their customers entered the cubicles through the doors leading to the alley. None of them was ever permitted to visit the back room where the girls lived.

Maryam caught the quick look Fatima flashed toward the covered dish and shook her head. Fatima smiled; they both had lamented with good humour that their periods did not coincide. A lamentation not shared by their customers, of course. With one accord, both girls walked to the garden door and held hands, leaning against each other to watch the first stars of the evening appear over the high wall and the many fruit trees which grew just inside. For the last few minutes of their silent hour, they turned toward one another and kissed. Holding each other closely, they communicated their deep love in the sharing gesture.

'Lie down and rest now,' Fatima said at last. 'This has been a very difficult period for you...'

'I'm sure it's over,' Maryam protested, not wanting Fatima to do all the work for yet another night, 'there are no more signs...'

'You will rest tonight...and tomorrow night if need be. Your face is drawn and you have no more strength than a kitten.' Maryam opened her mouth to protest again, but Fatima hushed her. 'You play mother to me when I'm unwell...now, no arguments.'

A heavy knock sounded at Maryam's door. The girls looked at one another, then Fatima led her friend toward the low bed and forced her down gently.

'It's that burly carpenter,' Maryam spoke apprehensively. He was a brute of a man and his demands were almost unthinkable. The size of his member matched his demented desires.

'It's all one to me. Now rest, I'll see if he will accept a substitute for his favourite plaything,' Fatima joked lightly.

Lying back with her arm propping her head, Maryam watched the darkening evening fill with many more stars. Drowsy as she was, it took an effort of concentration to blot out the sounds in the cubicle nearby. In all the time they had been here, neither had ever entered the other's cubicle when there was a visitor. It was one thing to learn the humility necessary to accept any debasement. It was another to see that happen to the one you loved.

One day we shall have to part, Maryam told herself, wondering how she could ever survive without Fatima. She did not understand how she knew this, but the premonition was increasingly clear. Their paths would divide, that was all. Will God grant me the strength and the will to face that? This life in Mecca was made bearable only because of Fatima. What life would be bearable without her? Anwar, is there no end to sorrow and suffering?

She closed her eyes and immediately a brilliant vision filled her inner sight. A shadowy, indistinct male figure, dazzling none the less, stood on a vast and empty plain. Only one feature was clear: a huge, golden phallus with a tip which glowed like a ruby. The face was blurred by coruscating light, the limbs shimmered and faded, only that one feature remained distinct and motionless. It was a vision she had had many times over. Familiar for that reason…but there was something else. A familiarity beyond the mere vision.

She had learned to accept the male organ in all its various forms: it was necessary, it was there, she could do anything with any of them now and not even an eyelash would flicker. If she no longer feared them, no longer loathed them, it was only because she had controlled all that. To her they were now simply appendages…and not very attractive at that. She had learned to accept, even make the owners feel she was fascinated. Flattering male pride and vanity was part of her vocation now.

She opened her eyes slightly and looked over the garden wall. She imagined she could still see the vision, as though it had transplanted itself to a rooftop across the rear alley. Hazy, ephemeral overall, but the impressive organ was clearer than all the rest, still golden and throbbing…as though it were mutely calling out to her. A positive shiver of desire coursed through her, increasing her astonished wonder. This one did not repel, did not leave her feeling indifferent. It touched something so deep inside her she could not plumb the abyss to its source. Why did she want *that* one so? A faint sigh of longing broke from her lips just as Fatima slipped around the heavy door-hanging. She paused on her way to the garden, noting that the girl's eyes were closed.

Squatting over a basin just outside the garden door, Fatima washed herself carefully, then threw the water over some flowers. As she re-entered the room, another sigh wrenched itself free.

'Maryam,' she whispered softly, 'are you asleep?'

'No,' a lethargic voice answered, 'it's just my waking dream again.'

'Oh?' Fatima commented. There was something about that golden phallus with the ruby tip that haunted her too. 'I'm jealous!'

'Oh!' Maryam echoed, her voice catching in her throat. She propped herself up on her elbows. 'Did he abuse you…the carpenter?'

Fatima reached out and pulled the girl to her, cuddling her in her arms.

'Your carpenter has gone most peculiar. When I disrobed, he made me sit on his knee. Know what he wanted me to do? Take his nipple in my mouth and nurse like a baby! He was most unhappy about something. He held me in his arms and rocked me, cooing like a motherly dove all the while.'

'I don't understand...you just washed yourself,' Maryam looked up and blinked.

'Neither do I. He rocked me, I nursed on him and then...Bang! It splashed all over my exposed bottom. Luckily, none of it got on the carpet. Now...look at this!' Fatima held out her hand, opening the fingers slowly and dramatically.

'Ten silver dirhams! No one has ever given us...'

'I know!' Fatima interrupted. 'Isn't it amazing?' She reached under the low bed and drew out a small wooden chest and threw the coins in it. 'You know, he was too embarrassed to suggest what he wanted at first. He told me the most amazing story.'

A stranger had come to the carpenter that afternoon with a broken saddle. He wanted new wooden pieces fitted immediately. The carpenter said he would have to charge a lot if he was to put all other work aside. The stranger threw twenty dirhams on the counter. With a smile! Not too many months ago, he told the carpenter, he had been a poor man, working as a driver for the richest man in all Arabia. One day, this mighty merchant decided to give everything he owned to the poor, to his servants and employees. The once poor driver was now a wealthy man, the owner of four camels and a very successful merchant in his own right. If that was not amazing enough, when his former master had heard that another rich merchant, an old friend of his who had borrowed one hundred camels from him, had been set upon and plundered by brigands in the Bactrian wilderness, he sent the man a message. He discharged his old friend's debt. He wanted nothing from him. When the stranger returned for his saddle, the carpenter had commented on the story, assuming the merchant who had been robbed must be delighted with such generosity. On the contrary, he was corrected, the beneficiary was furious. It was one more case of hating your benefactor. All he had for his pains was a sworn enemy, this saintly Ibrahim ben Yussef...

'Ibrahim ben Yussef?' Maryam exclaimed. 'I knew him...I mean, I knew him to see...in Bashtahal. The other man in the story must be Hassan...Anwar once looked into his heart and his hands turned blood red. The same thing must have happened to Ibrahim. He must have given everything away...I don't know, because of Anwar? It must be a miracle...'

Before she could finish, a pounding on Fatima's door silenced her. Fatima rose, settling Maryam on the bed. Shrugging her shoulders, she walked toward the cubicle.

'Duty calls. Now, please shut your eyes and sleep. No more visions.' She shook her finger sternly at Maryam.

Hearing the murmurs wafting through the heavy curtains, Maryam ignored Fatima's instructions; she sat up in the centre of the bed and crossed her legs, tucking her feet up on top of her thighs. In a few moments of enforced application, she screened out the room and all noises. Even as her meditation deepened, she felt the effort to draw her attention toward the rooftop beyond the garden. Ignoring that erotic call, she focused her thoughts on the hills to the west of Bashtahal. Soon, she visualized the area clearly. Anwar sat in his usual place atop the hillock. A tall, scrawny man was leading an old woman up the hillside. She recognized him at once as the sneering egotist who had stared at her once in Bashtahal. The old woman was crying. Below, at the base of the hill, hundreds of people were milling about. As the old woman and Najmuddin came closer to Anwar, she saw the elliptical arch of what appeared a great aura surrounding him. Instinctively, she knew it was artificial.

The old woman knelt before Anwar and her hands made gestures in the air; Maryam knew she was explaining something to the old holy man, but no words formed in her mind, only pictures. Now she visualized an oasis filled with pilgrims, merchants, camels and horses. Children were playing. One little girl ran off from the others, skittering among groups of camels. She saw a long arm snake down, catch the girl under the chin and, in a trice, the girl, the camel and the heavily covered driver disappeared in a cloud of dust.

When the woman's description ended, Anwar looked out over the desert and then closed his eyes. A few moments later, he addressed the woman. Again, Maryam's focus changed. She saw the interior of a lavish palace. The new, young caliph was striding through the main rooms of the harem. Finally, he arrived at the last room, smaller and more modestly furnished than the rest. One young woman sat on a large cushion in the centre, alone, her face hidden by veils, her head bowed low. The caliph reached down and lifted her to her feet, then removed her veils. It was the same girl, now a great beauty of sixteen. The woman kneeling before Anwar seemed transported with joy. She bent forward and kissed Anwar's hand in deep gratitude. The vision of the hill faded and Maryam uncrossed her legs, easing herself down on the bed.

Just as she was about to slip into sleep, she heard water pouring. Then Fatima's footsteps crossing the floor. A moment later and the sound of something being scrubbed vigorously reached her from Fatima's cubicle. When she opened her eyes, Fatima was standing in the garden door, wringing out a cleaning rag.

'Fatima, I just had the most wonderful vision...'

Dropping the cloth, Fatima ran to the bed and flung herself across Maryam's body.

'How many times do I have to order you to sleep?' Fatima demanded, pinning the squirming body down. 'You'll be exhausted with all this visualizing, don't you understand?' She opened her hand and ten silver coins dropped on the cover next to Maryam's head.

'The carpenter again?'

'No, not quite. This was a goldsmith we have never seen before. Everyone is so generous tonight! Think of all the food and clothing we'll be able to distribute…and what we'll be able to buy for Mother Farah.'

'Was he gentle with you?' Maryam feared that for so much money what had been asked must be dreadful.

'You will not believe this. First he exposed himself and stretched out on the carpet. He made me keep my robe, just stretch out my bare feet. Can you imagine? He wanted to suck my toes! The big toes. First one, then the other. Back and forth, as though he couldn't decide which was best. Before I knew what was happening, he leaped to his feet, wrapped himself up and threw the coins on the carpet in front of me. He was out the door before I could open my mouth. As you can well believe, there was quite a sticky mess on the carpet. I hope it's dry before the next caller arrives.'

'You can use my room, dear heart.' Maryam rolled Fatima off her and wrapped her arms about her. 'What a strange thing to want. When you think of the nights we got nothing but old clothes, some stale food, some fruit and one or two pieces of silver…for all of ten visitors each!'

'Oh, this one had a strange story to tell also. They find it so difficult to speak about their unusual desires at first.

'A tax collector from Bagdad was a regular customer of the goldsmith's. This very evening he had arrived from Bashtahal and regaled the goldsmith with the wondrous feats of a holy man there. This holy man had the power to locate people who had been separated from their families – for whatever reason. It seemed not to matter how long ago the event occurred. The tax collector had heard an old woman speak to the holy man about her granddaughter, a young child who had been kidnapped in an oasis…'

'She is now in the harem of the caliph…in Bagdad,' Maryam took up the story. 'She is beautiful, about sixteen and the caliph loves her very much.'

'What? Were you listening?' Fatima drew back and regarded her friend with amazement.

'No…nothing like that. I was meditating. Thinking

about Anwar. And I saw everything…just as plainly as I see you now. Fatima…' Maryam was genuinely frightened…'it was as though I were standing there, perhaps just where that tax collector stood. And how eerie. Not only was I there, but I was obviously back many, many days in time.'

Fatima pulled the cover over them and put her arm around Maryam's neck. No more than Maryam could she explain these phenomena. Maryam had taught her how to meditate, but she never seemed to go anywhere. As she stroked the face and brow of her friend who had already dropped off to sleep, she prayed the visiting was over.

Sitting on the rooftop beyond the garden wall, his legs dangling over the edge, Hawwaz watched the two girls with petulant wrath. Every time he got his hooks into that girl, something happened. Her friend would return from another bit of depraved promiscuity. Or that damned Maryam just took off on one of her visionary trips…who could reach her mind when it was gone?

He pulled his legs up and wrapped his arms around his shins, resting his chin on his knees. Mecca! Damn this city to dust and ashes! He muttered a few more ribald and horrific invectives. You couldn't even land here correctly…one slight slip and you'd end up in hell…or worse! Nothing works right in Mecca.

A terrific thud knocked Hawwaz off the roof. Landing lightly, he whirled and looked up. A surprised Hutti was sitting where Hawwaz had been, his face puckered up with embarrassed chagrin. Hawwaz bounded back up to the roof, snarling.

'Just what do you think you're doing?' he demanded.

'Sorry, something went wrong. I meant to land next to you.'

'I know…it's this place,' Hawwaz agreed. 'Did you follow me for a reason?'

'Just a bit concerned, that's all…'

'Concerned that I won't be there in time to help you? I *told* you I would. We have plenty of time. Now, why don't you let me get on with *my* project?'

88

'*Your* project?' Hutti scoffed. 'Your project, as you call it, is going to get you in even more trouble, the way you're going about it. Want to end up in a little urn again?'

'I know you got me out,' Hawwaz snapped back, 'I *owe* you, all right? Stop pushing. If it wasn't for you grabbing my pearl and yanking me back from the hilltop not so long ago...'

'You think you would have got her, don't you?'

'I *know* I would have got her...I was almost there when you ruined it all.'

'Hawwaz, little brother, you are such an egomaniac. If I hadn't pulled you back, Anwar would have got that precious pearl of yours.'

Hawwaz glared at his friend defiantly. 'He would? What makes you think he's *that* powerful?'

Hutti groaned and slapped his thigh. 'Don't you ever listen? I told you about that urn, about the stopper. When I released you I thought my arm had been burned off.'

'Oh, that ring of Solomon business again,' Hawwaz sneered with superior indifference.

'Laugh if you will, but I am older and know a bit more. That is a very powerful talisman. It sealed you in, believe me. You watch your step or Anwar will really do you in.'

'Dear, dear, threats and warnings. When I do sink my ranji, Anwar will beg for mercy. As you once told me, he has good reason not to want his precious little protégée mothering a demon.'

'If you had a demon son, neither would you.' Hutti muttered under his breath.

'I heard that! And how did *you* get one? And now you're preaching to me, old holier-than-thou Hutti?'

'Frankly, Hawwaz, I think Anwar has outsmarted you. With all the time you spend spying on that girl, trying to insinuate yourself into her mind, have you ever concentrated on that little dish over the bed?'

'No, why? What's in it?' Hawwaz asked with little curiosity.

'Just try it...you'll see.' Hutti yawned and stretched

out on his back, twisting until he found a comfortable spot.

Hawwaz focused an extending vision until he had brought the dish so close it was the size of a huge platter. He forced his special perception through the gauze covering and pinpointed the cloth-covered pill. A moment later, he felt his eye burning and smarting so badly he let out a small yelp. When his ranji began to experience the same sensation, he turned on Hutti and grabbed his shoulder.

'What is that diabolical thing?'

'I suspect it is something Anwar concocted...something that makes it possible for them to ply their interesting profession with absolute immunity. If my suspicions are correct, it is just as potent against unearthly sperm as against the earthly variety.'

'You're making this up,' Hawwaz huffed regally.

'Am I?' Hutti answered laconically. 'They why did your projected eye...and your ranji...begin to burn?'

'That old man is a fiend...say, why do they keep it in a dish? Is it supposed to drive us away?'

'Sometimes I think you're still a child,' Hutti groaned. 'It is in the dish because...well, human females have what is called a period every month of their time...'

'I know that!'

'Amazing, my dear. What else do you know?' Hutti's patience was taxed and his friend realized it.

'Come on, tell me the rest,' he cajoled, 'I'm sorry I sounded testy.'

'Logically, there must be two of them, correct? One for each girl? The raven-haired one seems to be doing the work, according to you, so it must be Maryam whose little amulet is resting in the dish, hmmmn? So, who is vulnerable for the moment?'

'Oh, Hutti!' Hawwaz clapped his hands for joy. 'You are the clever one, aren't you? If I can get at her tonight, without her protection, everything will be perfect.'

'Yes, but how?' Hutti asked reasonably. 'With her girlfriend next to her, how will you be able to manifest? Remember, we're in Mecca. You're terribly restricted.'

'You're so clever, haven't you got any ideas?' Hawwaz sounded desperate enough to promise anything.

'Well, I may. However, for one favour alone, you guaranteed to help me...'

'I will, I will...we have so much time left. The sculpture is built, everything is ready, what are you worried about? I promise you absolutely...'

'Enough, enough, don't overdo it. I'll do you one more favour, and that's all. If you fall on your face this time, don't haunt me any longer. Agreed?' Hawwaz nodded eagerly.

Hutti exclaimed: 'What is the one thing you need to get into that house, without arousing suspicion, get the girl's clothes off and overwhelm her before she knows what's happened?'

'The only way that could be done is to walk in there like any normal, corporeal human...a man. Is this some more of your dubious humour?'

'Your answer is correct, so leave my humour out of it. You need a body. And I'm going to tell you how to get one.'

'Are you joking? You mean, capture a human body at the very split second the soul is leaving it?'

'Exactly,' Hutti answered with great authority. 'I just happened to land here incorrectly *twice*. Very shortly, across from the great mosque, an old beggar is going to die. There is a curious irony in this that will appeal to you. He happens to be the very one who caught you in the urn...how do you like that?'

'I don't believe it!'

'Oh, you'd hardly recognize him...I didn't at first. In fact, when I landed on top of the wrong building, I didn't notice him at all. There was another man there, a very unusual type for a beggar. His aura caught my attention. Very strong, indeed...and it was reaching out toward the dying wretch next to him, trying to firm up his will to live.'

'What's the matter with him?' Hawwaz's question was quite transparent to his companion. He was fastidious

91

to a fault, and if the man were dying of some disagreeable disease, Hawwaz would shun him.

'Don't worry, he hasn't the plague fever. As you remember, I had to borrow my demon son's block of gold to trick the poor devil into releasing you. Losing that gold broke his heart. He's aged incredibly…just giving up the ghost…oops! We'd better be off, you don't want to be late for this one.'

When the inaudible twin Pops! occurred, Maryam's body vaulted on the bed. Sleepily, Fatima pulled the cover back up and nestled the disturbed girl closer.

XI

Hawwaz stretched out full length on the roof of the tall building opposite the great mosque. He watched the crowd of beggars with the choice positions just outside the wall surrounding the mosque. At this late hour, most of them were asleep, their legs stretched out, backs leaning against the wall. A few of them curled up like dogs; snores wafted on the still night air. The Djinn's nose wrinkled, testing the air for unsavoury odours. Near the gate, a small band of the fraternity were gambling. There was a wineskin being passed surreptitiously from hand to hand. The Djinn's handsome, though invisible, features did not hide his disdain for the conspicuous lack of righteousness.

Stretching his neck, he concentrated on one small beggar who picked up the dice with one hand, pointing across the road with the accusing forefinger of the other. In effect, Hawwaz extended his ears to catch the man's words. He was pointing to a tall beggar almost directly below the Djinn on the nearside of the road. He distributes all his alms to the poor, the man spat with contempt. Won't accept anything in return save a bit of food and water. But he has the evil eye. Every time he looks this way, I have a losing cast. It must be more than an evil eye, protested one of the others, or why else would so many rich pilgrims go to him. Just as they are about to enter the gates, they turn, as though guided by some strange power. They cross the street and they talk to him. He collects more than we do and he never shouts for attention, never waves his bowl and begs aloud. Curse him, exclaimed the embittered gambler, he is some sort of devil. None of them, it seemed, had the courage to approach the tall, powerfully-built man.

Curious, Hawwaz glared directly below him. It was just as Hutti had described it: one enormous aura emanating from that tall man who sat apart from all the others. Near him, with head bowed, legs and arms splayed out, was a decrepit derelict about to expire. The aura of the dying man was almost gone. Once or twice, as Hawwaz stared down, it would flicker slightly, trying to respond to the encouragement beamed to it by the brilliant aura close by.

Hutti was right, he's trying to keep that miserable bag of bones alive! With a deep frown of annoyance, the Djinn stretched his arm down the side of the building and batted at the extended aura the way a cat will strike an exhausted mouse. It had no effect. Withdrawing the arm, the Djinn began invading the man's thoughts, looking for clues to upset his concentration. First, he discovered the man's name: Ibrahim ben Yussef. He was thinking about two things at once. He sorrowed about the dying man next to him, though not in a consciously direct way. The extended aura was an involuntary reaction. His main focus concerned another man, one named Hassan, who had passed this way early in the morning. They had once been friends, Hassan and Ibrahim, but Hassan had scorned Ibrahim; as he rode by, he spat in the tall man's face with contempt and livid anger.

Hawwaz probed further, learning from Ibrahim's memory that he had discharged a debt, a very large one, as an act of charity for a man who had lost nearly a whole caravan. From that day forward, Ibrahim's hands had never turned red again. Hawwaz understood immediately that Ibrahim's nature was such that he could not conceive of hatred and vengeance as a reward for kindness. With a mischievous smile, Hawwaz winged a thought into the troubled mind: Is it possible that Hassan's hands have never been white since that day? Could it be that an act of generosity proved to be a curse in disguise?

No sooner had the last thought been transmitted when a shock wave smote the Djinn. Ibrahim's aura had drawn in protectively, screening the man from further interference. Vaulting up on his hands and knees, Hawwaz glowered down the side of the building. No matter how hard he tried, he could no longer penetrate Ibrahim's barrier. He puzzled about the bloody hands and this man's amazing powers of resistance. It was like...that's it! Anwar again! A link between this man and Maryam, between both of them and Hassan. And behind it all, that meddlesome old fool on the hilltop.

Hawwaz cocked his head and took a long, critical look at the tall man with so many luminous fibres now gathered tightly about him. Another damned Anwar in the making! he cursed quietly to himself. It was then he noticed a tiny pinpoint of white light just beginning to appear on the surface of the dirty bit of rag covering the head of the dying man next to Ibrahim.

Hawwaz locked his toes over the edge of the roof and let his body slide down the side of the building; with the stealth of a stalking leopard, he inched downward, all the while elongating his bulk until it was no thicker than a hair. The top of his head pointing like a needle just above the covered skull, he waited as the white light, visible to none but the Djinn, reached its brightest. Just as the soul was about to break its bond with the body beneath, Hawwaz arrested it momentarily, for just long enough to plummet through the psychic aperture. Once inside the deserted body, the soul was freed. With the soul inside, he could not have made the telling penetration. But the moment the soul broke free, the mystical aperture would have closed.

The emaciated beggar's body retained its balance for a moment longer, then toppled to one side. Ibrahim felt the man's passage from life to death; he sighed deeply, but did not turn. A body had fallen to one side. Across the road, nothing altered. The peace of the late and waning night was hardly broken by the occasional whisper, the light clatter of dice. Life went on, minus one small contributor.

In sorrow for the life that had passed, Ibrahim drew himself inward and prayed with sincere devotion. In only moments, he entered a trance so deeply that the world

95

about him no longer reached his senses. The shrunken corpse near him shivered, then jerked spasmodically. In ungainly and comic fashion, limbs straightened and the body rolled toward the roadway. Picking up speed, it spun silently along, hardly touching the ground as it careered grotesquely toward the end of the street. When lost in the gloom and far from the cluster of beggars, the body shot straight up into the air and landed uncertainly on the splayed feet. The first few steps were like a drunken dance, two measures forward to one back. By the time the macabre spectacle reached the corner, Hawwaz's skill as a puppeteer had improved. At the end of the next street, the possessed body was walking normally, if a bit stiffly and slowly.

The beggar's animated body stopped in front of the shop of one of the more affluent barbers. With the strength of a lion, he began pounding the door so loudly, the sound echoed up and down the street. When the bleary-eyed barber finally opened the door a crack, the beggar struck it with such force, the barber was bowled over on his back, halfway across the room.

'I want my beard trimmed and my head shaved,' a booming, stentorian voice informed the open-mouthed barber. 'Yes, and my body shampoo'd and made sweet-smelling. Send someone for the finest tailor, tell him to bring his best raiments. The best money can buy. Now!'

'But – but – we – everything is closed, everyone is asleep,' the barber stuttered. He looked up into the cold, fishy eyes staring down at him.

'Everything in this world opens for gold,' the beggar's hollow voice counselled. He held out his empty hand, palm up. Slowly, the hand turned; when it was palm down, there was a loud clinking and jingling. Before the barber's saucer-wide eyes, bright, new golden coins rolled across the floor. The barber had never seen the like of those strange coins before.

'Get up and get busy, I have no time to waste.'

Hassan ibn Mohammed paced back and forth over the

luxurious carpets in his splendid tent. His heavy body perspired even in the chill of night and his features clenched and unclenched themselves as he fed on a fury he could neither control nor vent. His caravan was well-hidden in the hilly territory a few leagues north of Mecca. Against his better judgement, he had chanced the detour en route from Bagdad to Alexandria, but now time was running against him. Still, he could not bring himself to desert the search for that infuriating girl, Maryam.

Looking guardedly toward the closed flaps of his tent, he uncrossed his arms and withdrew his hands from the capacious sleeves of his richly embroidered robe. Blood-red, front and back, the crimson colour making jagged marks at the wrists. The condition was now permanent, every hour of the night and day. The caravan had skirted the holy city, no purpose in letting it be known he was here. But he had not been able to forego a ride through the city himself early that morning. And who would be sitting there but Allah's new beggar, Ibrahim. What pleasure, spitting in that crazy fool's face. A lunatic, to be sure. His damned charitable gift had made these accursèd hands permanently blood-stained.

Maryam was the key. He had never been able to get that disdainful, loathing look of hers out of his mind. She would be humbled when he got his hands on her...she would unlock this curse of Anwar's. Not only that, but she would offer up her virginity to atone for all the mischief she had made.

A respectful clearing of a throat sounded outside the tent. Hassan thrust his offending hands back inside his sleeves and ordered the man in. It was the captain of the guard.

'Master, an old beggar has come to the camp. He says he has important news for you.'

'How did he get here? Who told him *I* was here? Are you not in charge of security?'

'Master,' the captain pleaded, 'you and a few discreet guards are the only ones who visited the city today. You sent advance guards to scour the city for that girl.

Questions are asked and people listen. This beggar says he knows where the girl is.'

'Bring him in…if he's lying, he'll leave his head here.'

A scrawny, bedraggled man of middle age was dragged into the tent, but not before Hassan had wrapped the folds of his cowl over his head and face.

Kneeling in front of the merchant, the frightened beggar explained that he had been approached by one of his lordship's men. This man described a girl with hair of a very distinctive shade, much like a roan or bay horse. There were two girls, and they shared rooms together near the mosque. He had seen them many times because they worked with the poor, feeding them and giving alms. One was named Fatima, but she had black hair. The other was Maryam, she of the burnished hair. They were very highly thought of by the men of the city.

'Thought highly of?' Hassan asked. 'Why is that?'

'They are great beauties, my lord. And they will accept anything their clients are willing to give…'

'You son of a whore, you lying bastard…' Hassan's jowly face purpled as he aimed a kick at the kneeling man. With amazing speed, the beggar flattened himself on the carpet and the leather boot passed over his head.

'Please, master, it is not my fault. They do what they do. I have never visited them,' the beggar whined.

'She is working as…a prostitute?' Hassan glared at the captain. He shrugged his shoulders.

'Shall we cut off his head?' the soldier asked calmly. The beggar screamed.

'Shut your mouth!' Hassan roared at the prostrate wretch. With a quick flip of the wrist which hardly exposed his hand, he tossed a small purse of gold and silver coins to the guard.

'Send the man who brought him and one other. But hurry, dawn is no more than five hours away. We must be gone from here swiftly. Use the fastest camels. Yes, send a third man to watch the camels and this wretch here. If he tells the truth, pay him. If he lies, cut his throat. No one kills beggars save other beggars.'

'How will they do it, master?' the captain asked, a dubious look crossing his face. 'There are two women ...they may be entertaining...'

'Use your head, damn you. One guard goes as a client to each woman. If the one named Maryam refuses to come here in her capacity of a pleasure-giver, then bring her in a sack...but bring her. And quietly. There must be no out-cry, no pursuit...is that clear?'

The captain called and two guards entered. He pointed to the beggar and they yanked him to his feet and dragged him out.

'Either way,' Hassan whispered, 'cut his throat.' The captain nodded and left.

As soon as he was alone, Hassan sank down on the thick carpet and pounded his crimson hands impotently against his chest. Tears of rage blinded him.

'Allah, how could this be? All this time I have thought of sweet revenge and she is a whore? Hundreds, maybe thousands of men have trampled down a virginity that belonged to me? It is that Anwar, I know it is...he is in league with the devil!'

With a sudden realization of how blasphemous he sounded, Hassan began praying piously.

As the night lengthened, reaching ever nearer the dawn, Maryam stirred, feeling first an undefined discomfort, then a more positive pain. Fatima's thigh was resting on her abdomen, pressing down on a full bladder. Easing her-self away in small stages, Maryam managed to settle her friend's leg on the bed and slip away.

In the garden, behind a row of shrubs, Maryam squat-ted to relieve herself; her mind still drugged with sleep, she tried to recover her dreams. In the quiet of her half-world, she saw the smiling face of Anwar. The smile faded and she felt some warning was being signalled; there was some-thing she had to do...a cat screeched and leaped up on the wall behind her, growling ferociously. Automatically, the girl stood and drew some water from the nearby cistern to cleanse herself. When she had finished and wrung the cloth out to hang on the line, she connected the action with the recent vision. Her period was truly over and Fatima would be able to re-insert the protective device in the morning. Suddenly, her skin began to pucker though the night was not cold; why had she come out to the garden naked? She looked toward the end of the garden, over the wall and the roof of the house beyond. Nothing seemed to threaten her from there... yet?

Inside, she tip-toed to the shelf over the bed and took the cloth-covered pill from beneath the gauze covering, inserting it deeply, wondering at her own anxious haste. Moving past the bed, she took her own light robe from the peg and slipped into it, even raising the cowl over her head. She began to pace the room like a nervous cat, or a vixen searching out some danger to her lair.

Her steps shortened and slowed until she came to a stop just behind the curtain to her own cubicle. Something beyond the curtain was pulling at her, drawing her and drugging her at the same time. Like a somnambulist, she drew the curtain and stepped into the empty cubicle, took two more steps and stood stock still. The outer wall vibrated; the house was caught in the eye of a terrible storm, the walls pressed and bent inward with the force. One more mighty squeeze and the room would fly up to the sky. Lips parted, her eyes glazed and fixed, she hardly drew breath as she stared at the street door.

Mesmerized, she watched the bolt move back as though drawn by an invisible hand. Soundlessly, the door was pushed open and, framed in the doorway, was a resplendent figure in a purple turban, white under-robes and covered from neck to foot with an outer robe of royal blue, all cinched by a wide golden belt which sparkled with jewels even in the soft light of the oil lamp burning in a niche in the wall. The princely figure took two paces into the room and the door closed of its own accord. A hand reached under the jewelled belt and withdrew a fine, bulging purse. It landed at Maryam's feet, scattering a few large, bright and newly-minted gold coins. The hand came forward until an extended finger pointed to

100

Maryam, then made a circular gesture to indicate she was to remove her robe.

Totally dazed, her numb fingers fumbled with the closures; the robe dropped, caught in her hands midway between hips and knees. She watched the splendid robes before her part and, from a white and lifeless groin a huge phallus rose. Golden in colour, it glittered more brightly than the coins at her feet. Fully extended, the ruby tip expanded until it seemed the very sun was imprisoned in its flashing depths. In her fogged consciousness, she felt rather than saw the compelling vibration in the glorious gem; a feeling more intensively erotic than she had ever imagined enthralled her entire body. She had the distinct impression of turning into a seething pool of roiling liquids. The ruby touched her and the liquids turned to living flames.

With a piercing scream, Maryam jumped clear of the floor and landed on her feet at least three paces back. She drew the robe frantically about her and crouched like a trapped beast. The burning she felt came from the cloth-covered amulet she had inserted a few moments earlier. Fully alert, she at last recognized her adversary.

A hollow voice rang loudly in her ears: 'You may refuse no man, Maryam. I have paid you handsomely. Do as I will.'

'No man!' she hissed. 'You are no man. I know you, sender of foul visions, Satan's tempter. Out…and the vengeance of Allah on your hellish head!'

A crack of thunder struck the cubicle, the door rattled and a terrible wind swept through the house. In the next moment of absolute silence, Maryam watched the man before her slowly keel over, stiff as a stick of wood. He crashed to the floor on his side, then rolled to his back, the legs crossed and sticking up in the air. Speechless and aghast, Maryam knew intuitively that he was dead, in fact dead for some time. She turned and ran into the back of the house.

'Fatima, Fatima, please help me…wake up!' She shook Fatima's shoulder and listened to the querulous sounds of the waking girl.

'What is it?' Fatima sat up, suddenly alert.

'A dead man. In my cubicle. Hurry, we have to do something.'

Clutching each other, they stood on the threshold and stared at the lifeless apparition in splendid robes. Explaining between sobs, Maryam recited the drama of the unearthly visitor. Fatima listened to the description of the protean penis...yes, the same one that appeared in the unbidden visions and dreams. Whatever evil monster had been here, it had used the dead body as a vehicle.

Gathering her courage, Fatima crossed the room and pulled back the flap of the open robe. Shrivelled and bent against the lifeless white skin was a small, shrunken member no larger than a kitten's tail. She then gathered up all the spilled coins and stuffed them in the open purse. Placing the purse securely under the wide belt, she then arranged the robes to cover the naked corpse.

'We must find help,' she advised Maryam. 'He may be – have been – a person of great consequence. If he is found here...'

'I'll go,' Maryam volunteered. 'Surely, some of the beggars we have helped will help us now. They will know what to do...then there is all that gold.'

'No, it isn't safe. I won't have you wandering about alone. We'll both go,' Fatima insisted.

'No, my dear, you can't. One of us has to stay here. The dead man is in *my* cubicle. You must wait for any possible caller. I am known to be indisposed...so it will be natural if you answer for both of us...'

'Maryam!' Fatima's hand flew to her mouth and her eyes opened wide in terror.

'Hush,' Maryam kissed her, 'my guardian angel must have warned me. I put it back in just before the fiend arrived.'

They both left the cubicle and Maryam wrapped herself in her street robe and lowered the cowl well down over her head and part of her face.

'I will be back as soon as possible.'

Ibrahim drifted back across limitless heavens from a brilliant white void filled with everything and nothing, an experience unlike anything he had known before and thus totally undescribable. The aeons of bliss he had felt followed him like trailing comet tails as his consciousness slipped back into his physical body. He felt the reluctance to leave all that bliss tugging at him, but he resisted the urge to dwell upon it. Nothing is to be grasped, nothing is to be coveted or desired. Atom by atom he became aware of the world about him and accepted it without regret. To be in this world, but not of it, requires accepting everything, including the time, the place and the conditions. As Anwar said, after a life-time of learning, one begins only then to understand how much there is to be learned.

He opened his eyes and looked about. The little wretched beggar was no longer beside him. Surprised but not unduly disturbed, he reasoned that, as the man was dead, what difference did it make where the body was? When the essence has departed, it matters not where the container is cast away. Still, who would covet a bit of skin and bone wrapped in rags?

Who will steal my empty parcel of rags when the time comes? he wondered. Or young Abdullah's? He thought about the boy and yearned to know what happened to him. Anwar had sent him wandering in the desert...each path the same, each path different. There is one grain of sand in that endless tract, one grain which is wisdom. Find it. Ibrahim grimaced. One thing for a man over fifty: give up the world and all desire, become a wandering fakir and accept every harshness, the fasting and privation...you have one goal, find yourself. That Self with a potential beyond most men's wildest dreams. Anwar repeats the claim of the Brotherhood of Love: Man is moving along an infinite line of evolution. His duty to God binds him to do everything in his power to push his own evolution forward. But poor Abdullah, so young, knowing nothing of this world, must eschew it all...No, another voice in his head answered, not poor Abdullah. Most fortunate Abdullah.

The wool-gathering stopped as abruptly as the snap of fingers. Ibrahim rose to his feet with lithe ease, in spite of the many hours of immobility. Something was happening, had happened. He knew he was needed, but didn't know how or why. Or where. But he followed his head and strode rapidly to the corner, unwittingly tracing the route taken by Hawwaz earlier, inside the beggar's corpse.

As he rounded the corner at a dog trot, Maryam crashed into his chest and would have fallen breathless on the path if his strong arms had not caught her. He recognized her immediately as he waited for her to regain the breath he had knocked out of her. Although she had passed close to him but twice, that faint but delightful scent identified her with utter certainty. The crackling energy coursing through his nerves and sinews was associated with nothing but her presence.

'Maryam, tell me, what is wrong?' She wobbled, struck by the impact of her name on a stranger's lips. But the voice was so kind and gentle, it seemed incongruous coming from such an awesome frame. The thought produced the answer.

'You – you are Ibrahim. Ibrahim ben Yussef?' she asked, trying to discern his face in the dark alley. 'The richest man in the world who gave away…'

'Shhh, we can discuss that some other time,' he warned. 'You are in some trouble – please tell me.'

'Yes…oh, yes. But how did you know?' She realized how foolish she was being. She described everything that had happened as briefly as she could, albeit blushing and hesitating when she came to the part about the extraordinary organ.

'Hurry, the night is our only ally…and that not for long.' He took her arm and they raced toward Farah's house.

Ibrahim looked at the corpse for one brief moment before righting it. It leaned against the wall, legs crossed and head bent, the same position in which the small beggar had died. The trimmed beard and splendid clothes altered nothing for Ibrahim's sensitivities. Fatima stood pressed into the wall near the lamp, her eyes still wide with terror. Maryam had collapsed on the floor at Ibrahim's feet where she sat crying softly. Fatima extended her hand. She forced herself to cross the room and present the two gold coins to the tall man. He took one and stared at first one side, then the other.

'I have never seen coins like these,' she whispered.

'Few have. Your fiendish visitor must have a horde of strange treasures. The clean-shaven man whose head is engraved here is Alexander The Great. These coins were minted in Alexandria, but I cannot read enough Greek to tell more.'

'They are brand new?'

'No, certainly not. He founded the city over one thousand, one hundred and fifty years ago. Where do they belong?'

Fatima pointed to the broad golden belt; Ibrahim searched under it and found the purse. When the coins were securely inside, he returned the large leather pouch.

'Can you help us hide him somewhere?' Maryam pleaded, her tear-stained face looking terribly haggard.

'I will take him back to the spot where he died. No better place to put him.'

'What about the clothes?' Fatima's voice squeaked.

'Just as he is,' Ibrahim assured her. 'The other beggars will find him and his gold. There will be a terrible battle. Many will be seriously punished by the authorities. It is in the nature of things. None of this had anything to do with you or Maryam...so it must not be traced to your doorstep.'

'But they will punish you too,' Maryam cried, clutching forlornly at the ragged hem of his robe. He reached down and stroked her fantastic hair reassuringly.

'They cannot punish a man for proclaiming the miracles and wonders of God. Get me a large sheet quickly, the night is fleeing fast.'

He laid the sheet on the floor and picked up the stiff body with ease, placing it in the centre of the cloth and gathering the four ends up to make a sack to sling over his shoulder. As he worked, he told them a story about the dead beggar.

Maryam interrupted him, recounting how she had been in a caravanserai at just about the time he was talking about. Anwar had spirited her away because he feared something would happen to her.

'It is all fitting together,' Ibrahim surmised. 'This one's friend is lost in the desert searching for a block of gold. Each time the dead man here told his story, he got a beating. And driven away as a madman. There is a Djinn at work here…one who is trying to possess Maryam…but why? I believe it is to do something terrible to Anwar. Blocks of gold, and no one believes it. In order to release a captive Djinn? Captured by whom, Anwar? No doubt. Probably to keep him away from Maryam. Now, these gold coins. You two must be on your guard every moment, do you understand?'

The girls looked at each other, then back to Ibrahim. They nodded in assent.

'Good. Maryam, come with me. Walk ahead of me to the corner. If all is clear, signal with your hand. In this manner, you will lead me until we round the last corner near the mosque. Wait there until I have positioned our friend. Then I will come back to you with the sheet. After that, you are to come back here as fast as you can and stay in the house.'

Again the girls nodded and he slung the sack up on his shoulder. Maryam covered her face and peeped through the slight opening in the door. She hurried out and Ibrahim followed.

As soon as they had rounded the first corner, a form emerged from the shadows near the far end of the alley-way. He reached out his hand and plucked someone from the recess of a doorway. Pushing the shorter and slighter form ahead of him, the larger man approached the two doors marked with initials. He whispered softly to the man whose cowl he held firmly.

'Who was the giant with the sack?' The little beggar cringed and shook his head. 'All right, which girl went with him?'

'Maryam,' the beggar answered. 'Hers is the door marked M.'

The taller man dropped a silver coin into the beggar's hand. 'Go back and tend the camels. Send my young guard back here. Wait until we call you. There will be two golden coins for you then.'

The old beggar scuttled down the alley and a few minutes later, the young guard joined his companion. They nodded to one another, then crossed the alley and knocked on the door marked with F.

'It is very late,' Fatima whispered, holding the door slightly ajar.

'Never too late for fun,' the larger man laughed, pushing the door open. 'Five pieces of silver each, my young friend and I are easily and quickly pleased. In five minutes you'll be rich.'

Fatima backed up, watching the large silver coins fall on the carpet. The large man circled her waist with his arms and the younger one moved behind her, pressing his body into hers. Before she knew what was happening, her wrists were caught in an iron grip and a strong hand was clamped over her mouth. Two minutes later, bound so tightly at ankles and wrists she could feel the circulation cut off, and a binding gag covering half her face, she was unceremoniously dumped on the bed at the back of the house. The two invaders moved softly from the room, entering Maryam's cubicle without a sound.

Ibrahim closed his eyes and settled back in his usual position against the wall of the house opposite the mosque. The night was still pitch black, but he sensed the approach of dawn...perhaps less than two hours off. Maryam should be safely home by now...with the doors bolted, may it be Allah's will. He thought about the resplendent figure propped against the wall near him. Who across the way would open his eyes first and exclaim? Would any of them recognize the man, or would they pluck his corpse clean, knowing or caring little or nothing? Clean, neatly trimmed and richly bedizoned, they would soon know he

107

was dead. Then they would tear at him like frenzied vultures. When the purse was discovered, how many would be dead or injured before the troops arrived to put down the riot? Perhaps he should have buried that accursèd gold.

Ibrahim had not dozed long when he heard the thud and shuffling gait of camels on the move. Three of them came around the corner at the end of the road in single file. When they neared the building against which he rested, they turned that corner. Heavily cloaked riders on the first two beasts and a large sack tied to the saddle of the last, which was being led by the second rider who held the last camel's reins. Was it an illusion that the sack moved just before the camel disappeared?

A sudden panic gripped Ibrahim's midriff. He turned and crept the few yards to the corner on his hands and knees. Slipping around it, he rose and took a few paces out into the road. The three camels were already swallowed up by the night, but he could still hear them. Something was not right, but what? Standing indecisively, hands on hips, he listened, hoping some sound would reach back and inform him. Even as he waited, an uproar on the road behind him shattered the night's peace. Shouts and running steps, curses and screams, roars and blows all mingled. He turned and edged back along the building until he reached the corner again. Just as he did, a beggar holding a torch screamed as a purse was torn from his hand. The mêlée rolled back into the road, the purse flying from hand to hand. Another roar filled the night as the leather tore apart and a shower of golden coins flew out to litter the road.

With the sounds of wounded shrieks and cracking bones filling his ears, Ibrahim ran from the conflict as fast as he could. When he reached Maryam's house, he pounded on her door. He waited and pounded again, his panic rising. Still there was no response. Then, he heard a groan from a doorway on the far side of the alley. Leaning over, he crept forward cautiously. Lying in a dark doorway, a collapsed heap of rags made a sickening noise. Ibrahim made out a form that moved and gurgled horrifyingly. Lifting the head, he cradled it on his knee. One bloody hand pressed the top of a dirty garment to the area beneath the chin. A voice croaked something and he pressed his ear to the fetid mouth. Hardly intelligible words and broken phrases reached him, constantly drowned in the terrible noises of the severed throat. His butchers had been bad ones or they would not have been so careless.

The girl with the burnished hair had been abducted. Would the stranger pray for a poor fool of a beggar who led the villains here for a promised reward, only to have his throat cut? Where…where had she been taken? Gasping his last few breaths, the beggar described Hassan and the location of his camp, then slumped forward. He was dead, Ibrahim knew, as he wiped his bloody hands and arms on the dead man's garments.

Running across the alley, he threw himself against Maryam's door with all his might. The frame yielded and he tumbled through, hardly able to arrest his headlong flight until he reached the curtain at the rear. Tearing that apart, he saw Fatima's trussed figure struggling vainly on the bed.

When he had untied her fetters, he massaged her ankles and wrists as she winced with pain. Lifting her off the bed, he placed her feet on the floor and, half dragging her along, made her walk as best she could, knowing the circulation would begin to flow. As he listened to her story, he saw a short, robust woman dressed in black enter the room.

'Who broke the door down?' she demanded.

'I did.' Ibrahim turned, still supporting Fatima, and stared into the eyes of the old herbalist. 'Two men have abducted Maryam. They tied up Fatima. I had to break in. As if that was not enough evil in one night, an old beggar has just died across the alleyway. The same men cut his throat.'

'Soldiers will come here,' the old woman gasped.

'Do not worry. Many other beggars may have died. There was a riot in front of the mosque. The soldiers will think he was one of them.'

'Ibrahim, what can we do? Do you know where she is?' Fatima cried.

'I believe so.' He turned to the old woman. She was staring at him in a very strange way, as though she were seeing something not visible to others. She nodded her head a few times and smiled.

'Who are you?' she asked simply.

'Ibrahim. A friend. Who are you?'

'I am Farah, also a friend. You will need a very healthy and strong camel.' She looked him up and down. 'No one will believe a beggar on a camel. A good robe is needed.'

'I have no money,' Ibrahim offered lamely.

'I have!' Fatima reached under the bed and took the twenty silver pieces from the coffer.

'Keep it for good work,' Farah advised. 'I am owed the use of a camel. Who abducted the girl, Ibrahim?'

'A man who was once a…well, a merchant I knew well. I believe he has become a very dangerous man. I have great fears for what he may do to Maryam. He thinks Anwar – a friend of ours – put a curse on him. As a result, I dread what he may do to Maryam.'

'Do you know anything about herbs and healing potions?' the old woman asked.

'I think I can manage…why?'

'Just in case,' she answered non-committally, 'it pays to be prepared. Will you take Fatima with you?'

'I will endanger no one.'

'Good. I will return as speedily as I can.'

XII

POSING LIKE A KING ON a throne, Hassan relaxed against silken cushions piled up on the two-tiered dais, his paunch rolling over his groin, his jowls quivering with anticipation, as he watched his two guards up-end the large sack. The trussed body of Maryam landed awkwardly on the lush carpet before the dais. One of the men extended the purse he had received from Hassan.

'Keep it, it is your reward for a job well done. Share it with your comrade-in-arms.' Hassan pointed to a glowing brazier near the tent entrance. 'One of you slide a dagger through the side of that. I want the blade red-hot, but the hilt cool. Tell the guards on duty they are to ignore all sounds from here. Unless I call, I don't wish to be disturbed.'

The taller guard pulled a long, curved dagger from his waistband and thrust it carefully between cross-pieces at the side of the heavy, iron basket. With a bow, he ducked out of the tent with his companion.

Maryam struggled for quite some time on the floor before she could roll herself over and jerk herself up to a sitting position. Her head was bare, her clothing twisted about her, exposing most of her legs; disordered hair tumbled down over her shoulders. She looked at Hassan with no expression. The cloth in her mouth and the thick windings of a dirty turban around her face were making her gag again. She had nearly suffocated on her own regurgitation bouncing along on the saddle, stomach down.

Hassan tilted his head to one side, his eyes hooded as he took in every detail. He smelled the hint of stale vomit. She'll need a good cleaning, he told himself. Yet he couldn't dawdle, the caravan had to be under way by dawn's first light. With a casual slowness that belied his

111

excitement, he edged his bulk off the raised platform and walked to the far end of the tent. When he returned, he carried a silver ewer filled with rose-scented water and a shallow bowl. Over his shoulder he had placed a cloth and a larger towel. He set all these before Maryam on the carpet and proceeded to untie the gag. Rolling the smelly cloths together, he tossed them in a corner.

Still with eyes that gave no hint of her feelings, she accepted mouthfuls of water and rinsed with it, spitting into the bowl as directed. Hassan soaked a cloth and carefully washed her face and neck. With the dispassionate air of a surgeon, he unfastened her clothing, pulling and yanking until only her arms were covered, imprisoned in the sleeves. Without a word, Hassan retrieved the dagger from the brazier; it was beginning to glow with an ugly rufescence. He slit the sleeves of her robe, judging the distance of the knife from her arms with great precision. The heat scorched her and she stifled a scream. Hassan returned the knife to the fire and continued with Maryam's ablutions. He missed no part of her and she gave no emotional concessions until he parted her thighs. She clamped her legs together and inched back. But she didn't open her mouth; she was determined not to break down and plead.

Hassan shrugged mildly and retrieved the dagger. When the point was so close to her sealed thighs she could smell her own flesh burning, she gasped involuntarily and snapped her thighs as far apart as the bindings on her ankles would permit. Hassan held the ugly weapon in his left hand as he washed her secrets with diligent care. When he was satisfied, he dropped the cloth and towel and put the dagger back in the brazier. He took a few pillows from the dais and placed them in front of the girl, then lowered himself to a comfortable sitting position.

'Well, Maryam, at last you are here. What expense, what time lost just to track you down. Surprise you?'

She continued to stare at him blandly, determined not to show fear or loathing. Not even for his blood-red hands. She refused to look at them.

'Yes, I can see you are wondering why. You are so

determined to give me no satisfaction, are you not? Oh, you would have. I had to do no more than arrive at your door with a few pieces of silver. I could have anything I wanted, yes? Maryam would do all the tricks of her trade just to please me.' He smiled with a reptile's mirth, his voice honeyed. Then he spat venomously, 'Just as you do for every filthy beggar who comes to you, you bloody whore! And I bet Ibrahim gets it any time he wants...for nothing!'

She shook her head with incomprehension and pity. He is rich, but he is mad. Is it because of his hands? She would not cast down her eyes, but began praying instead.

'Don't you look down your pitying nose at me, you filthy harlot! That's not why I had you brought here.'

Her eyes opened wider. 'Then tell me why you did all this injury to me. I don't even know you.'

'Oh, yes you do.' He thrust his hands out, holding them within inches of her face. 'Don't tell me you never saw these hands before.'

'You hate me, you revile me because I am a prostitute? Yet you bring me here because your hands are bloody? Either I am terribly stupid or you are mad.'

'Mad...yes, you're right. Before the dawn, you will find out just how mad. And who drove me mad? Come on, who drove me mad?'

'Certainly not lusting after me,' she answered reasonably. 'You just said, you could have bought me anytime for a few pieces of silver. I would have accepted *one*.'

'Why? Why?' He seemed genuinely distressed. The truth began to dawn on her. He believed she had bewitched him.

'To learn something important. When this trial is over, I hope to be a different person. Is it so strange to search for one's soul? Admittedly, the path itself may seem strange. But I assure you, it was not to steal anything from you.'

'Don't you taunt me!' He picked up the wet cloth and slashed it back and forth across her face until ugly, red welts appeared. She didn't flinch, turn away or cry out.

'Why should I taunt you? I'm your captive.' Her voice was breaking and she fought hard to control it.

'Do you do all this to please your friend, Ibrahim? Do you give him the filthy money you earn on your back?'

'I have spoken to Ibrahim but once in my life, and that most briefly. He has never been my client.'

'Do you think I'd believe a lying whore like you?' he screeched.

'If you will not believe me, then it seems such a waste to have done what you have done.'

He held up his hands again. 'That's why you are here, that's what you have done to me.'

Her head moved slowly from side to side with incredulity. With candour and not rancour, she studied his eyes, hoping for some clue to his madness. All the time, one part of her mind was praying ceaselessly.

'A man named Anwar once pointed to you in the darkness. He said, "That man's hands have turned the colour of blood. Please pray for him, perhaps he will understand what he has done to himself in the sight of God." He did nothing to your hands. I did nothing…they were already red when I looked. And what has Ibrahim done to you? Extended a kind and generous hand in your misfortune?'

Don't you lecture me, you holy harlot. Ibrahim put a curse on me. These hands turned red once or twice…then he disgraced me with his charity and pity. My hands have never been white since.'

'Do you really blame everyone else for your own misfortunes?' she chided softly. 'The one time I did meet Ibrahim, I felt he would exchange hands with you and ask nothing in return.'

'I'm through playing with you, Maryam.' With an ungainly struggle, Hassan pushed himself to his feet. He walked to the brazier and pulled the dagger loose, checking the blade. It was nearly white-hot. Maryam turned her head and bit her lip so hard it bled.

'What are you going to do?' she asked. 'I have no power over your hands. I have no power over anything on this earth.'

'No?' he snarled, thrusting the blade back into the fire. 'I, for one, don't believe that. You have power you share with that sorcerer, Anwar. You're a witch, and witches have strange ways of communicating with their masters…'

'That is simply not true!' she broke in.

'We shall see. When I am finished with you, no man will ever want to look at you again. *If* you live. And if I were you, I would pray to Allah that you die. You'll talk. Oh, will you talk.' He crossed back and stood in front of her, leaning over. 'You will contact that demon master of yours and tell him to take away this curse, or I will burn every bit of flesh off your body.'

'I swear, and may God be my witness, I have no power to do this. You are the author of your own disaster and I doubt if Anwar or any mortal can change that…save you.'

'How…by giving my money away like that fool friend of yours did? By taking the begging bowl and howling for alms? You are a bigger fool than I thought.'

'How can you do a thing like this? I am a defenceless woman and have never wished you harm or evil. Why?'

'I never wanted a woman as I wanted you. And what did you do? Sold it to every filthy lout in the market place. Before I force you to talk with a white-hot dagger, I will repay you for that rotten slight. Have you ever been enjoyed in the way young boys are enjoyed, Maryam?'

'You know that is a terrible crime in the sight of God!' Her lips trembled as she spoke and he smiled with glee.

'So there *is* a virginity left. Isn't that wonderful. The hatred you inspire in me now will see to it that I am not tender with you. Perhaps after the first time, you will contact your devil-master before I am ready for the second ravishing, eh?' As he opened his robes, he pushed her over rudely with his foot.

XIII

IBRAHIM REINED IN THE CAMEL and swung around in the saddle to take his bearings. The blinding white turrets and minarets of the city had slipped from view behind a tall dune. Permitting himself a sigh of relief, he pondered about the guards stopping people leaving Mecca. Only the new and long white robe Farah had brought for him saved that fraught moment. How wise she is, he breathed. And poor, distraught Fatima. Would he face Hassan and his entourage without a sword? A man waving a sword would impress them? Farah had asked. What would he wave then, he wondered?

A distracted and anxiety-ridden man becomes lost all too easily, he counselled himself, sweeping the horizon from left to right. He altered course slightly, aiming the animal's head a bit more toward the north. There is desperation in what Hassan is doing. Why else would he have a poor beggar's throat cut? Because he knew about the quest for Maryam, had probably seen her pursuer, could lead others to the caravan. Yes, and Hassan had skirted Mecca carefully, as though he wanted to cover his tracks. At that, he may have broken camp before the night ended; now, the sun was up nearly two hours. Find the camp and there will be enough signs to tell you that. Stop asking yourself why he wanted to do this, what he wanted with Maryam. Concentrate on the job to hand, one thing at a time. When you understand what the problem is, then think about solutions.

It had taken a good deal of intensive practice, but he had taught himself how to turn off the interior dialogue in favour of a calm state where only the most necessary thought-processes existed. The sun struck him, glaring fiercely like the red eye of hell. He forced his eyes ahead

116

until they discovered the telltale wisp of smoke on the horizon. Even from that distance he knew the overnight camp had been deserted for hours. Raising up to search the sand and sky behind him, he realized the dead beggar's description had been quite accurate.

Half an hour later, the man walked through the deserted camp, the disgruntled camel tugging at the reins behind him. Scraps of food, trodden camel's dung and the ashes of a few fires corroborated his earlier prediction: the caravan had got under way before dawn. Circling the area once more, still searching for clues, he saw the light breeze lift a scrap of white cloth. A human foot stuck out grotesquely. Dragging the reluctant camel after him, he raced to the spot and forced the camel to kneel. The scrap of cloth proved to be a large woollen coverlet. Maryam was half-buried in the sand.

When he had finished delicately wiping the sand from her naked body, he could no longer hold back his tears. From her face to her feet, the deep, ugly burns glared back at him, oozing sickeningly in the merciless brilliance of the sun. The soles of her feet were the worst; he forbade himself the thought that she would never walk again.

With fury and quiet desperation, Ibrahim cast aside the fears; she breathed, she was alive, that was all he could ask for now. Do something, he commanded, and stop shaking like a sick child! When he had washed down her body with a powder of herbs dissolved in water, he searched through the bag Farah had given him till he found an unguent. It was only when he had turned Maryam over on her stomach that he discovered the rest of the damage. He braced himself, summoning all his courage for that intimate and terrible examination. And forced himself to pray ceaselessly in order to thwart the temptation to curse Hassan to eternity.

The damage was so brutal, so fiendishly vicious, the man fought with his rebellious stomach as he prayed, applied lotions and bandaged her as best he could with the clean cloths Farah had supplied. Through all this, he made note of the things the old woman had put together. It was

117

as though she knew...or was his imagination running away with him? Uncanny, all the same. When he had wrapped Maryam completely in the white coverlet, he rested her head against his chest and moistened a cloth to wipe her lips. They were swollen and cracked and he feared she would become violently ill if she tried to swallow water too quickly. Patiently, he squeezed the cloth so her tongue and mouth would become moistened drop by drop. When he had repacked all the gear and tied the bundle to the saddle, he lifted the girl in his arms and remounted. When the camel rose and began the long trek back, he loosed his own robe to cover his patient as the sun neared the zenith. Near the dunes he'd passed soon after leaving the city, there were deep troughs and some rocky overhangs; they would have to rest there until nightfall. In the dark, a tired traveller carrying his pregnant wife would be less conspicuous.

Through the long hours of the afternoon, hidden from the sun in a gully, he nursed the delirious girl. In very small amounts, he administered water and pressed cloths, cool and damp, to her feverish brow. He prayed that the shock had temporarily paralyzed her normal bodily functions. He was not sure he had the strength to steel himself against her pain. In the late afternoon, the soft moans and little cries diminished; her body became less tense and she seemed to enter a real sleep. The first evening drop in temperature came rapidly to the unlit gully and he held her more closely, rocking her softly in his arms. As he did, all his feelings for her filled his mind like a song, extending through a limitless time. She seemed to have been a light inside himself forever, a lamp that could never be extinguished.

Maryam, I have loved you and desired you with such devotion it has consumed me. I have dreamed of you and longed for you in such depth and breadth that I cannot imagine a time when you were not there, like a lamp burning brightly inside me. And as I was consumed with love, so did I have to take those ashes and create a new kind of love, one of rededication. You are not diminished, only I

118

am reformed. I can now offer that love up to God also. When the self that was once fully there is no more, even the desire will be reshaped, but you will still in no way be diminished. For me you describe the very essence of love and you are the most perfect symbol of love. Through you, I have been able to see into a realm where no veils are left, where all is clear and pure, where perfection can dwell.

Ibrahim discovered the night; he had dozed, caught up in the rhythm of her deeper and more peaceful breathing. Even as he stirred, a memory struck him. He had dreamed that she heard everything in his heart and had answered him, telling him that she loved him as he loved her. If in truth her ordeal was now over, that love would be for her what it was for him, the vehicle of a perfect vision.

XIV

IBRAHIM CARRIED MARYAM OUT TO the garden every afternoon. He had built an ingenious contraption with parts of saddle frames, cushions and folded cloth which supported her comfortably while elevating her legs. Farah had decreed that she must not attempt to walk until healthy, new tissue had replaced the scarred tissue. For each of them, the old life had come to an end. Fatima spent her time caring for Maryam and working among the sick with the old herbalist. Quick and capable, Fatima proved herself not only a keen student of medicines, but of many more esoteric subjects as well. Ibrahim worked for the saddle maker; it was he who had lent Farah the camel.

After that first fearful day, when Ibrahim arrived in the middle of the night with the stricken girl, the past had been dropped from all references by silent and mutual agreement. Hassan and Maryam's ordeal were never discussed. After the first two weeks, men stopped coming to the doors on the alley to seek the favours of the girls. It was as though an invisible hand had turned a page in their book of life. The four of them formed a tightly-knit community in which all their different strengths were combined to attain Maryam's recovery.

When the girl was propped comfortably on the cushions, Ibrahim gazed around the garden before seating himself. The last rays of the sinking sun filtered through the leaves and upper branches of the trees; soon they would bear fruit again and the thought warmed his heart. Folding his legs under him, he sank to the ground beside the makeshift couch and opened a battered copy of the psalms. Maryam's eyes were closed and she held her face up to the warm sunlight. As he read, from time to time he glanced at her face, his eyes lingering for a moment or two. The scars were now pale, almost colourless. Many women, he reckoned, would have spent the rest of their lives behind veils. She did not display her scars, merely accepted them.

'Am I terribly ugly?' she whispered, catching him off-guard at the end of a psalm. Her eyes were still closed; he could not credit the question for she was certainly not vain.

'When beauty has depths greater than the ocean, only a fool would let his eyes float on the surface,' he chided gently, admonishing a pointless question.

'Come closer, Ibrahim,' she pleaded, 'I feel suddenly...so lonely, so far away.'

There was something strange in the light as it played with her damaged beauty, something extraordinary in her impassioned expression that seemed no part of her own personality. He turned sideways and edged closer, settling his body against the couch and resting his elbow on one of the cushions. She moved toward him and pressed her face against the arm. He closed the book of psalms and placed it on the ground, watching her from the corner of his eye. She had been serene and calm and now an odd turbulence was making her quiver. Her back arched and her thighs strained upward. A sigh reached him as her brow rubbed against his sleeve.

'You're so far away...leagues and leagues. You're way out there somewhere and I need you in here, close to me,' she murmured.

Her eyes were now distorted and out of focus; she was looking past him, it seemed, to some point in the distance. As he concentrated on her face, her expression became more intent. It radiated a deep, unfulfilled longing and the abrupt twitches, the quickening breath and gasping sounds in her throat spoke of something deeper...almost a lust, he thought. Appalled, he felt his own heart pounding. Frightened, yet fascinated, he watched an incredible metamorphosis: the scars faded to nothing and in a few seconds he was gazing into the face of the girl he had first seen walking past the mosque in Bashtahal. Sounds blending the cooing of a dove and the heat of a cat gurgled in her throat.

It is a fit of madness, a delayed reaction to all the horrors she suffered, he told himself…it must be. How else could one account for what seems a wanton display? He felt her hand reach out and touch his leg, move upwards to stroke his thigh. He wanted to jump to his feet but couldn't move.

'I want you so,' she called out in pain, 'and you deny me. Why do you spurn me so?'

He looked down in horror to see her small, delicate hand free his penis. It thickened and expanded so rapidly, he gasped involuntarily. The colour changed from swarthy olive to a brighter golden hue and the purple became ruby red. Growing larger and larger, he realized with extreme shock he was seeing an actual monstrosity being formed from his body.

A soundless voice struck the back of his head with the impact of a hammer blow: 'Look, Ibrahim! Now you must actually "see"!'

Unerring guidance forced his eyes toward the rooftop behind the enclosed garden. He narrowed his eyes and crossed them slightly while moving the effective centre of his focus minutely to one side. A vague shadow took on substance so rapidly the vision nearly shattered. But he held it forcibly. The gigantic naked Hawwaz stood there on the rooftop, hands on hips, head thrust back laughing soundlessly. Rising with majestic, arched splendour, the golden phallus with the ruby tip quivered and flashed in the rays of the setting sun.

The most ear-splitting screech he had ever heard shattered the silence and reverberated from every wall. There was an explosive flash on the rooftop and the image of Hawwaz was gone.

Maryam's rigid body levitated straight up from the couch, then crashed back with a sickening crunch. She was totally unconscious, but her hand was blood-stained. As he closed his robe, he saw that his penis was covered in blood. He knew instinctively it came from no specific wound. Another ringing screech started and he whirled.

Naked herself, Farah crouched in the upper window

of the house, her body straining forward. Kneeling on her left knee, the right was pressed tightly to her chest, one hand beating against the leg with a large, polished bone, the other thrusting a strange amulet out the window. When her incantation of power against the Djinn ended, she rose and stood on her toes for a second, then leaped back with such stupifying speed and lightness, it seemed she had been yanked by invisible strings.

'Bring her in here immediately,' the old woman's voice thundered from the remote darkness of the room.

Ibrahim sprang to his feet and lifted the girl in one sweeping gesture. His whole body shaking, he climbed the difficult ladder, carrying her on one arm. Farah helped him stretch the girl out on her own small, neat bed. Unconcerned, she slipped into a loose, brown garment and mixed some powders in a bowl with fresh goat's milk. Nodding, she directed him to hold Maryam's head while she coaxed the fluid down her throat. He wondered at the ability of the woman; many a sleeper would have choked. Putting the bowl down near the window, she beckoned Ibrahim and gestured for him to open his robe. He hesitated for a moment, then did as directed. The blood was gone, but his penis remained a deep crimson colour.

'You told me about your hands and those of her torturer,' she indicated Maryam with her head. 'Has anything like this happened before?'

He shook his head. 'What does it mean?' he asked unhappily.

'You are Anwar's disciple and have to ask that question?' she countered pointedly.

'In my search for God, it was necessary to cleanse my heart of greed. What has that to do with the enormous fiend who transplanted his penis on me in order to...'

'You actually saw him, then?' she interrupted. 'Good, you are finally beginning to "see".'

'You haven't answered my question,' he began, but she cut him off once more.

'Don't be so impatient. Complex things do not have simple answers. That fiend, as you call him, is a young and headstrong Djinn named Hawwaz. His object is not you, not Maryam. He is after Anwar's soul.'

'What?' The man was visibly stunned.

Patiently and indulgently, she reminded him of the path he had chosen for himself and the red hands that had moved him in that direction. His search was for the real, not the phenomenal...to accomplish that, he had to put passion and desire behind him. It was no good to protest that he had done so. Hawwaz had been able to reach him and tempt him. Only with such a vehicle, could Hawwaz reach Maryam now. If Farah had not intervened, had Ibrahim not finally opened his eyes and "seen" the Djinn, Hawwaz would have won. Anwar would have given his soul to save both of them. He could not have done otherwise, being Anwar. Maryam would now be invulnerable, if Ibrahim could become invulnerable also.

'I don't understand fully,' he cried. 'Why does he want Anwar's soul...is he really the devil?'

'No,' she answered tersely. 'Just a bored, mischievous Djinn. If he can capture and absorb a soul as great as Anwar's, it will enhance his power enormously. Now Fatima will not be back for about an hour. Help me and I will try to answer you questions.'

Puzzled but silent, Ibrahim helped her spread a large, circular black cloth on the floor. She then centred a smaller white cloth circle on the black one and began arranging a number of wooden and metallic objects around the white circle. From the back of the room, she fetched a wide, shallow blue bowl filled with clean, white sand. This she set in the middle of the white cloth and arranged small containers of brilliant powders on one side. Bright red, deep blue, golden yellow and sparkling green. When she was satisfied that everything was correctly in place, she pointed to a spot on the black cloth where he was to sit. She eased herself into the place next to him, on his right, and took his right hand in her left. He felt an amazing flow of energy from her hand inundate his entire body.

'She was in a trance when that happened outside,' Farah muttered, 'and now she is enjoying wholesome sleep. She will remember nothing when she wakes, and that is as it should be. It will unsettle her terribly if any of us mentions the incident. We will tell her she fell asleep and you carried her here, that is all. Agreed?' He nodded his assent.

Concentrating on the sand, whispering in a low but powerful voice, she described the Djinni. In that obscure, primordial time before matter, many spirit forces existed. When Lucifer rose against God, it was a battle of Creation versus Destruction. In terrestrial terms, every action creates an equal and opposite reaction. Not necessarily so in the world of spirit or mind. The great release of energies in that battle transformed primordial spirit essences. Neither good nor evil, light nor dark, the Djinni in many ways resembled their unintentional creators, the angels. Value terms were useless in a realm where moralities did not exist. It was a realm suspended between heaven and earth, belonging to neither. To those adepts who could travel outside their bodies, it was part of the astral plane.

Because paradise was part of their race memory, the Djinni attempted to create a facsimile paradise of their own. In material terms, many would say they succeeded. Trees bearing large jewels fed them forms of nectar and ambrosia. As an existence, it most resembled a place of Limbo. It came from nowhere and went nowhere: a pointless existence, lacking goals. In part, this explained the mischievous meddling in human affairs. Mind and spirit, without the objectives of faith, become immersed in boredom and frustration.

Due to a natural superiority, the female Djinni fared better than the males. Wingèd and more powerful, they subjugated the males. Their realm was divided: at well-spaced intervals, the females invaded the male zone. They overwhelmed the males for lust-fulfillment, not for procreation. The females were invariably hostile toward childbearing and woe to the male who tried to accomplish pregnancy. Few ever succeeded for few were clever enough for the superior females. Thus, the frustrated male ego singled out human females. To succeed, he must make her call out for him or dupe a man as his intercessor…as Hawwaz had with Ibrahim. The result of such a union was a sad and terrible thing. This demented offspring, known as a demon, was a creature without a soul and belonging to no world. They grew more rapidly than human children, ravaged their mothers' nipples as infants, bullied their way in the world until the peculiar green skin began to show. Then they were off, having discovered many great powers beyond the ken of men. They built palaces for themselves below the earth and preyed on human women. Fortunately, they could not reproduce, but they did have prodigious sexual powers. Once captured, few women escaped them. Few really wanted to, accepting the wanton life with no question. Like crows and magpies, they were great collectors of treasure. They tricked humans easily and, since they were virtually immortal, they controlled treasure hordes that would fascinate an emperor. The coins Ibrahim had identified as minted in the time of Alexander were an example. Undoubtedly, they had been stolen, perhaps from the Macedonian himself, and put at the disposal of Hawwaz. Another Djinn named Hutti was Hawwaz's friend. Hutti had a demon son named Musa who probably had the coins and gave them to Hutti. Djinni tended to love their demon sons, but the sons did not reciprocate that love. The realm of the Djinni was forbidden to demons and no Djinn father could visit his son's underground palace. To go under the ground was fatal for a Djinn. Lucifer was not so forgiving.

When Farah leaned forward to sprinkle coloured powders over the sand in the bowl, Ibrahim realized belatedly that he had not heard her voice for some time. Just when the communication ceased to be oral he could not ascertain; he felt himself to be in a strange trance, not of his own making. She had found a direct path to his mind…then he remembered: she had already done that in the garden. Her unspoken voice had struck him at the crucial moment, forcing him to look up and discover the Djinn.

They would now visualize some things together, she

126

advised him in their new communication, which might help him define his path for the future more clearly. What they would see could be part of the past, the present or the future. But he could ask no direct questions: particularly if those concerned the future and persons he was close to. One reason, obviously, was that it could do more harm than good. Equally important, vibrations of a tense or negative nature could scatter the scrying. When that happened, they would both be extremely vulnerable to powers suddenly unleashed which they were attempting to harness and use. In a sense, spiritual entities which could turn against them.

Before he could even consider this thoroughly, the sands in the bowl began to shift subtly, redeploying the colours and forming the first hint of a vague picture. Farah squeezed his hand and he narrowed his vision and crossed his eyes in the manner she had taught him.

A beautiful vista opened before his eyes and he found it difficult to credit such a possibility. The ground was like lavender silk and an endless panorama of gorgeous fountains and tall trees laden with jewels stretched to the horizon in all directions. The long view condensed and he watched a tall and supremely handsome Djinn engaged in building a superb sculpture. In the shape of a huge lotus flower made entirely of large precious stones, it put every legendary human work of art to shame. With no warning, there was a flash of light and the visual effect of an explosion; a second Djinn stood next to the first. Ibrahim recognized the newcomer as Hawwaz. He knew intuitively that Hawwaz had just returned from the earth plane. Now, his ears became attuned and, in a difficult and extremely ancient form of Arabic, an argument ensued. Catching only fragments at first, he understood that the older Djinn was demanding that the younger stay and help him with his monumental project. The younger one, Hawwaz, was furious because his last attempt to reach Anwar through Maryam had been foiled. Seemingly, he did not blame this on Ibrahim or Farah, but on Hassan. Hassan's outrageous act of unnatural rape had altered something primary and

Hawwaz wanted immediate vengeance on the culprit.

Hutti argued on, reminding the impetuous Hawwaz of his obligations and promises. Hawwaz chided Hutti, telling him he was a silly old woman, that there was endless time to spare before the females arrived. In despair, Hutti finally relented and picked up the largest diamond lying on the ground at his feet. It was flat, with a large face and stretched from one of the Djinn's elbows to the other as he cradled it in his arms. With a gesture of his head, he sent Hawwaz to stand behind him. With one accord, both their impressive penises rose, bent at right and left angles, closed in on the edges of the diamond and attached their magnificent ruby tips to the jewel.

The table surface of the diamond began to shimmer like a lake under blinding sunshine. Ripples moved from the centre to the edges as though a stone had been cast in a pool. When the motions finally ceased, a picture began to form. With a sense of overwhelming awe, Ibrahim realized that he was looking into one scrying device to see yet another picture form on a different apparatus in a completely different realm of existence.

Their eyes fixed intently on the surface of the gem, Hutti and Hawwaz kept up an argument at a furious pace. Hutti insisted it would be no problem to trick Hassan into being the author of his own punishment. Hawwaz was worried about interference from Anwar. Ridiculous, Hutti answered, after what Hassan had done to Maryam...not even Anwar could be that mistakenly saintly. All they needed was the huge block of gold which had tricked the camel drivers into releasing the captive Hawwaz. Hawwaz winced at the jibe, then complained that it was buried somewhere east of Mecca and Hassan was now leaving Egypt en route to Jerusalem. Hutti reminded him that Musa, Hutti's demon son, had managed to move the huge block to its present location and would find no difficulty in transporting it to a point in line with Hassan's march. Hawwaz was admonished to stop fretting and leave the logistics to Hutti and the mechanics to Musa.

Hazy outlines on the huge diamond clarified and Ibrahim looked into a lavishly furnished chamber. The walls and ceiling were completely covered in exquisite mosaic work. Persian carpets were butted side to side and end to end over the vast floor. Near the centre of the room, hundreds of silk cusions formed an enormous bed and, in the middle, a tall, incredibly muscular male reclined, his green skin luminous in the subdued, underworld glow, a shock of red, unruly hair making for a grotesque effect. Reaching halfway to the ceiling, a thick, sturdy phallus of deep vermillion quivered in the eerie light. As Ibrahim gaped and held his breath, a spiral band of frosty white wound itself around the huge shaft from tip to base.

Spellbound, Ibrahim saw two lovely girls enter the vast chamber from behind the large bed of cushions. They were totally nude and as young or agelessly perfect as nymphs. With cries of delight, they stared up at the striped, erotic column, extending their arms toward it with uncontrolled desire. The demon extended his arms sideways, the palms raised. Each girl stepped lightly on the offered hand. One arm flashed and a girl rose high in the air to wrap her thighs tightly about the unbelievable pole. Hugging it with her arms, she began to descend with dizzying speed, spinning in a spiral as though guided by the white stripe. Before she was halfway down, the other girl was catapaulted aloft to begin the same giddy descent. Ibrahim divined, without knowing how, that a vibration was causing the strange glow, a vibration so high it was invisible. As fast as the girls struck the demon's body, so fast were they thrown back to repeat the downward voyage. Screams of animal abandon filled the chamber as the two young bodies began glowing with perspiration that shimmered from the intense vibrations.

Hutti called out, shouting Musa's name. An angry green face loomed up, wreathed in a snarling grimace. The two girls fell headlong into the cushions. In a placating, almost pleading voice, Hutti apologized for the disturbance; he would never have been so bold if there was not an immediate, urgent need for the demon's services. Musa roared back like an infuriated lion. If his grand and glorious father could see he was busy, what right did he have to snoop? Or, for that matter, destroy the beautiful and enchanting spell Musa was weaving. As though to back this complaint, the two girls sat up and began crying inconsolably.

Hutti apologized again, even more profusely. Musa was needed for a very important assignment. It wouldn't take long, he could come back and play again very soon. With a grumpy expression, the demon asked, pointedly, what was it *this* time? As Hutti launched into his plan concerning Hassan, Ibrahim watched the huge phallus shrink down to its normal twelve or so inches. The two girls stopped crying and reached out to grab it. In a twinkle, it contracted and disappeared, lost in a secret cavity. The girls pouted for a moment and listlessly began making love to each other.

Farah waved a hand and the scene shifted. A large caravan was threading its way up from Egypt and entering the narrow strip between the Red Sea and the Mediterranean, aiming for Jerusalem; it was a clear night, a full moon rising in the east and millions of stars twinkling overhead. Flanked by two heavily-armed guards, Hassan rode at the head of his small army of vigilant men and burdened camels as they neared some craggy hills in the eternal wilderness. Rounding the first outcropping, the leaders halted, staring with disbelief at a huge, square mass that blocked their path. Expelled air whistled past Hassan's thick lips. The obstruction seemed half the size of the base of one of the great pyramids. He rose from the saddle and held up his hand. Camel by camel, the train came to a disorderly and somewhat lethargic halt. He called out the names of the nearest men and they rode forward. Dismounting, a group of ten men moved out cautiously to inspect the outlandish object; taut, swords in hand, they appeared to be stalking a dragon.

While still over two hundred yards from the huge block, a voice like thunder from the heavens rolled across the sands. On pain of instant death, none were to approach save he who was called Hassan ibn Mohammed. Startled, the men halted and held a hurried conference. When they looked up again, a corner of the square mountain broke loose and came hurtling toward them. Before they could jump back, it landed at Hassan's feet. With only the stars and moon for light, Hassan did not have to look closer to identify the object. Curtly, he ordered the guards back to the caravan. When they were far enough away, he crouched and touched the jagged piece, stroking it lasciviously, as though it were a woman's thigh. In a hushed and restrained rumble, the voice beckoned him toward the mountain. Why play with a small piece when the whole mountain was there? In fact, his for the asking…if he could fulfill one simple condition.

Hassan's ponderous body jerked forward as though drawn by powerful magnets. When he stood before the magnificent block of gold, an invisible presence spoke to him, pouring verbal honey over his peerless greed. He had over two hundred pack camels, did he not? Loaded with what? All sorts of merchandise he would have to sell…all in all, endless hours of bickering, bartering, wrangling and trading…for what? *One* camel load of gold…if he were lucky? Dump all that useless rubbish, free the camels to carry nothing but gold. Over two hundred camels, loaded with all the gold they could carry…just think of it! He could forget about the long march to Jerusalem, he could return now to Bagdad, the world's richest man. And he would not have to worry about brigands or even the caliph's men, he would be protected by supernatural powers wherever he went. What king or emperor – from Cathay to Córdoba – could boast such wealth?

Tremulously, Hassan reached out and touched the unbelievable mountain. Maybe what could not be transported could be hidden; how many journeys would it take to get it all? As though in answer to his insatiable lust, the gold sent a current of warmth through the hand to permeate his entire body. It was so warm and powerful he nearly fainted. What, he asked craftily, would he have to do to gain this unique fortune…what was that simple condition his would-be benefactor had alluded to?

Simple, indeed, the voice answered soothingly. All he had to do was seek out a woman he knew well, a woman named Maryam. When he found her, he was to ask…no, beg her forgiveness so sincerely and profoundly that it would be granted. By his penitence and his piety, he would wash away the disfiguring wounds he had inflicted. He would have to atone for his sins, nothing more. To accomplish this, he would have to renounce and banish every bit of desire. One iota of covetous passion would be his undoing. If he could agree to this, the gold was his.

Shifting from foot to foot, his body swaying and his head bent, Hassan created the picture of a worthy penitent deeply contemplating his unseen benefactor's offer. He could hardly believe his ears. A Djinn had come to him like this, his heart sang happily? He would build Maryam a house of solid silver. A mosque in her honour, beautiful in every detail. He would appear before her in rags and covered in ashes, repentant. The world had never seen the like of such piety. The total cost would surely not be greater than the gold one camel could carry. Out of two hundred and twenty camels? Why, it was less than one-half of one percent! Adopting an aspect of great humility, Hassan bowed and agreed.

Pictures raced across the bowl of sand below Ibrahim's eyes. Sensing his disquiet, Farah squeezed his hand reassuringly. As the sun rose over the scene he had been watching, the wilderness appeared to be littered everywhere with piles of cloth and merchandise of every description, all of it abandoned with haste. In the distance to the east, the long train of camels struggled along, burdened to the breaking point with their new cargo. In the foreground, the huge block of gold seemed hardly diminished by the crazed onslaught of Hassan's men, though the surface was no longer smooth and square. Musa, clearly visible in the sunlight, sat on top of his golden block, holding his sides and laughing hysterically.

The old woman passed her hand over the bowl and the tiny particles of pigment began to form a new picture.

132

In the deep of a new night, Ibrahim saw Hassan's entourage camped at an oasis. He picked out Hassan's tent, set off by itself and nearly dwarfed by the piled up baggage of two hundred and twenty camels. Fires burned brightly everywhere and guards on duty paced the perimeters as the rest of the company dozed uneasily.

The picture altered focus until only Hassan's tent stood out. Musa's image, all but invisible, leaned against a palm tree; the demon's attention was riveted on the tent's entrance. Like a wisp of vapour, he suddenly slipped between the flaps. The exterior of the tent disappeared and Ibrahim saw Hassan sitting on his carpeted and cushioned dais, a huge lump of gold resting between his splayed legs. His pudgy hands stroked it lovingly; it was obvious from his attitude he was completely unaware of the demon's presence. With a villainous sneer, Musa dropped to his haunches at the edge of the rolled out carpet and crossed his legs. The sneer became a concupiscent smile and he wove patterns in the air with his hands, the gestures wafting alluring subliminal impressions in Hassan's direction.

This new psychic force went through Hassan like a discharge of lightning. Abruptly losing all interest in the gold, he raised a leg and pushed it to one side. His gross thighs and midriff began quivering uncontrollably; astounded, he looked down to see an unusually large swelling rising up under his robe. Startled, he heard a slight scratching on the tent flap. Like a small boy caught masturbating, he threw a few cushions over the lump of gold and placed one on his groin to hide the protuberence. Regaining his composure somewhat, he called out imperiously that whoever was there might enter.

A slender, delicate hand slipped around one of the flaps, held it tauntingly for a moment, then pulled it back. The next instant, Maryam stood inside the tent, her body covered from neck to feet in a thin, gossamer garment which enhanced rather than hid her splendid body.

With a gasp rising in his throat, Ibrahim leaned forward, straining toward the revealing bowl of sand and its disturbing image. Farah's strong fingers warned him: such negative vibrations would obliterate the picture. He must control himself.

Calming himself, Ibrahim watched the image of Maryam remove a thin veil to reveal the scars on her face. She loosed the gown and let it fall to the ground, displaying the ugly wounds on her body. In a voice soft and sibilant, she told Hassan that he alone could undo the evil he had wrought. If he were truly contrite and sincerely wanted her forgiveness, let him bathe each of her wounds in his tears of remorse, that they might be washed away by genuine atonement.

The image flickered, as though in tune with the torches stuck in the sand. Ibrahim watched varying shades of emotion played across the fat man's face. In the wavering light, suppressing his laughter, Musa's hands gestured again. Maryam's body began to shimmer with an unearthly glow, undulating, sending irresistible messages to the wide-eyed Hassan. Only then did Ibrahim realize that this Maryam he watched was a fantastically life-like illusion created by the demon. With a twinge of annoyance, he knew he had been as gullible as Hassan; how else would she appear from nowhere in that wilderness?

Hassan crossed the carpet on his hands and knees, drawn to the shimmering illusion like a fish on a hook. When he knelt in front of her, she asked if he had any tears at all to shed. The pudgy face puckered ludicrously as he forced tears to his eyes. When his eyes were swimming, she pointed to a scar on the inner part of her right thigh, swinging the leg out to reveal it. She moved closer to him, angling her body invitingly. Hassan pressed his tear-stained face to the scar. As he did, Maryam shifted her weight again, moving the other leg out to expose the hidden inner recesses of her womanhood.

Hassan's rapt expression told Ibrahim that a scent so heavenly was being exuded from the facsimile of the girl's body, the hypnotized victim's wits were being deranged thoroughly. His head lolled and he whinged and whinnied like a confused, frightened child. Maryam's legs inched further apart and opalescent drops glistened on the fine, ivory skin of her thighs. Gibbering wildly, Hassan plunged forward desperately, burying his face in that stunning, overpowering chalice of joy.

A tremendous clap of thunder struck the tent, shredding the cloth into millions of fragments. A howling wind smote the camp, raising thick clouds of sand that sent men screaming in terror in all directions. In another illuminating flash, Ibrahim saw the illusion of Maryam disappear and, in her place, stood Musa, fully visible, shrieking like an avenging fallen angel from the pit of the damned.

Crying in panic, Hassan rubbed his eyes with shaking hands, unwilling to accept his own perceptions. Musa struck the defending hands down and pointed two glowing, fiery fingers at Hassan's face. They shot forward like striking serpents and bounced off Hassan's terror-stricken eyeballs. He recoiled in pain and horror. As he rolled blinded, screaming and helpless on the carpet, Musa stepped out into the opaque night.

Ibrahim could no longer see Musa, but the fiery trails he left in the sandstorm clearly indicated he was flying through the air, creating the impression he was everywhere at once. Men, camels, baggage and all the camp equipment rose up into the violent tornado and shot through the air with blinding speed. As quickly as it had appeared the storm died, the sand settling on a landscape calm once more. There was nothing left but a deserted oasis and no sign that a huge caravan had been quartering there. Save for one desperate fat man crawling blindly along on his hands and knees, crying out for help that was no longer there.

In the bowl before him, Ibrahim watched the illusion of sand flying across the dark wilderness; it came to rest finally at the spot where Hassan had first seen the huge block of gold. All the pieces which had been cut away were back in place, the whole as smooth as it had been at the start. To the southwest, in the direction of Egypt, men and camels were picking themselves up and wandering about in bewildered confusion. All about them lay strewn the scattered cargo that had been dumped to make room for the precious gold. Not one man among them retained an inkling of memory; it seemed they had been struck by an horrendous wind storm which had denuded the camels of their burdens. As they set about the task of repacking, Ibrahim sensed they would accept Hassan's absence as a casualty of the storm.

Musa sat like a shimmering shadow atop the huge gold block. He laughed as the gold began sinking under the sands. He too disappeared as the sands closed over him. There was a minute flash and the picture was gone.

Just before Farah released his hand, he felt a tremor go through her body. She reached out and ran her hand over the sand. It broke a spell of sorts; he felt the room brighten, the light normal again. Birds were singing and the sounds of the city's teeming life reached him.

'Why did you show me Hassan's fate?' he asked haltingly, his voice husky.

'You saw but one stage of what you call his fate,' she answered calmly. 'He is not dead. Why? That you might see and understand the Djinni...especially the one who torments Maryam.'

'Many things could have illustrated that,' he countered doggedly. 'Why particularly Hassan?'

'It seemed more relevant. Are you not pleased that Maryam's terrible defilement has been avenged?'

He placed his hand over hers and his head bowed with deep consternation. 'I am appalled. Would that I could have helped him. This will teach him nothing, it will only increase his senseless hatred. He doesn't need punishment...' Ibrahim looked at the old woman. She saw the tears and smiled softly.

'I had hoped you would say that. You are truly ready for the next stage of your journey. Dear Ibrahim, the path is shortening.'

He smiled sadly and squeezed her hand. 'You sound like Anwar.'

'And so do you...that is why I know the path is shorter, the end in sight.'

136

'I believe you must know him,' Ibrahim brightened, looking into her dark and fathomless eyes. 'Do you? You have never said so.'

'I will tell you a story that very few know,' she answered simply. 'But briefly, for Fatima will soon be here.'

'Very many years ago, there was a devout and gifted cobbler who lived and worked in Mecca. When he was still quite young, a marriage was arranged for him by his father. As was his fashion, he approached his bride with the same unquestioning acceptance he applied to everything in life. His love for her was as enduring as his faith. His trade thrived for a fundamental and simple reason: he made the best shoes that could be fashioned by the hand of man. More, he never turned a person away because he could not pay enough. Many were those shod freely, for he was a compassionate and charitable man. By the example of his own upright life, he warmed and enriched the lives of all who knew him. Many came from near and far just to seek his advice. None went away empty-handed.

This singular yet simple man and his wife had but one child, a girl. When the child reached womanhood, she was married to a kind-hearted youth who chose to follow his father-in-law's trade. Soon after, they too had an only child, again a daughter. A few months before the cobbler's grandchild reached her fifth birthday, his wife died as one of the victims of a fever which spread throughout the city. He buried his own sadness in order to give strength and courage to the others. On the day his granddaughter was five, he took her for a walk to the centre of the city and pointed to a spot on the road. There, he told her, my father stood holding his father's hand when the Prophet passed by with his companions. Mohammed detached himself and crossed the road to lay his hand on my father's head. He was exactly five years old. When I was five, my father brought me here and repeated the ceremony. Today, this transmission of bakara or grace I will pass on to you.

That afternoon, he announced to his daughter and son-in-law that he was leaving them in the morning. His apprentice was now a master cobbler and could easily get along on his own. He would take nothing with him, for he would be seeking a new life of the spirit; his old life was finished and the greatest gift they could give him was to accept his decision and remember him as he would always pray for them.'

Farah stopped speaking and turned to Maryam who had just stirred for the first time.

'That was Anwar?' Ibrahim whispered. Farah looked at the tall man seated next to her. His eyes told her that he could hardly accept the crone before him as Anwar's granddaughter. Then the acceptance was there, beyond any doubt.

'An extraordinary man,' she answered. 'One day, you will be too.'

'Extraordinary in the case of Anwar is an understatement, Farah. Now, of course, I see many things.'

'Yes,' she agreed cryptically, 'you are beginning to "see" in a new and better way. Before Maryam wakes, tell me if you can see when your journey begins.'

'Tomorrow. I cannot tell you in words how I know. Just that the time has come. I cannot see clearly to the end of the road. But the road does lead back to Bashtahal. For all three of us. Yet, how Maryam can travel...'

'If a man who wishes to beat a dog can always find a stick, we who have better things to do and higher purposes, can always find a camel.'

'That reminds me of something...a story you might wish to hear, as Maryam still sleeps.'

After he had given away every last bit of his worldly goods, Ibrahim had said, rather naïvely, 'Now, Anwar, I have nothing.' The old man's laugh had been kindly and indulgent. How, he had asked, could Ibrahim know what it was to have nothing? Why not, he suggested, undertake to teach himself what the word nothing meant. To do that, he must now search for the poorest man in the world. He might well be surprised to discover how relative that could

138

be. If he could find that man, then he must surely also find at least one thing he could give that man. One thing which would make Ibrahim even poorer.

For many days Ibrahim wandered, accepting the quest without reservations, yet puzzled. He had nothing but the burnous on his back, the staff in his hand and the sandals on his feet. He knew Anwar was trying to teach him something more profound than that. At first, he had fasted voluntarily, hoping that even his body would understand total impoverishment. Fate took that decision out of his hands. He misjudged the distance to the next village; when he finally arrived, he was delirious from lack of food and water. His altered state offered him one bit of insight: if he could not reach that final goal of being poorer than the poorest, he would never be able to mine the riches in his own heart.

He stood gaunt and mute before the tiny, mud-walled dwelling; the suspicious woman saw him sway from side to side, hardly able to raise a supplicating hand. She looked into his eyes for seconds on end. Then, without a word, she turned and disappeared. A moment later, she returned with a chunk of stale bread and an old dipper filled with water. He tried to croak his thanks, but couldn't until he had swallowed some of the water.

Stumbling uncertainly, he moved off down the road, breaking off but a small mouthful of bread. Before his hand could reach his mouth, he saw the small pile of human wreckage at the side of the road, leaning against a garden wall. A light breeze fluttered the ancient mendicant's flimsy, tattered garment; Ibrahim saw the fragments of sandals still attached to the skeletal feet. Next to the old man, a staff rested on the ground. The head moved sparingly, just enough for the sunken eyes to find Ibrahim's. He neither looked at the bread nor held out a begging hand. Ibrahim leaned forward and placed the larger piece of bread on the resting hands. As he continued down the road, he stuffed the small morsel in his mouth and began chewing. He worked very hard to force his mouth to retain the bread as long as possible, to let the juices trickle slowly down his gullet.

Just before he turned a corner, he looked back. In front of the old man stood a dog. Or a few sticks of bone wrapped in dried parchment representing what once was a dog. The animal's mouth was open and the old man put all of his bread into the dog's mouth.

Ibrahim clutched his staff in both hands, sinking to his knees on the dusty road. His heart ached terribly and he could not be sure that he heard cries coming from deep inside himself. Even worse was the terribly bitter taste in his mouth. For a very long time he wandered, his dream-like state seeming to extend forever. The days were filled with his own rancour, reviling himself for that one morsel of bread he had kept. Finally, he accepted that the lesson was valid. He had much to learn and could not allow himself to be destroyed for one failure. Even more finally, he saw how pride itself was the destructive force. His remorse and self-anger were merely vestiges of the pride he still had not exorcised. He looked into the hypocrisy and self-deception and felt truly ashamed.

In the end, he returned to Anwar and told him the story of his failure. Again, Anwar smiled lovingly. From behind him, he took a dry, rock-hard piece of bread. To his surprise, Ibrahim recognized every angle, depression and contour. It was burned into his memory: there was no other chunk of bread like it in the world. Anwar placed it in his hand, saying: 'Keep it with you always. It will teach you that you succeeded. Whenever your footsteps falter and your purpose is in doubt, smell that bread. It will remind you of the moment when your heart was the most impoverished heart in the world.'

That day, Ibrahim set out for Mecca. He pondered his strange adventure endlessly. The bread was real, but how had Anwar come by it? The old man and the dog he had seen in the road, were they mere illusions, all of it halluci-nation caused by his delirium? Until this day, when he had seen the illusion created by the demon…

'Do not jump to conclusions, Ibrahim,' Farah warned him, rising and taking the bowl to the back of the room.

Ibrahim followed with the cloths and the powders; the old woman stored them all in a cupboard.

'I was merely speculating...' he began.

'Speculate always on the lesson, not the manner of the teaching,' she advised.

A sudden clatter on the ladder announced Fatima's arrival. When they turned back to greet her, Maryam was sitting up, her eyes shining and fixed on the door.

XV

Ibrahim held the camel back as they approached the last oasis west of Bashtahal. The crazed animal scented the water, but the man knew she would plunge into the pool and stir up the sand before any of them had a chance to drink. Usually the most tractable of beasts, she was now berserk with thirst. With strength and patience, he calmed her down and made her kneel, still many yards short of her goal.

Holding the reins in his teeth, he helped Fatima ease Maryam off the special, deeply padded saddle he had made for her.

'Drink and wash at this side of the pool,' he told them, 'and I'll manoeuvre the camel to the opposite side, away from the spring.' He looked up at the first stars, the light failing rapidly. 'It will be dark soon. When I have the fire started and our bedding arranged, I suggest both of you bathe...it will be the last chance before we reach Bashtahal.'

He watched Fatima take Maryam's arm and guide her slow footsteps toward the water. Each day, Maryam's walking improved. There was no longer reason to doubt her full recovery, except that, when questioned, Fatima admitted the wounds caused by her vicious, unnatural rape stubbornly refused to respond. Ibrahim shuddered to think what the long hours in even the softest saddle did to her. Or how much excruciating pain the normal daily functions of her body caused. He always managed to absent himself when the time came; he would have done so for motives of delicacy and consideration, yet he knew he could not have borne to hear her cries.

By the time they returned from their bath, he had a cheery fire blazing and a frugal meal prepared from nearly the last of their supplies. It was enough, he told himself, for surely we will reach the city by tomorrow evening.

When the meal was finished, he helped Fatima settle Maryam on the extra, warm robes Farah had supplied. He unfastened the camel's tether and moved her on so that she could continue to forage in the sparse undergrowth.

'Ibrahim,' Maryam called, 'you have done enough for one day, please take your bath now before you fall with exhaustion.'

On returning, he brought more sticks to keep the fire going and settled himself between the two sleeping girls. Listening to the cropping of the camel and the soft hissing of the fire, he took one last look at the glorious canopy of stars overhead and fell into a deep sleep.

Maryam woke to see a thin crescent moon suspended above the oasis. Her body trembled unrestrainably and the heat radiating from it was greater than that coming from the embers of their cooking fire. She tried to focus on the bright stars and the moon, but everything blurred, refusing to stay put. She felt Ibrahim's back pressing her from one side, Fatima's body curled up tightly on the other. Had one of them changed places to keep her warm? The way she was burning and shaking, surely she would wake them both. She closed her eyes and made a supreme effort to rise. Something contracted, there was a bright, shimmering light behind her eyelids, then she seemed to expand, rising into the air and floating away.

Standing at the edge of the pool, Maryam looked back at the peaceful scene. Ibrahim's long shape didn't move. Fatima rolled over and then backed up to the body in the middle. That body was...her own. She looked down along the body which stood by the pool. It too was her body...at least, it looked substantial enough. She looked up at the trees, then toward the sky. It all seemed right, if a bit misty. Deeply perplexed, she looked back at her own sleeping form. All three bodies, the trees, the pool at her feet began to evaporate.

No, her foggy mind argued, that can't be it, for it feels as if I'm travelling somewhere, everything is slipping by so rapidly, I can't even see it. She felt consciousness sliding away from her and fought with all her might to retain it. When she opened her eyes, she was standing on the plain of Bashtahal, about fifty yards from Anwar's hillock. She looked up and blinked.

Anwar was seated in his usual place, but he was surrounded by a great aura of bright light which twinkled and changed colours, flashing and pulsating enough to dim the stars overhead. Suddenly, it went out as a stone struck the old man's chest. Gasping, Maryam looked down. Hundreds of townspeople were milling around, waving their arms angrily and shouting. A troop of soldiers on foot and mounted on horses and camels moved about. Three men were tied together at the base of the hill and foot soldiers were protecting them from the angry crowd. More soldiers appeared from behind the hillock. Each group of four laboriously carried a huge jar. When eight of them stood lined up in front of the three trussed-up men, the commander of the troop rose up in the stirrups of a cream-coloured thoroughbred and shouted instructions. A group of soldiers clambered up the hill and began tearing at something behind Anwar. A few moments later, a large tangle of thin metal strips rolled down the hillock to come to rest near the jars. When the group of soldiers descended, another angry roar went up from the mob and Maryam saw many stones fly through the air. Two of them struck Anwar's chest, a third smashed into his face, just below his right eye. The old man's body rocked, swayed forward uncertainly, then righted itself.

Distressed to the breaking point, the helpless projection of Maryam saw a huge, shadowy figure materialize on the pinnacle behind the beleaguered sage. Even in her shocked state, Maryam recognized the huge Djinn. She saw him stretch forward until his body was parallel to the ground and stretched so far he could begin to wrap his arms protectively about Anwar. Immediately, Anwar stretched his arms out fully on either side and blocked the Djinn. In her mind, she knew his name to be Hawwaz and that he was pleading with Anwar, assuring the old man that he wanted nothing in return. Before that registered fully, she saw a huge hand streak down from the sky behind the pinnacle and jam itself between the Djinn's thighs. It wrapped itself about the enormous golden penis and yanked it back. The hand, the captive penis and the Djinn disappeared as through a hole in the sky.

Another shout from the crowd diverted her attention. From the west a large cavalcade of horses, camels and men rode at breakneck speed toward the tense scene. With a shout, the commander mustered his troops, all of them mounting save two guards with the prisoners. They wheeled and fanned out to intercept the new threat. She saw the commander's face blanch when he recognized the imperial banner.

When the new troops drew up, a dignified man with white robes and a flowing white beard rode to the head of the company on a splendidly caparisoned horse. Ignoring the glowering captain of the opposing entourage, the dignitary gazed up at Anwar, then signalled to some of his people. Three men rode up to confer with him, then dismounted. Detaching bags and pouches from their saddles, the triumvirate ascended the hillock rapidly. For the first time, individual voices reached Maryam distinctly. The angry captain shouted that any interference with the soldiers of the caliph would not be tolerated. They were here with express commissions from the caliph to capture a gang of thieves, swindlers and heretics. He pointed to the three men who were tied up, then to Anwar.

'Captain,' the princely older man called back, 'I am Sheikh Ahmad El-Sayed, Director of the Collegium of the Faithful in Jerusalem and personal emissary of the caliph. The most honoured member of our fraternity seems to have been wounded…under your protection, I might add. While my physicians are attending to those wounds, perhaps you would specify your case against him?'

The commander hesitated, then called for a man Maryam had not noticed before. He was not a soldier, she discerned from his rich robes and headgear.

'That honoured member of your fraternity,' the

captain called back, 'has been guilty of representing himself as a prophet. With these jars, stolen from the caliph's treasury, and the aid of this metallic tangle, he created a saintly aura of lights about him to fool these innocent people and swindle them of their silver.'

'I see,' the sheikh answered gently. He turned in his saddle and faced the gathered townspeople. 'Has anyone here ever heard Anwar say he was a prophet?' After a moment's shuffling and doubt, heads began shaking from side to side. 'Anyone who has heard Anwar claim to be a prophet, please step forward,' he called out loudly. None stepped forward. 'Has any one of these three men,' he cried, pointing to Najmuddin, Hakim and Mirza, 'ever said Anwar was a prophet?' The crowd roared affirmatively. 'Has anyone seen mysterious lights surrounding Anwar?' The entire crowd shouted yes.

'Captain, on behalf of the worshipful caliph, do you claim that Anwar went to Bagdad and stole these...uh... things you claim have magical properties?'

'This man is one of the caliph's alchemists,' the captain rumbled petulantly, 'and he has identified them as the very ones stolen. They are *here...with* your saint and his three accomplices...'

'Now, captain,' the sheikh admonished, 'you have not proved that Anwar stole them or that these men are his accomplices. It is true, however, that he might have been their unwilling accomplice...another matter entirely. Now, for the sake of justice and the satisfaction of these good townspeople – and surely you would not want a blood-thirsty mob on your hands as he is *their* saint – would you ask the alchemist to demonstrate how these magical lights work?'

The commander leaned down for a hurried conference with the alchemist. When it was over, the man did not seem all that sure of himself. A quarter of an hour and more went by as, with the help of a few soldiers, he connected, disconnected and reconnected the copper strands to various combinations of jars. In the end, he had to give it up in complete chagrin.

'*They* made it work,' the captain called back angrily, 'you just heard these people, they all saw it.'

'No, captain,' the sheikh remonstrated mildly, 'the people said only that they saw an aura of light, not that these jars created it. How could that be if your own soldiers, with the help of the caliph's esteemed alchemist, cannot produce even a flicker? Are you saying that your prisoners are wiser than a man of science?'

Rattled, the captain scowled. 'There can be no question that these good townspeople, as you call them, have been swindled out of a fortune.' He turned and raised himself in his stirrups. 'Is that not true?' he shouted to the crowd. 'Did they take your silver or didn't they?' A rumble began to build as the crowd exhibited fresh anger.

The sheikh swung his horse about and rode to the nearest man in the crowd. He asked him to move toward the hillock, then selected two more men and three women, requesting they do the same.

In the hush that followed, in answer to kindly questions put by the sheikh, each person told his own story. Miracles of healing were described. Lost relatives found. Unhappy marriages restored. Barren women conceiving. More people pressed forward, each eager to add his testimony. It took the sheikh many minutes to calm them and restore silence. The captain was no fool; his men might have been a match for the sheikh's troops, but not with the crowd solidly on their side.

'What did Anwar do with all that money?' the emissary from Jerusalem called out. As with one voice, they bellowed back that most of it had been distributed to the poor.

'Well, captain?' the sheikh called out. The confounded officer looked about, then silently fussed with his bridle. 'As you would surely regret creating unnecessary unrest or insurrection, you will have no objection if we ask Anwar to accompany us back to Jerusalem. Incidentally, I strongly suspect you will find your prisoners' portion of the townspeople's money where you found the jars. Do distribute it among them,' he added, loudly enough for the crowd to hear.

When the sheikh had dismounted and made his way to the top of the hillock, he sat before Anwar and bowed deeply.

'Master, will you come with us now? Please share your knowledge with us.'

'Thank you, Ahmad. Your arrival is timely indeed…in more ways than one. It just so happens I will soon have something of great importance to attend to in the holy city. As to my knowledge…you flatter me, Ahmad.'

'We will prepare a litter for you…'

'Not at all,' Anwar answered, shifting the bandage that covered his eye, 'I am not that infirm…yet. If you will leave me for a few moments only, I will join you.'

The sheikh had not reached the base of the hillock before Anwar started down. As he passed the silent crowd, one man stepped forward with tears in his eyes. He kneeled and extended a hand beseechingly.

'Before you ask,' Anwar laughed, 'forgiveness is not important. Learn charity and compassion and remember how fortunate you are that you didn't stone a prophet.'

The old man mounted the offered camel and when it rose, he turned his attention to a point beyond the crowd, focusing his good eye intently. Maryam felt the glance pass through her like a physical force. Warm fibres of silvery light wound themselves about her and lifted her from the ground. She felt herself vibrating in tune with the force as a clear triangle of light formed on the sand beneath her feet; immediately, another one formed and the two triangles moved until the apex of one touched the apex of the other. It seemed all the vibrations now formed an emanation that went out from her and infused the nearest triangle. The second was imbued with Anwar's essence. Then Anwar's triangle moved and did not stop until it was superimposed on her own, forming a six-cornered star.

The glowing star moved up, bearing her with it. She felt herself float over the groups of people below; she was aware that the caliph's men were heading east with their prisoners and the jars while the sheikh's entourage headed west. The people of Bashtahal watched mutely as the camels and horses moved off. Anwar still sat stock still in the saddle, his gaze trained on the top of the hillock.

The scene faded from Maryam's view. She came to rest on the shallow pile of carpets, the star still glowing brightly beneath her. Suddenly, she started receding backward, though at first it seemed the hillock was racing away from her. As the night enclosed her more and more, she could still see that one star, separate from all the rest, shining on the no longer visible hilltop. She was aware then of the light trickle of the spring as it struck the pool. Palm fronds, dry and parched, rattled in the pre-dawn breeze. The camel strained at its tether. A faint glow in the west indicated the departure of the moon. Three bodies were stretched out in a shallow depression beneath the protective trees and bushes. She saw a very fine silver cord stretching from the body in the middle to her other self at the poolside. Drawn by the cord, she moved forward and down until surrounded by that still form. Inside, it was so hot with fever she could not think clearly. What dreams, she wondered, would this cauldron of flesh not cast up? She felt herself sliding down into endless flames, her throat so sore it could have been a nest for scorpions.

XVI

'YOU TRAITOROUS LITTLE FOOL, YOU nearly ruined everything...how dare you slip away like that? Look at them!' Hutti pointed to a dark magenta cloud just beginning to form on the far horizon.

'They're leagues away!' Hawwaz stamped his foot with frustration. 'Don't you understand? They were stoning him...they may kill him.'

'You and your obsession with Anwar! I'm warning you, any more of this foolishness...' Hutti stopped speaking and crouched, peering at the enlarging cloud. 'Get under there and stay there this time. You owe me, understand?'

At the base of the gorgeous lotus sculpted of precious gems which Hutti had built to conceal the Fountain of Forgetfulness, an invisible rent had been made in the lush, carpet-like ground. He reached down and lifted the flap, pointing significantly with the forefinger of his other hand.

'What if the fountain sprays on me?' Hawwaz whined. 'I'll be in fluffyland for hours...'

'That's nothing compared to what I'll do to you if you try one more trick. Now, you promised...in you go.'

Hawwaz stretched out on his belly, his heels toward the upraised flap. Hutti worked the feet through, then walked back to push the rest of Hawwaz's body into concealment. Just before the head disappeared, Hutti grabbed the lobe of his friend's ear.

'You keep your hands just inside...at the ready, understand?'

His only answer was a resigned twitch of eyebrows. 'And you leave one finger sticking out...right?'

'I don't understand that...'

'I am going to place my heel over that finger. If you so much as move it, so much as try to slip away for one second…'

'Oh, Hutti, I'm not going anywhere…'

'You bet you're not! Now, when I say, "Oh, darling," that's your signal. You reach out and grab her ankles. You hold on with all your might so she can't fly away…understand? A moment later, I push her in. The sculpture collapses and she is in the land of forgetfulness.'

'And you talk about people being obsessed,' Hawwaz muttered.

'Just get in there and stick that finger out, they're nearly here.'

Hutti rested his heel on the finger and tried to compose himself. He cocked the knee above the finger-holding heel and turned slightly to the side, offering his best profile. Too posey, he decided. As self-assured as Hawwaz when he discovered his ranji was not just for playing diamond hockey with. He lifted his head and arched his neck with great hauteur. Reaching down, he grabbed his ranji and stretched it out; squinting down his nose, he strove for the most attractive balance, then draped it alluringly over his left arm.

Looking up, he saw dozens of Djinni gathering along the far horizon; the steady, churning magenta cloud was developing solidity and heading toward him at breakneck speed. Suddenly, he saw individual females spin out of the cloud and pounce on waiting males. His skin tingled giddily, he could hardly contain himself.

'"Aysha," I will say,' he whispered to himself, '"you are the most beautiful creature in existence." When she steps closer and reaches for me, I will say – "Look! I made this for you." When she cries out with admiration, I will say, "Oh, Darling…" and push with all my might.' As he said this, he raised up on his toes and bunched his magnificent muscles. In that split second, Hawwaz popped a moist date stone from his cheek and slipped it under the descending heel. A split second later, he was straddling the pinnacle over Anwar's hilltop.

Anwar was gone! Everyone was gone! Blinking with disbelief and misery, the Djinn stared down at the hilltop, his vision swooping in for a closer look. He saw the now dimly glowing, six-pointed star and scowled.

'It isn't true!' he screamed at the sky overhead. 'The Pillar of Islam, practically the leading authority, and all this time a secret Hebrew?' Then something clicked in his mind. The Seal of Solomon, that was it. It had been burned into the stopper of the urn in which Anwar had imprisoned him for those stupid camel drivers. Snarling, he grabbed his ranji and began swinging it over his head with such speed it became a dim, golden blur in the night. Extending further and further, it at last became long enough and with a roar of fury, he dipped the lashing motion and struck the star. The shock that struck his body forced a howl of pain from him; the ranji came flying back, shrivelling and twisting like a snake that has been dropped into a fire. It struck his body so hard, it knocked the air out of him. When he recovered, he lifted it tenderly and kissed the ruby tip. Venomously, the shaft lashed out and the tip struck him so hard on the bridge of the nose, he was momentarily blinded, seeing nothing but stars. When he recovered, he bit his lip. In all the pain, his only comfort was that the star was no longer visible.

'Hutti!' he roared... 'oh, no.' The Pop! sent him hurtling back to the hiding place under the fountain. He reached out and grabbed the ankles. Muffled screams reached him, but he held on doggedly. No matter what, he hissed to himself, I must not let go.

The next thing he knew, he was lying on the ground, face down, with two unattached legs in his hands. A foot in the middle of his back kept him pinned down. Raising his head, he looked balefully about him.

A few feet away, Hutti's motionless torso greeted him. Then he saw the dismantled arms. He turned his head and saw Hutti's face twisted into a horrible grimace. The separated head was lying on a carefully arranged mound of jewels. With a shudder, Hawwaz tossed the two legs away from him.

'Poor Hawwaz,' a delightful, musical voice tinkled, 'always ready to do anything Big Brother asks. Don't you know he'll never get you into anything but trouble?'

The foot in his back flicked and he was lying face up, staring into the eyes of the most beautiful creature in existence. Blue hair cascaded down to her waist in front, framing the magnificent breasts that swelled and throbbed with unbearable invitation. The slender legs tapered down to small, elegant feet and he stared at the one placed on his belly. How could they have so much strength? Her skin was like the inside of a pearl oyster shell and shimmered in the soft light. The smallest triangle of golden dates did nothing to veil the incredibly lovely secret beneath. But the tiny roseate orifice that pouted at him from the spot where humans have navels was the most fascinating aspect of all. Only through that precious entrance could she be fertilized.

'You have the same foolish thoughts as your over-confident and self-styled genius over there, don't you?' Aysha demanded. 'Such supreme egotists, all of you. Inferior in every way, yet you think you are heaven's gifts to us. Never satisfied with the pleasure we offer you, you all want to turn us into breeding machines just to inflate your miserable little egos. My, my, my, the two of you are some pair.'

With a flip of her foot, she sent Hawwaz up in the air, catching him by the ears when he floated down. Holding him like that, she extended her four small translucent wings which began beating in opposite directions with a speed at least ten times that of a humming bird. When her breasts were level with Hawwaz's goggle-eyed face and his feet a few inches off the ground, the breasts began to change colour. One went chocolate brown, the other a strawberry red. Hawwaz's eyes darted one way and the other; he couldn't make a choice.

'You're such a typical little boy, simply can't make up your mind,' Aysha chided maternally. 'Go ahead, you may have both. But don't be greedy and make yourself sick.'

With a delighted gurgle in his throat, Hawwaz fastened his mouth to the chocolate breast and closed his eyes, sinking into blissful oblivion. When his ranji became fully erect, she clamped her thighs on it and released his ears.

Humming absently, Aysha began twisting one of Hawwaz's arms counter-clockwise. A moment later, she dropped it on the ground. She removed the other arm in the same way. Next, she removed both his legs and separated each at the knee. With happy abandon, she tossed each limb in a different direction, scattering them as she had Hutti's. When Hawwaz had nearly emptied the second breast, she drew it back gently and unscrewed his head. Gliding over to the mound of jewels on which Hutti's head reposed, she hovered just above the ground, holding Hawwaz's torso to her with one arm. His ear was caught in her teeth and she held it there while she built another small mound of precious stones. She set the head on top so that the two Djinni could see all the pieces of their bodies and look each other in the eye at the same time.

Aysha folded her wings and came to rest facing the two heads. With the preoccupation of a surgeon, she carefully removed Hawwaz's ranji from the torso, assuring that the pearl remained attached to the ranji. She laid the torso next to Hutti's and the ranji snaked along the ground and coiled up behind Hutti's, trembling in terror.

For the first time, Hawwaz saw the Fountain of Forgetfulness fully revealed. Hutti's elaborate masterpiece which had concealed it was nothing more than a scattered pile of rubble. With incredulity, he watched Aysha ignore the occasional drops that splashed her.

'Not talking to each other?' she asked, laughing, her hands resting lightly on her splendid hips. 'As soon as I leave, you'll be screaming at one another, won't you? I can just hear it now: "It's your fault, it's your fault," and you'll go on like that until you put yourselves together again. Well, it may one day sink in: we're just too smart for you.'

'The fountain doesn't work any longer,' Hutti wailed.

'Be more precise,' she advised. 'It doesn't work on me. Don't you think I knew what you were up to?'

'You were spying,' Hawwaz accused.

'Don't flatter yourselves. You're both so transparent, why bother spying?' She shook her head and picked up Hutti's terrified ranji.

'I'm not even going to enjoy it,' Hutti howled, 'I won't feel a thing.'

'Nobody's fault but your own,' she reminded him. 'If you must play the fool, then you have to pay the penalty.'

'It's simply not fair,' Hutti groaned. 'You make it seem so unnatural to love and want children. I brought Hawwaz up as though he were my own son. I miss all that. I just wanted a son of my own...'

He paused to squeeze the tears from his swimming eyes. 'Oh, never mind, you wouldn't understand. No more than you'd understand how much I love you.'

Aysha cocked her head and regarded the miserable Djinn as though she were seeing him for the first time. The seconds ticked by as she fondled the large pearl in her hand, the ranji itself dangling nearly to the ground, still terrified. Her brows were furrowed as she concentrated on her own thoughts. Finally, she shrugged, threw her shoulders back as a look of resolve crossed her divine features. She drew the tip of the ranji up and inserted it in the roseate orifice at the centre of her abdomen. Hutti gasped.

'We're not exactly heartless, you know,' she said in response to the shocked gasp. The entire ranji disappeared and only the pearl, quivering as it pressed into her flesh, was visible.

'You're actually going to...' Hutti's voice broke down with the emotion and he could not finish the sentence. Hawwaz's eyes were opened so wide, they accounted for nearly half his face.

'Yes, I'm actually going to let you have that son,' she finished for him. 'Not only that, I'm going to make a twin brother for him – or, I should say, a half-twin. With Hawwaz's life force.'

'Really!' Hawwaz's head bumped up and down on the pile of gems.

'Yes,' she drawled philosophically, 'and perhaps I should have done this a long time ago. The responsibility will do you both good. You might finally grow up.'

Both Djinni watched the deep magenta cloud begin to reform. In the distance females winged their way toward the vortex, singly and in groups. They watched Aysha join friends before she too disappeared inside the mass. In no time at all, it seemed, the cloud was gone, as though the females had never been there.

Hutti's eyes were closed tightly, his eyeballs rolled back. Hardly audible at first, the humming from inside his head began to increase by imperceptible stages. Somewhat like an advanced form of meditation, the Djinn was using the power it contained to concentrate a dynamo effect. With such unbroken concentration, the effect would become pure energy and in that form, discharge under his control to knit his body together again. Eyes wide open, Hawwaz bent his own forces on drawing his ranji to a point directly in front of his eyes.

'Did you enjoy that?' he asked, but not in words. He was transforming the same basic energy Hutti was using into a vibrational thought pattern, one to which his ranji could respond with fluency.

'Not particularly, I was too scared,' it answered, the thought crackling with fury.

'What are you so peeved about? we got taken apart, not you,' Hawwaz vibrated back hotly.

'Exactly! You two idiots will never learn. Now, look at you! Some other stupid plot up your sleeve. At least Hutti's doing what he's supposed to. By the time you get yourself together again...'

'Shhh, pay attention.' Hawwaz narrowed his eyes, trying to force unquestioning obedience. 'I have a mission for you. All on your own and time is precious. You and the pearl are going back to the earth plane...'

'Oh, no you don't!' the ranji warned. 'You don't care what you use me for, do you? Trying to blast that star Anwar left behind, you nit-wit. I'm still sore.'

'Calm down and pay attention,' Hawwaz ordered. He explained that Maryam had witnessed the scene of Anwar's stoning and his departure. She must have, because Anwar hadn't been there the second time, only the star. And Maryam had been travelling out of her body; her body must be at that oasis west of the city. No matter where Anwar was, he would have to capitulate if the ranji could take possession of her body. Under the right circumstances he could, all on his own. He would have the power to read her mind, to send thoughts into it, to influence her. It would be a creative milestone, he would be the first ranji in history to accomplish this on his own...

'You must be absolutely deranged,' the ranji snapped at him. 'Off on my own, indeed. And what if I can't get back? Fine fix you'd be in, to say nothing of me.'

'Will you please have a little faith?' Hawwaz closed one eye and concentrated the persuasion in the other. He knew ranjis understood a one-eyed approach. 'If you defy me, when I am together again...well, you know. I have my methods...'

The ranji trembled. 'Look, I'm exhausted. That sex-mad monster you two think is the be-all and end-all nearly wiped me out. I need some rest. Maybe a bit later we can discuss it. In the meantime, get smart, Hawwaz. Look at Hutti, he's almost there.'

Hawwaz shifted his gaze, opening the other eye. Like a cobra, the ranji shot through the air and landed behind Hutti's. Hawwaz gritted his teeth with vexation. Once again, he'd been outwitted. He closed his eyes and drew inside himself to build up the power he needed to catch up with Hutti. As he went into the trance, he allowed himself one reassuring thought: Hutti assumed he had merely grabbed the wrong pair of ankles. After all, that could happen to anyone.

'Feel like a little game of bash the diamond?' Hutti's ranji asked affably.

'Are you crazy too? I am exhausted. I've had all the action I need for one day, thank you.'

'No need to get huffy. We'll be half crazy with boredom waiting for those two, mark my words.'

'Until then, let's just have a long, refreshing nap, shall we?'

157

XVII

IBRAHIM HEARD THE QUICK, DARTING movement of a lizard on the dry bark of a tree. Again the silence was punctured by the sad cry of a distant bird – bird? he wondered sleepily. Then the camel grunted and yanked despondently against her tether. A small breeze fluttered, bringing the warmer breath of a new day rippling over the oasis pool. He sat up and rubbed his eyes, trying to chase the all-pervading fatigue. He looked down at the sleeping Maryam and his body was jolted into complete wakefulness.

He pressed his lower lip to her cheek, then her brow, feeling the dry heat radiate from her skin as from an abused anvil. Fatima was lying with her back to Maryam. Ibrahim rose quickly as Fatima began to turn over, seeking the warmth of her friend. Stepping over Maryam, he scooped Fatima up in his arms and trotted to the opposite side of the pool. He deposited her near the lusher undergrowth by the spring, easing her into a shallow trough. She woke as he straightened.

'What is it? Why did you take me away?'

'Shhh.' He squatted and placed a restraining hand on her shoulder. 'Maryam is ill with a very high fever. I don't want you to catch it, that's why I carried you here.'

'You don't want *me* to get it?' she retorted, struggling against his hand, 'what about *you*?'

'I will care for her. Somehow, I know I won't be infected. Or if I am, I am the stronger and I will get through it more easily than you. If it becomes too bad, you will have to ride to Bashtahal for help.'

'What can *you* do for her?' Fatima lowered her face into her hands and began crying.

'My dear, please don't lose your courage and strength. Don't you remember all the things Farah packed

158

for us in case of emergencies? There is a strong herbal tea and an unguent that penetrates the skin. After all,' he chided, hoping to firm her resolve, 'you are the expert now. You must instruct me from here.'

She wiped tears away with the back of her hand and looked up at him, ashamed for her momentary weakness.

'There is one thing you simply cannot do,' she began, but he pressed a finger to her lips.

'You will have to instruct me on changing those dressings, I am afraid. She will undoubtedly be delirious, so she will not be embarrassed.'

'Oh, Ibrahim,' she cried, clutching his arm, 'that is the *only* thing you have been spared.'

'Please rest and conserve your strength,' he counselled, 'I have to rebuild the fire quickly and boil water for the tea.'

Maryam whimpered softly but never became fully conscious, even as he fed the tea to her. She trembled violently as he rubbed the strong unguent into her body. As he worked, he practised a form of breath control Anwar had taught him; he also kept his mind clear, forcing it to transcend the circumstances. Although he was unprepared for the shock waves that rolled over him when he removed the dressings from between her thighs and buttocks, his face remained calm and serene. If compassion and sorrow filled his heart, his mind remained devoted to the task, to the immediate needs of the woman he loved so deeply. His own identity he distanced to infinity. In no way could he allow himself to hate Hassan ibn Mohammed.

A splash in the pool behind him turned his head. Naked, Fatima stood at the water's edge holding her dripping light robe toward him. Ibrahim picked up Maryam's robe, the twin of the other, and walked toward the pool.

'I will leave this here so it can be immersed in boiling water before I rinse it in the cool water. Throw me that one and go back to the other side.' He caught the wet robe and averted his eyes. 'Do you have anything else to wear?'

'You will have to change her at least once an hour if the wet robes are to bring the fever down. Don't worry about me, I'm quite comfortable…oh, I'm sorry, does it distract you?'

He smiled but didn't answer as he wrapped Maryam in the wet robe. Fatima was right, they were the only ones here.

As the sun set, Fatima prepared a meagre meal for Ibrahim and herself out of the last few bits of dried vegetables, supplemented by whatever edible shoots she could find near the spring. Instinctively, she knew Ibrahim had kept the camel away from there, saving the more nourishing plants for the beast's last meal before they pushed on. As she worked, Ibrahim prepared more of the herbal tea; he insisted Fatima share it, guaranteeing there was more than enough to see the patient through.

By the time it was dark, he had made a new bed for Fatima on the near side of the pool as the spring area would be too cool at night. It was far enough away for her safety, yet close enough for her to feel less isolated. He tethered the camel close by for what warmth she might supply the sleeping girl.

Before stretching out himself, he washed Maryam down one last time and rubbed the unguent into her body. His hands told him the crisis was not far off, the fever might even break that night. If so, they could be under way by the second day. He wrapped Maryam tenderly in a dry robe and covered her with his own heavy travelling burnous. Methodically, he relaxed his body, but not his mind. He needed sleep badly, but he felt he could not afford to be oblivious when her fever did break.

When the crescent moon was directly overhead, he stirred himself and put more sticks on the dying fire. In the silence, the whole world seemed to be standing still. Then Maryam sighed deeply. Another sound rumbled deep in her throat, hesitated for a moment, then words poured from her lips in a husky voice not at all like her own.

'I am standing before the hillock,' she recited in a stilted monotone. She went on to describe the scene in quite minute detail; as she did, the mysterious quality of her voice activated direct visualization for the man. Eyes open, he gazed past the fire and saw it all re-enacted over the surface of the pool. The voice went on, intoning the events with the steady dispassion of a youth reading a lesson from the Traditions. She was describing a journey she had made – both to the heart of her fever, then beyond, leaving that fevered body behind.

When the story ended, she sighed once more, drew a deep breath and sank into a deep and more wholesome sleep. He felt her brow without taking his eyes away from the pool. It was cooler. He ran his hand down her arm and the muscles were relaxed. As he started to pray, the persisting visions before him created a profound distraction. Even as the vision of Anwar turned and the camel started off after the sheikh's entourage, even after Maryam had returned to her body, he continued to see. First, the huge Djinn materialized atop the pinnacle again. He saw the great phallus lash out like a whip and smite the glowing, six-pointed star. After the Djinn disappeared, the star brightened once more. Or was it an echo in his own mind?

The vision finally faded and he was once again looking at the fire and the pool beyond. Maryam was sleeping soundly, the fever definitely broken. God be praised. He rose quietly and lifted the robe over his head and walked to the water, depositing the robe near the edge. When he had bathed and wipe himself down with his hands, he donned the robe again and walked away from the oasis, setting his steps toward a rather high dune some half mile away. When he had climbed to the top and reached the centre, the oasis was no longer in sight. There was no sound, but the night's quavering vault sang to him. He prostrated himself and began praying with his heart and soul, thanking God for one more deliverance. In a very distant corner of his consciousness, he knew he had the fever now. But he would fight, he would break it by morning through sheer will. He prayed that this would be God's will too.

Finishing his prayers, he drew himself up on the cold sand and folded his legs under him. Quickly, he started easing himself into a deep meditation. Controlling his body through his will, it did indeed seem he was holding

161

the fever at bay. Just before he cleared his mind entirely, he went back over Maryam's visions. As in the pictures Farah had showed him, there was something important being told, something they must understand. The two triangles merging…it must be that Anwar was handing on his retreat on the hillock to Maryam. But what of the rest: Anwar, Fatima, himself? Even there, a piece seemed missing, the picture was not yet complete. They had come to Bashtahal to see Anwar and now he was moving toward Jerusalem. Should they follow? Or was it time they had to answer all their own questions.

By the end of an hour, every vision was gone, every thought stilled. Nothing remained but an absolute void. The void filled with light until it was brighter than a million suns. With no awareness of the forces at work, or indeed, how they worked, Ibrahim rose up in the air over the dune and hung suspended there, swaying very slightly in the windless chill. Of its own accord, his body relaxed and straightened until he was lying flat, his back a few inches above the sand. After another hour, the body settled on the sand with total lack of impact. Deep inside, the brilliant void sustained itself as he battled quietly with the fever sweeping over him in its soundless fury.

Fatima rolled over, conscious of the cold; she tried to wrap the robe more tightly about her, unable to locate the focus of her discomfort. The camel's breathing disturbed her and then…she felt a hot needle penetrate her skin just below her breast. Quick fingers removed the flea and tossed it in the direction of the camel, its rightful host. Turning on her side and drawing her legs up, she squirmed, shifting the sand beneath her shoulder. Why, she queried, would a bird be singing like that at this time of night? Her head raised slightly; what a wonderful melody! In a sultan's garden, filled with cages, yes…but not in this wilderness, not in the dark. When the pattern climbed in complex arpeggios and then cascaded down through a series of glissandos, she sat up abruptly. It couldn't be a bird!

Her throat parched, she thought about walking to the

spring. She feared waking Ibrahim who needed all the sleep he could get. Morosely, she sipped the dregs of cold herbal tea. Suddenly, a new melody reached her from the distance. It came from the direction of Bashtahal, to the east. Slipping out of the natural shelter, she walked carefully to the far edge of the deserted oasis to listen. Straining her eyes, she looked toward the horizon and saw a tiny figure poised on top of a dune, barely outlined by the sinking crescent moon behind her. The poignant song climbed the scale and ended in an incomplete crescendo. She gasped as the figure rose into the air, suspended itself there for the blink of an eye, then hurtled down the side of the dune, its headlong flight lost in the sandy trough below.

She ran out into the open landscape and halted, her ear straining. It must have been a flute, she told herself, but what happened? The plunge itself seemed so fatally final. The music had been so beautiful, so moving, she was still transfixed. The tragic way the man...it must have been a man...had tried to reach heaven only to fall so piteously. And wandering alone in the desert at night...what did it mean? She hesitated one moment longer, then raced back to untie the camel. The beast balked reluctantly, but she pulled the halter, urging it along.

The camel stood obediently in the deep depression, watching the woman bend low over the still figure. Fatima clucked persuasively at the animal to calm her while noting the tattered, shredded clothing which hardly covered the emaciated body on the ground. Lying next to the unconscious form was a small tambour attached to a leather thong. A few feet further off a long flute stuck up, its end buried in the sand. There was nothing else, not even a waterskin. It took all her strength, once she got the camel to her knees, to lift the body and sling it over the rump. All the way back to the oasis, she ran back and forth, pulling the camel's head, then holding the man's ankles. Even so, he nearly slipped off the perch a number of times.

She tethered the camel closer to the spring, hoping Ibrahim would not chide her for letting the beast near the lusher plants. Settling the man in her own bed, she found the scraps of raiment so rotten they came away piece by piece in her hands. She shook her head and began bathing the hot body with cold water. She covered him in her own robe, leaving only the thin under-robe to protect her from the chill night. It will soon be dawn, she told herself; in the heat of the day, you will have the lovely memory of this coolness. Creeping on her hands and knees, she found enough of the herbal tea, still warm, to fill her empty cup. It took some time, with the lad's head on her knee, to coax him into swallowing it. When he had the last of it, she laid him back in the shallow depression. The moon's descent reached the point where light now filtered into the bower. As she bathed his face again, she was struck by his youthfulness; the fine beard was hardly full grown and even the hardships of the desert hadn't covered the vulnerability of such tender years. He tugged at something inside her so deeply maternal, tears filled her eyes.

With no warning, the youth sat bolt upright and stared at her with eyes so wild they could hardly focus. His arm shot forward and an accusing finger pointed to a spot just past her head, in the direction of the pool.

'So, you're here to tempt me again, are you?' His voice was clear and lucid for a man with a raging fever. 'Well, you're wasting your time...'

'Hush,' she warned, 'you are not the only sick person here. Keep quiet or you will waken the others.'

His extended finger began shaking violently; Fatima couldn't tell if he had heard her or not.

'He sent you to make me break my vows, I know you, temptress. Never, never, never. Desire and lust are behind me, conquered, destroyed. I desire nothing, do you hear me?'

'Yes, I hear you,' she answered calmly, pressing his shoulders down. 'And lust or desire did not send me out into the night to rescue you, you simpleton. Now rest, will you? You are sicker than you know.'

Desire and lust are behind you, indeed, she mocked him silently as she bathed his head and face. What have you, twenty summers at most? You have yet to face desire, no less conquer it. Wait…just wait until life bursts upon you, like a storm exploding in your face. She covered him with the warm robe again and sat back wearily to keep her vigil.

Yet, something about him was enveloping her heart. Beneath her worldly and superior reaction to his outburst, there was a good deal of admiration; not for the supercilious words, but for the dedication and sincerity she detected behind them. A hoarse croak drew her head down to hear his request. Water! While tethering the camel, she had filled a waterskin at the spring; as he gasped, she emptied the dregs of herbal tea and filled the cup with water.

Even after he had taken two full cups, his lips kept moving; once more, she leaned forward to hear what else he wanted.

'When he asked me what I was seeking, I told him knowledge,' she heard his rasping whisper, no longer the strong voice of his brief respite from delirium. 'He smiled and asked me where I would search for knowledge. Surely, among the learnèd, I answered. The learnèd, he told me, are usually scholastics, mostly theologians who memorize thousands upon thousands of "learnèd" words. They seldom "experience" those words, they seldom really understand the meanings. From time to time, one may glean useful information from them, but information does not become knowledge of itself. Any more than knowledge can become wisdom without the proper direction and effort. In the end, what we are seeking when we use these words is Truth. In these realms, mere words no longer suffice – transmission takes many forms beyond spoken or written words. In music and dancing one may learn; there is timeless truth at the heart of great poetry. Even in dull work – if one detaches himself from the fruits of that work – can be found the essentials of a knowledge which leads to wisdom. Only in his own heart, eventually, can the seeker find valid answers.

'He sent me forth on my search, reminding me that our conditioning makes us prone to obsessions. Nothing

165

in itself contains all the answers and thus no one thing should become a fixation. If I felt impoverished when I arrived, I left him understanding even less. And I had come to him knowing nothing. Wanting nothing of this world, I wandered off consumed with a great thirst in my heart. North of Bagdad, I wandered through Persia, seeking great teachers. I heard many men speak. Some were accounted great poets, others wise and holy men.

'One teacher asked me to stay, he said I was born to dance. And so I danced. I worked hard as a weaver's apprentice during the day to earn my bread. I learned to share that bread with others less fortunate and through the nights I danced. When I no longer knew I had legs, I danced. When I no longer cared if I had body or legs, I danced. Many came to praise me and admire my skill. They told my teacher there was none like me, that he must be proud of his prize pupil. He told me to leave his group, I had become obsessed with dancing. I said I had become selfless in my dancing, that I had emptied my personality. Yes, he scolded, and the vacuum has been filled with pride. I cried bitter tears: Who told me to dance? He shook his head. Who told you to become obsessed? he asked.

'Once more I wandered through villages, across mountains and plains, often sleeping in the wind-swept crags where only eagles dwell. I had danced and still knew nothing. I slept too in rich groves and did any work that was asked of me. One rich orchard owner tied me to a water wheel and made me work with his camel from dawn to nightfall. He said I was an escaped slave and, until my owner came to claim me, there I would stay, chained to the wheel. Eventually, his kindly daughter interceded, shaming her father for his heartless exploitation. I left with no more than the clothes he put on my back, as mine had rotted with sweat and sun, labouring for him. I would take nothing more. Along the road, his daughter appeared from a place she had hidden herself among the young trees. She had prepared fine food for us, a jug of wine and sweetmeats too. I thanked her, refusing. When I departed, she cried out, cursing me for a heartless ingrate. I owed her my life and my body, she believed. She could not comprehend that in stealing my body, then returning it, her father gave me nothing that was not mine. She called after me, tearing at her clothes to expose herself, offering me all of her. What was it I wanted, what more could I demand? she screamed after me. She did not understand that I truly wanted nothing.

'In the next town, a kindly old man looked at me and asked if I could play music. I told him I could not, but wondered why he had asked. He said I appeared to be a haunted man, one who searched for something he could not find. Perhaps that something could be found in music. He took my arm and led me to the far end of town. There lived a teacher in a fine house. My benefactor said nothing more to the teacher save: Here is a hungry lad, a lad hungry in many ways.

'With hardly a word, the teacher led me to the gardens in the central court of the house. There, he had food brought and many dishes were placed before me by his servants. As I stared at the wonderful dishes, I felt embarrassed to devour them alone. Smiling, the teacher produced a long flute which had been lying behind the cushions on which he sat. He placed it beside the dishes in front of me. My gaze was drawn away from the food. I could not resist picking up the instrument to inspect it, wondering how it could make such intricate sound patterns. He seemed pleased and said I would become his pupil. Would I mind, before I had my meal, showing him how I danced…it was obvious to him somehow that I was a dancer. I hung my head, admitting I could no longer dance. Because you became obsessed? he asked gently. My head dropped lower in shame. Would it not be a pity should the same happen to the wondrous music you will learn to play? His question chilled me and I thought my heart would stop beating.

'When it came time to leave, my teacher told me that I had truly learned to make sounds more beautiful than the birds. Such music can be a great joy to the hearts of men. It can move the consciousness up to new levels of awareness.

Thus, the player must always be mindful of the appropriateness of time and place, of the proper conditions. When such music can be played in the presence of those capable of such experience. Evoking the wrong response is far worse than no music at all. And always, one must play more from the heart, not just with the lips and hands. When such conditions did not exist, the musician plays only for God. From the very core of his heart.

'Heading homewards, I again passed through Bagdad and wondered what more I could learn from the lips and books of men. I longed to return to the wise man who had sent me on my journey, but what could I ask him now? What guidance could I ask that had not already been given? It was up to me to achieve the goal. If I said he was the only teacher from whom I could learn, would he not chide me, saying: It is not the teachers who fail to teach, it is the disciple who fails to learn.

'So, I continued to wander, stopping now and then where work could be had so that I could put flesh on my bones once more. Then, with only a waterskin, my flute and drum, I would take up the seemingly endless journey once more, a journey more in time than space, a journey to the centre of me. Light-headed for want of food, one night I found myself high in the air, looking down at my body lying in the lea of a dune. You are like a worm trying to burrow into itself, I said aloud. There you are, turned inside out. Your skin is on the inside, your bones on the outside. Then I knew: inside out or rightside out, God was always on the inside. I had found the path.

'When I was once more united with my body, I began to play as I never had before. I found patterns which never existed before, the melody racing off on its own, moulding itself through some new power within me. I called it the Song of God. I was happy, for I had found prayers more powerful and profound than any I had ever heard or spoken.

'This new power lifted me, speeding my feet, filling me with tireless energy; and with no thought for the next town, the next oasis, I raced on toward the great plain from whence I had commenced these wanderings. When I arrived the hillock was bare. The song in my heart was stilled and I wept like a child who has lost his mother. But my heart and mind fought against those childish tears. Is this not just one more obsession? I demanded. If what you have found is on the very verge of the real, why are you clutching after illusions? He told you what you needed to know, was that not all and everything? On the ring that could banish the depths of despair and the peaks of happiness is inscribed: This too shall pass.

'Through the town of Bashtahal I walked, but doors were bolted everywhere. One old beggar told me about the fever, the most severe in living memory. Not one of my family had been spared. I asked, with trembling lips, about the holy man who once sat on the hillock. A proud day in the history of our city, he told me. We had a saint in our midst and would have stoned him to death. An emissary of the caliph had arrived just in time to save Anwar and take him to Jerusalem.'

Fatima held her breath as the voice died, the body racked with great heaving shakes. Her hands moved automatically, pressing a damp cloth to the brow. As she calmed him, her own brain was in a fever. The semi-conscious litany had gripped her so, it was only at the last moment she realized he had been speaking of Anwar. Anwar is gone! And they had undertaken this perilous journey to Bashtahal...now what? Turn back, strike out for Jerusalem, obviously.

When the youth's seizure passed, Fatima leaned back against a tree, closed her eyes and wept.

XVIII

Anwar sat bolt upright in the soft bed which had been made for him in the luxurious tent he occupied alone. His dream was so shattering, sleep had left him abruptly. He peered toward the entrance flaps, straining his ears. The sheïkh's encampment was calm, nothing stirred in the night. The bandage drawn tightly across his chest seemed to irritate the broken rib and he wished to remove it. This thought was merely peripheral to the anxiety the dream had caused. As he could control his own dreaming, he did not doubt that the sleep-like vision of the oasis was completely accurate. If what was bound to happen next could be averted, there was no time to lose.

From the meagre parcel he had brought with him when he left his hillock, he drew out two small squares of cloth, one white, the other black. As he reached for the pouch suspended from his neck, he felt the air stir near him.

'Where do you think you're going now?' a disembodied voice asked him. 'With all due respect, Anwar, your very life is in peril.'

'Every human's life is always in peril,' he answered calmly, wrestling with the stubborn drawstring. 'With all due respect to you my dear, don't you think you're being a bit meddlesome?'

A pained gasp sounded very close to him. 'Not a very generous response to my concern, saintly one. After all, I am your guardian angel.'

'Aysha,' he scolded gently, 'we have discussed this many times already. I know you are very fond of me. I am very fond of you. I am very grateful for your concern. None of this, however, proves the theory of the guardian angel. You're not really an angel anyway, you know that.'

A radiant, heavenly form materialized, poised demurely on the edge of the bed. Aysha's body was covered with flowing folds of fine, gossamer material, her hair golden rather than blue, the skin glowing with a soft shade close to the colour of a peach. Large blue eyes stared at the old man; they shone with a divine light. He looked at her and shook his head. Two very large wings formed of white feathers sprang from her shoulder blades.

'You are truly beautiful, Aysha,' he admitted with reverence, 'but I haven't time to elaborate right now.' The drawstring relented and he wriggled two fingers inside the pouch. 'Better close your eyes, this may prove painful.'

Aysha snapped her head to one side, averting her face. 'You're not going to wear that ring, are you? You *never* do!'

'I have to now, for you were quite correct, my life is in great jeopardy. Your friend Hawwaz is about to make another desperate attempt to snatch my soul.'

'You're joking!' she exclaimed. 'Hawwaz is not about to do anything of the kind...he can't! I left him in little pieces and he has a long way to go.'

'I don't doubt you,' he answered, slipping the ring on his finger under the bedclothes, 'but he is about to send – what shall we say, an emissary? A rather potent one, at that. Maryam, his target, has been weakened by fever. If he succeeds this time, it will take my soul to undo the damage.'

'Are you serious?' she asked with incredulity. 'That is unheard of, he wouldn't take such a chance...do you realize...'

'Don't question me, just close your eyes and look. An oasis about ten leagues south east of here...the one near Bashtahal.'

Aysha faced the indicated direction and closed her eyes. Anwar stretched out on the bed and initiated the process to free himself of his body.

'It's true,' she whispered with awe. 'I can see it clearly, pearl and all. It's sending an erotic, hypnotizing impulse to her, making her stir in her sleep. It is an overwhelmingly

171

powerful force, I don't know how that stubborn, pig-headed Hawwaz can...'

'He can and he is,' the old man intoned from his developing trance. 'I have no time to lose.'

'Wait! Nearby a youth is stirring in his sleep. He is suffering with a fever too. The waves being sent out have caught him up...' she coughed fastidiously, somewhat embarrassed...'those waves are having a telling effect on him too. Another girl is approaching him...'

'I have to go now, Aysha. It was very kind of you to visit...'

'No! I'm going with you. I will take you and protect you.'

Anwar opened one eye a mere crack. 'Why do you want to do that? You know, you too may never come back.'

'Many reasons,' she answered cryptically. She could tell by his expression that he would wait no longer. 'One is a secret...I'm making sons for Hawwaz and Hutti. And that is why I am so angry with Hawwaz for what he is doing. I disapprove totally. There is another reason. You must be able to complete your journey, it is of great importance. It is imperative you complete your spiritual transmission in this world...'

'Nothing will deter you from being guardian angel,' he surmised with a touch of irony. 'Well, then, perhaps you can help me with that transmission...more than you imagine. Please change your wings first. Those are very pleasing and quite traditional, but they are far from functional.'

Anwar and Aysha arrived at the oasis with the first pale hint of the dawn to come. Standing in the shadow of a tree near the spring, they saw Fatima leaning against a nearby tree trunk, her eyes closed. The youth she was attending had broken his fever and now lay sweating pro-fusely; he was clothed in nothing but the robe thrown over him and now that had fallen to one side. Although he was in a deep sleep, he had just spilled his seed over his exposed torso in response to the erotic vibrations created in the area.

172

Aysha's arm extended and she pointed to a figure moving slowly and painfully across the sand toward a dune in the distance. Maryam moved like a somnambulist, completely oblivious to the tenuous outline moving before her like a serpent. Hawwaz's ranji and the attendant pearl were fully material to the watchers.

Aysha gripped Anwar's arm, pressing him to follow Maryam, but he covered her hand with his own, nodding his head in the direction of the two sleepers. Freeing his hand, he made a few gestures to Aysha. With a shrug of her shoulders, she moved forward. Lifting Fatima - who became almost weightless at Aysha's touch - she suspended the girl in mid-air over the prone figure of the sleeping young man. Delicately, she raised the girl's light gown and then lowered her until she sat, legs outstretched, on the youth's abdomen. She then created a psychic vacuum in the girl's womb, a vacuum so strong that when she lifted Fatima a moment later, the boy's abdomen was dry. When the sleeping girl was leaning against the tree once more, Aysha turned a quizzical face toward Anwar. He took her hand and they drifted across the pool and out to the desert just as Maryam reached the top of the dune.

Aysha screened Anwar's body with her own when they arrived at a spot a few feet behind Maryam's back. Back to back, they sank to the ground, Anwar facing the horizon, Aysha staring at Maryam and the golden phallus that had led her to Ibrahim. Still with the slow, deliberate movements of a sleep-walker, Maryam disrobed.

'I thought Maryam would be the vehicle of your transmission,' Aysha whispered silently into Anwar's mind.

'And so did I. A man named Hassan made that impossible. You will see why in a moment or two.'

'Who are the other two, then?' she asked, her curiosity by no means satisfied.

'Fatima and Abdullah, who do not yet know each other, though both have asked my guidance.'

'Could they not have done as you wished in a more natural manner?'

'It would have been very difficult for me to be present

at the exact moment of conception. With your help, I was able to imbue that conception with all my spiritual blessings. Now, pay attention, our timing here must be precise to the split second.'

'Seems rather bizarre all the same,' she commented. 'Is it possible that you secretly adhere to some more flamboyant faith?'

Anwar sighed. 'No, my dear, it was practical, that's all. This way, a very special relationship will result...' He felt Aysha tense and he braced himself.

Maryam detached the bandage and dressings and let them drop to the ground. Aysha shuddered with empathy, then steeled herself as the golden phallus superimposed itself on the sleeping man's body to rise up alluringly. Maryam stepped forward, placing one foot on either side of Ibrahim. The phallus shivered and recoiled slightly and just as Maryam began to lower herself, Aysha reached out.

A condensed tempest struck the desert, sending sand flying, but Aysha held fast to the wriggling shaft as Anwar reached back to grab the pearl. The pair vaulted up at the same instant and came to rest in reversed positions. Aysha glared at the buffeting storm, protecting Anwar as he wrapped the pearl, first in the white cloth, then in the black. He tied it off with strands of woollen thread from the hem of his robe, then ran the star-crested ring around the heaving parcel, impressing it in four places, aligned to the cardinal points of earth. With the last impression burned into the cloth, the pearl became quiescent. He nudged Aysha with his elbow and she blazed skyward to disappear into nothingnesss with her awesome squirming burden.

Anwar began to dematerialize when Maryam pitched forward to lie huddled at Ibrahim's side.

When the sun rose, the bright light struck Abdullah's eyes with a blinding impact. He sat up, feeling dizzy and faint, trying to orient himself to his surroundings. The voice of a beautiful girl in his dreams still echoed in his ears. Something stirred near him and he turned, blinking to clear his foggy vision. It was the girl he had seen in his dreams! The light striking her face made the sleeper wince.

Struggling to his feet, Abdullah lifted her in his arms, fighting desperately with his own weakness. He saw the protected bower with empty bedding on the opposite side of the pool and struggled toward it. Panting, he fell to his knees, nearly dropping the sleeping form. He had just enough strength left to ease her down in the shade. Seated on his heels, he controlled his breathing, commanding his body to regain strength and serenity. As he watched her lovely face in repose, the dream came back to him: through narrowed eyes, he watched as the visualization formed. Abdullah lost all track of time as he listened to the words the girl had spoken, heard himself tell her the story of his wanderings, of his hopes and quest. A shadow fell over him and he looked up. A man stood there, holding a girl in his arms.

'Ibrahim!' the youth called out. Ibrahim smiled and deposited his burden next the other girl. Abdullah rose and the two men embraced each other warmly. Ibrahim pressed a finger to his lips, and gestured toward the far end of the pool. When they reached the spot which was a deep bowl separated from the rest by a slender bar of sand, they stripped and immersed themselves in the cool water.

'What a joy to see my old master again,' Abdullah exclaimed happily. 'Often have I thought about you – I must confess, more often than my own father who now, alas, is dead. This terrible fever took so many in the city.'

'Abdullah, I have thought about you more often than my own sons. You are a very real son to me.'

When they had each told the stories of their wanderings, Abdullah related his strange dream. He had not realized how bad his own illness had become. A strange girl he had never seen before carried him back to the oasis and nursed him. He had told her about Anwar, how his first teacher had been taken off to Jerusalem. And that now he must follow. The girl had simply said they were meant to meet, that now their destinies were one. He did not question this, feeling it to be so ordained himself. Something strange and wondrous had touched them both in the night, linking them together, not in the ordinary sense of man and woman, but in a spiritual way, fully consistent with their own mystical development.

'By the way,' Abdullah added shyly, 'what is she called? I don't even know her name.'

'Fatima, my son. And she is devoted to her friend, Maryam.' Ibrahim gazed at the sleeping girls and tears filled his eyes.

'Father of my heart, what is it?' Abdullah sensed deeply the other man's sadness. Intuitively, he felt this might be their last meeting.

'Their paths will part here, I know this now,' Ibrahim answered. 'Maryam is mortally ill, she has been wounded and will never heal. She knows a place has been chosen for her…by Anwar. She will spend her days as Anwar's successor and spiritual heir, in that place he occupied for so long. A star calls out to her. You and Fatima will journey back to Jerusalem, as you have already divined.'

'And you,' Abdullah asked tremulously, 'will not come with us?'

'No, my journey ends here too. I will look after Maryam. I grieve deeply that, having found you, I will lose you. Moreover, I grieve for the sorrow of those two when they part.'

'Shall we go away for a while, so that they may share that sorrow alone?'

'They may need us, son. It might be unbearable for them otherwise. If we cannot look into the face of sorrow, how shall we ever understand love?'

XIX

SHEIKH AHMAD EL-SAYED LOOKED AROUND the pleasant gardens of the collegium's inner court as the school's dignitaries gathered to greet him and form an audience for the provost's report. In their light white robes, they reminded him of so many fluttering doves. It was practically nine months to the day when he had delivered Anwar to the faculty, instructing them to allow the old man to create his curriculum without restraints. Mustafa, the provost, bowed low before seating himself with an armload of scrolls. The sheikh had never trusted this Alexandrian of Greek descent. If a man chooses to convert to Islam, it must be a good thing. Yet, having changed his affiliation once, could he not do so again? He was a stickler for form, a severe disciplinarian, but an uninspired human being. His colleagues had been unanimous in putting him forward when the old provost died; Sheikh Ahmad was too well-versed in subtle politics to oppose a popular decision.

When the report had been read and the sheikh approved it, he sipped the cool water he had been offered with the sweetmeats he had declined and fixed his gaze on the provost.

'You have mentioned everything but the progress of your new teacher, Mustafa. In fact...' Ahmad's gaze swept the assembled staff to make his point...'he's not even here.'

The provost looked pained and his colleagues looked everywhere save at their guest.

'I assume you mean...' Mustafa halted, coughing and clearing his throat'...Anwar,' he finished at last. 'Anwar has *chosen* to live in a garden near the Mount of Olives. He seems to have developed a fixation on the man called the Christ, the prophet of the Christians, the one we call Isa ben Maryam.'

177

'I know the name Christ, Mustafa. I also know his mother's name. Furthermore, Mohammed revered him as a great prophet. You make Anwar's interest seem unnatural...perhaps even...heretical?'

'I did not mean to imply that, my lord,' Mustafa countered hastily, 'it is merely that he is so preoccupied...'

'I am sure his teaching duties occupy him more, do they not?'

'Well...' Mustafa cast a baleful eye at two deans sitting near him, but they offered no refuge... 'you see, Anwar has *chosen* to give up teaching.'

'Anwar has *chosen* to give up teaching,' Ahmad repeated, pacing the words slowly for emphasis. 'Under what particular circumstances?'

For nearly an hour, the dignified sheikh listened to what must have been a well-rehearsed litany. Started with carefully selected words by the provost, the subtle damnation went from one august teacher to the next, avoiding such direct words as 'apostasy' or 'heresy', but the accusations could hardly be misinterpreted.

Anwar had interviewed every one of the five hundred students. When he had a band of twenty to his liking, he refused the use of classroom facilities, saying buildings were too cramped, too full of books to allow ideas to penetrate. He took them walking...they brought nothing with them save enough water. They were gone well over a month and what had they been doing? They went to Bethlehem and there they danced in Christ's honour. He taught them to dance! They went to Mount Hebron and danced for Moses. When they returned, the students were ragged and skinny, as though they had been half starved to death.

When questioned, Anwar laughed. Of course: they had all been too fat. They didn't know how to take care of themselves. Dancing and walking had made them fit. When asked what dancing had to do with faith, which was the cornerstone of their collegium, he had turned to one of the students and asked him if he knew what faith was. As if Anwar did not know. After all, was it not the noble sheikh himself who had called Anwar the Pillar of Islam? Ahmad did not miss this careful honing of sharp blades. Anwar was taken, with his students, to the great library. It was filled with tomes on the subject of faith. The meaning of faith, its true inner meaning, cannot be found in words, cannot be explained by words, no matter how beautiful, how noble, how inspired, the old man said. Turning to one of his students, he asked him did he think words were important. The student answered, yes, up to a point words illuminate meanings; after that, they tend to obscure meanings. The words being discussed, the provost interjected with grave disapproval, just happened to be the words of The Prophet.

When another student asked him, pointing out that the library was one of the finest between Spain and India, did he not think some value resided there, did he think there was nothing to be learned from books, Anwar thought a moment before answering. Of course, he replied. The only problem is knowing *what* to read. Take, for example, the prophet who had lived and died here eight hundred years earlier. Did he write anything down? Very unlikely, but according to the traditions which apply in his case, his disciples recorded everything he said. However, there is no known manuscript clearly accrediting even these authors. It would seem that words purporting to be those of Christ's disciples might well have been put down in written form as long as two hundred years after his death. If we are non-selective about words and books, if we put too much emphasis on them, we keep repeating words and missing the essential message.

When he was asked why he had chosen such an eccentric way to teach, walking and dancing around the countryside, he told them he had asked the advice of Abdullah. It turned out that this Abdullah was none other than a mad dervish living on a ledge near the top of the Mount of Olives. He had a woman living there with him, in a virtual wilderness, a woman who had just recently given birth to a baby. These are the people Anwar acclaims as his close friends! And he asked a mere boy what he should do with the students of this collegium! With no loss of aplomb, Anwar answered this accusation by asking who better to advise on youth's needs but a young man? Abdullah said, make them walk and dance until they are thin and hard. It would open their minds and lungs, help them to breathe better. Abdullah should know, Anwar concluded, for he is a very fine dancer and musician in his own right.

They had made many allowances for Anwar's eccentricities...they understood that so many years as a recluse, a hermit in the desert, could have an idiosyncratic effect, but when he started describing such things as Djinni to his students...in shamefully intimate detail...well, he was threatening the foundations of the school.

Young and impressionable students would follow him on walks about the gardens, asking him questions about these exotic and bizarre creatures. Anwar ascribed names and all sorts of strange doings to them...as though they were friends he would meet as a normal part of any day. And the students took these hallucinatory ramblings seriously. He even told them there were laudable lessons to be learned in observing their behaviour: for instance, learning not to accept things on surface appearances. He described a huge block of gold, saying it was almost as large as a small mountain. The gold, however, was not as deep as the length of a man's arm. And why was this? Djinni and demons had no difficulty in duplicating the alleged feats of the alchemists...turning lead into gold was simple for them. But like small children, they were easily distracted. They had very little attention span, as he termed it. So, the job was forgotten before it was finished.

Mustafa cleared his throat nervously. 'Naturally, when he began describing the nasty sexual inclinations – or should I say, his fantasies about them – of these creatures, we had to put a stop to it...for the sake of the school, in the best interests of the students.'

'I assume,' Ahmad commented dryly, 'that was the point at which Anwar "chose" to stop teaching.'

'It was his idea, I assure you,' Mustafa replied. 'Ask anyone.' He extended his hand, indicating his colleagues.

They all nodded affirmatively. 'He said this was no place for him, all he wanted to do was meditate in that garden he is so fond of…and visit those unwholesome friends of his.'

Ahmad stood and the assembly fluttered to its feet. 'As we have covered everything, I will take a walk now. I will return to spend the night, then I will be off in the morning.'

'But we hoped you would dine with us…' Mustafa began, halting as Ahmad raised his hand.

'Thank you, but I would like to visit with Anwar. I know you will offer me an escort, but I shall have to decline that also. The least he is disturbed right now, the better.'

When he had seen that his entourage was satisfactorily taken care of, he over-rode his captain's protests. He would go on this walk all by himself. He was certain no harm would come to him. The provost saw him to the outer gate and pointed to a hill he would reach through the distant gates of the city. Ahmad's enigmatic smile did little to reassure old Mustafa. Through no fault of his own, having done his best to contain that demented old self-styled saint, his days as provost seemed numbered.

The sheikh was deeply occupied with his own thoughts on the long walk; he hardly noticed the constant stream of traffic on the road. If the local farmers and merchants found it odd to see a dignitary dressed as a high-ranking official of the caliph on foot and unattended, they hid their curiosity. As he climbed and breathing became difficult, he brought his mind back to his surroundings…and to his own poor condition. Would Anwar recommend a long walk to Bethlehem and a course in dancing for him too? He was grinning wryly when the path turned a corner around a large outcropping of rock. The path broadened, passed a high pinnacle and began its descent. As he crossed the open area between the two masses, he heard a baby cry. On a ledge about ten feet above the path, a woman sat, her bare legs and feet dangling over the edge. The protective overhang above the ledge cast a deep shadow into what seemed an open-faced cave. The woman drew her ragged robe aside and the infant closed his hungry mouth over the exposed nipple. As Ahmad continued his walk, he noticed for the first time that a man sat apart, well behind the woman. His legs were crossed, his head bowed, hands resting on his knees; Ahmad felt he could have been carved of wood, his spirit dwelling on another planet.

Silently, he continued his journey, descending the rather steep path carefully. Passing the last of the high rock formations, the hillside opened out and he saw the city far below. Traffic on the road beneath looked much like hordes of insects creeping along; no sound carried, making the vista, sharp as it was, very dream-like. Perched on its own plateau, the sparkling white collegium came into view. It was at this point he felt something unusual in the air. He found it hard to describe, but he felt engulfed in a warm and peaceful cocoon. A few steps further on, he felt he was entering a different world. On the far side of a low garden wall, he saw the object of his search seated on a carpet in a tiny clearing surrounded by wild flowers.

The sheikh approached to within a few feet of the ancient, still man who seemed more wraith than flesh and blood. Anwar held up a hand in greeting.

'Poor Ahmad, you've had a difficult day with those scholastics of yours, listening to all the terrible stories about a wicked old man.'

Ahmad laughed, seating himself on Anwar's right; he bent low and kissed the gnarled, parchment hand.

'I did hear that you found a sure cure for overweight and unfit students,' the sheikh admitted, 'even though it shook the foundations of the learned academy.'

'I am sure you know the story of the academics who were blindfolded and led to an elephant?'

'Yes. Each one felt a different part and described an elephant. The one who touched the leg said it was a tree.' Ahmad laughed again. 'They never *knew* you, did they?'

'It isn't important, Ahmad. Real teaching will be done in a different way. Soon, I believe, you too will opt for that way. How does one explain this to dogmatists

182

like Mustafa? He scorns men like Abdullah, yet that boy knows what can never be put into books. He has learned to see a reality which is anathema to scholastics. Abdullah actually experiences his faith.'

'Is he the young man I saw above, the one who sits with his wife and child in an open cave?'

Anwar shrugged. 'Yes, that is Abdullah. He sits with Fatima. The infant is Maryam's...in one sense. Fatima's and Abdullah's in another sense. Yet, none of them actually made the child...in the sense we normally mean when we speak of "making" a child.'

'Is such a thing possible?' the sheikh asked, his face and voice echoing his surprise.

'It has been known to happen, I believe. The universe is larger and more complex than we can measure with our ordinary perceptions, Ahmad. What is possible is limitless. As God is limitless and immeasurable.'

'Knowing this, I am still confused,' the sheikh declared.

'Eight hundred years ago, an extraordinary man spent many anguised hours in this garden. I am still trying to understand his agony. The Prophet had great reverence for the man who gave his name to the Christian faith, the one we call Isa ben Maryam. Perhaps, through Mohammed, I may yet learn to understand. In the last few days, I have felt his presence here in a very real way. I had to work for it. Not by reading a book,' he added mischievously.

'They are your disciples...Abdullah and Fatima?'

Anwar nodded. 'And the infant is my godchild. Now you will ask me who is the one named Maryam. Perhaps I had better tell you a story.'

When Anwar had finished the tale of the four wanderers and Hassan, the worldly sheikh was stunned; in a state of shock he repeated phrases inside his mind. Mountains of gold. A horrendous rape, forgiven by all, including the poor girl who would never be healed. Djinni and demons.

'You will soon be wondering if Mustafa is not correct to brand me as a dangerous heretic, Ahmad. Remember what I told you. The cosmos is greater than what we see.

There are forces in it which normal men merely suspect, giving them names such as good and evil. If the possible is limitless, we still say a thing is reasonable or unreasonable. Not so. That merely describes a man who has not, or cannot, find the reason. To a very great extent, those mysterious forces are shaping our own evolution. If it has not been said yet, one day it will be: Angels are the powers hidden in the faculties and organs of man. Our goal is to activate those forces.'

'You have frightened Mustafa...I must admit, I am not without fear myself,' Ahmad confessed.

'Fear is the executioner of those who speak their minds, those who defy establishment...in other words, those who are called heretics. If my truth is different than the established truth, I am dangerous. Thus, dancing is dangerous. Writing love poetry to the glory of God is dangerous.'

'That story about the demon with a mountain of gold...is it really true?' Ahmad appeared about to lose his grip on reality.

'Musa? Yes, I'm afraid it is. Shall I tell you why I know this with such certainty? It is a terrible thing to know, Ahmad.'

Anwar watched the usually self-contained man struggle to control his momentary weakness.

'Yes, indeed,' he nodded slowly. 'Tell me.'

'Musa is my great-grandson.'

Anwar watched the many images flicker across the stunned face. He analyzed fear, loathing, disbelief in all the possible combinations.

'How could that be?' the sheikh asked at last, his throat so constricted, his voice squeaked.

'When my granddaughter Farah was young, I did not have the knowledge or the power to stop it. In a sense, she became a true martyr. She turned her back on the pleasures of this world and became a saint, one who devoted her life to others and lived with a sorrow few can ever understand. When Maryam was imperilled by the younger Djinn, I was able to intervene...my development, as it is, enabled

184

me to. Unfortunately, with a man such as Hassan, I could do nothing.'

'Does this Djinn still threaten you?' Ahmad whispered hoarsely.

Anwar reached his hand under the edge of the carpet and drew out a small black cloth bound with thread; he smiled at it and replaced it.

'Not for the moment. Not till I return this to him, at least.'

'You can do that?' Ahmad didn't understand his own question...everything was so outrageous, what question could he ask?

'Very soon, I will be undertaking my last voyage. In terms of my responsibilities to my brethren and my own teachers, I have completed my work in this world. On the way, I will return to Hawwaz that which is his.'

These last words banished everything in Ahmad save a deep sense of loss and sadness. He knew there was nothing he could ask or offer, yet offer he did.

'Is there anything I can possibly do?'

Anwar pointed to the mountain top. 'Give them your protection, Ahmad. On your way back, stop and tell them so, it will comfort them.'

Ahmad bent to kiss Anwar's hand. For the first time, he noticed the peculiar silver ring, the six-pointed star raised from the surface. He stared at it briefly and felt something actually penetrate his eyes.

'Will you give me your blessings, Anwar?'

'I already have. Goodbye, Ahmad, and don't be too severe with Mustafa. He does the best he knows how.'

By the time Ahmad reached the top of the hill, the sun had dropped below the horizon west of Jerusalem. Even with the approach of twilight, the world looked brighter than he ever remembered seeing it at the approach of evening. He rubbed his eyes and stood still, listening to the song of a bird. It didn't seem reasonable, but his hearing seemed sharper than ever. From behind, he heard stones loosened in the path. He walked on until he reached a large boulder directly across from the ledge of the young people. Leaning against it, he gathered his thoughts and tried to dispel the sadness he felt before he approached them.

A howl of pain preceding a loud thud made Ahmad turn his head quickly. A tattered beggar heaved a heavy man to his feet and picked up a staff, pressing it into the well-dressed, portly man's hand. The sheikh understood with the first step he witnessed, by the way the staff probed the ground ahead, that the fat man was blind.

The beggar led his charge to one side of the ledge where crude cuts had been made to form primitive steps. Pushing and placing the man's feet, bit by bit the beggar got his man up to the ledge. The meditating youth never moved; Ahmad couldn't tell if he was aware of this new and unbidden presence. But the woman! She clutched the baby to her with a look of incredulous alarm the like of which the sheikh had never seen before. That look sparked something in his own mind. He did not know how, but there was no question of the fat man's identity.

The beggar eased the big man down until he was seated safely on the ledge. Then he whispered something.

'Are you sure?' the fat man cried out. 'How do you know?'

Although the beggar spoke softly, Ahmad heard every word clearly. 'You said you would give me two pieces of silver if I brought you to the holy man on the mountain. I have done so. Now, pay me.'

With an annoyed and disdainful expression, the blind man reached inside his handsome robe and extracted the coins. He held them out and the little beggar snatched them and dropped back down the steps, raced across the open ground and down the path.

'Anwar? Are you here, are you listening?' the fat man shouted. The girl rose and walked to the back of the ledge; she sank down on her haunches behind the meditating youth and drew her knees up, protecting the baby with her body. Ahmad saw her shoulders heave as she began weeping.

'Anwar? I have roamed the earth looking for you. When I reached Mecca, they told me you were here. Look

186

what they have done to me, it isn't fair. You have no right to punish me like this, give me back my eyes. I was crazy then, I didn't know what I was doing, do you hear? Is there no understanding, no compassion for a man who went insane? I am truly contrite!'

As the gloom deepened, Ahmad saw something radiating from the ledge. It grew until the whole area under the overhang was bathed in a strong but eerie light. It bathed the man, woman and child, creating a strong aura that actually hurt the sheikh's eyes. He climbed up on the boulder and leaned against the embankment.

The youth rose as though drawn to his feet by invisible ropes. Slowly he crossed the ledge and stood before Hassan. He bent at the waist and place his hand over Hassan's brow. The light intensified for a moment, then the hand was removed. The man turned, walked back to the woman and took up his seated posture.

Hassan opened his eyes and roared like a stricken elephant. He lumbered grotesquely, forcing himself up on his feet. Swaying, he rubbed his eyes, held his hands over them for a moment, then snapped them down to his sides. He roared again, trying to look in every direction at once. He began shaking so badly he nearly lost his balance and collapsed.

'Who – who are you?' he croaked, staring at Abdullah.

'You don't recognize me?' the youth answered calmly. 'I am Abdullah, the servant of your esteemed friend, Ibrahim ben Yussef. You might say, I am also his adopted son.'

'You are – what kind of son – who? Ibrahim's? I don't understand. I came here to make Anwar – I mean, beg him to...'

'You came here to ask for your sight back. Anwar has given it to you, though he certainly did not take it away. He has given it to you through me, so I am your benefactor ...' As Abdullah spoke, Ahmad sensed that his own voice did not sound like that. The expression on Hassan's face made it plain that he didn't hear what was happening: Anwar's voice was issuing from Abdullah's mouth '...and now there are three things you can do. You can slip that dagger under your robe from its place of concealment and stab your benefactor to death. Or, you can take your sight and run with it as a thief runs with his stolen gold into the arms of night. Or again, you may genuinely repent and devote yourself to your own atonement…and Maryam's forgiveness. Which shall it be, Hassan?'

The fat man took a hurried step backward, his face contorted. He turned, looking at the steps and began tumbling down wildly, groaning and wheezing. When he reached the open ground, his fat body swayed ludicrously as he ran down the path.

The ledge was dark again when Ahmad climbed down from his perch and crossed the level ground. He climbed up the steps and walked to where the couple sat. Fatima was nursing the baby again.

'Anwar has asked me to be your protector, which I gladly undertake. There will be official and explicit instructions concerning your welfare issued to the collegium. Just tell me your needs.'

'You are very kind, my lord,' the youth answered deferentially. 'However, we need for nothing. We have visitors every day and they bring many presents for the baby. Really, for our simple task, we have everything we could ask for.'

'Your task? What is that?'

'To love the child,' Abdullah answered, turning to Fatima. She held the baby up and Ahmad gazed into an extraordinarily beautiful face with wondrous eyes. He held his breath with a sense of happiness he had never known before.

'Did you name him Anwar ben Abdullah?' the sheikh asked as Fatima put the infant back at her breast.

'That was the name we chose,' Fatima smiled, 'but in the end, we deferred to Anwar's wishes.'

Ahmad looked into her eyes before speaking. 'You named him Isa ben Maryam.'

'Anwar has blessed you, noble sir,' Abdullah said softly. 'He has touched your eyes and your heart.'

There seemed nothing more the learned and important man could say. He looked down at his feet and shrugged self-consciously.

'I shall tell them that you are under the caliph's protection. He who harms you, harms me.'

'Thank you,' Fatima responded sincerely. 'And please tell the caliph that he who harms him, harms us.'

'Be careful on your way,' Abdullah added, 'for the path is not a kind one in the dark.'

'Let us hope I am fitter than your last guest,' Ahmad replied, walking to the stairs.

'You will soon know how true that is, my lord,' Abdullah assured him. 'You are about to discover many wonderful things.'

Ahmad turned, pausing on the top step. 'I envy you your youth, Abdullah. Suddenly, I feel as though I had slept my life away.'

'Envy me nothing, great sheikh. Everything must happen at its appointed time, in its appointed place. Bring a loaf one day early and the man who receives it will call it a fish. I know.'

When Ahmad reached the road and turned toward the city, he glanced behind into the night. High above, at the place he imagined Anwar to be sitting, he could just discern a glow in the sky. He looked about him, at the many people passing on the road, concerned only with their own footsteps.

'They can't even see it,' he whispered to himself. 'They don't even bother to look.' He still didn't reckon fully on the breadth and scope of Anwar's blessing.

XX

Naked and sitting on his heels, Ibrahim dipped water from the shallow pool behind the hillock and washed his body with studied diligence. If one is fortunate, he thought, the fruits of age can count burgeoning wisdom as one of them; if one lives long enough to replace conflict with resolution, anger with serenity, ignorance with perception. Age in itself is not a gift, for it wears a tired wrapping. Still and all, your body, like that tired and tattered robe, serves the purpose. Where is there room for vanity now?

Drying himself with his hands, he picked up the tattered robe and moved from the shade to face the rising sun; eyes closed, he silently spoke his gratitude for a new day. The breeze and heat dried him rapidly; he slipped into the robe and climbed to the top of the hillock and kneeled to pray. He took a long look at the glistening city first, his eyes memorizing details as if he might never see its outline again, inflamed by the rising sun. Today I must go and beg again. Food there will surely be and perhaps a flower for Maryam. Please, Lord, let there be a flower for Maryam. He prayed steadily into the fierce youth of the sun, not in words but in thoughts so deep that love became an abstract concept before entering a white void of purity in which nothing but his heart communicated in a unity of oneness. Still, he felt the aura of Anwar surround him, blending with Maryam's. Into the unique oneness, three seemed blended. Two flowers for Maryam, one from Anwar.

Eventually, prayers finished, Ibrahim straightened; he was aware of something unusual in his psychic state. With his eyes still closed, his head turned slowly, his mind scanning the horizon from northeast to southwest. His head began to turn again, but before it had moved five degrees, his attention was forced back toward the south-west. His mind was looking at the oasis nearest Bashtahal, on the road to Mecca. Nostrils pinched, hardly breathing, he concentrated for minutes on end.

In some way, as yet not clear, he told himself with equanimity, Fate is crossing the desert. Soon enough, its face and form will be known. With a slight shrug of the shoulders, he rose and descended the hillside. At the base he sat down, leaning against a boulder, his legs crossed. He put the momentary flash of precognition out of his mind, emptying it so that the day's meditation could begin.

To the southwest, two tired and hungry camels balked as they left the oasis and its shade; the dark-clad rider's impatience turned to wrath as he yanked viciously on the baggage-laden beast's halter, jabbing his mount's flanks simultaneously with a long, pointed staff. The long, cold night in the oasis had not improved his temper – he was in no moon for rebellion. The wretched camels were unhappy because there was hardly any forage at that miserable water hole? Who picks an oasis to suit a stupid camel? The shrewd buyer selects a well-bred, even-tempered beast that has been taught to endure hardship. Stealing a camel or two is another matter entirely. What else can a man do when he arrives in Mecca on foot, not a coin left to his name? He certainly cannot pick and choose.

With a scowl cutting into his sagging jowls, the rider watched the city of Bashtahal rise like a shimmering gem from the sand. It stood upside down, its towers piercing the desert, still golden in the early morning. He squeezed his eyes tightly closed to eradicate the mirage vision. The next time he looked, the towers had righted themselves, but a halo image in reverse still glimmered faintly above the real perception. Cursing under his breath, he yanked the lead rein, forcing the camel's head northward to where the foothills rose toward the pinnacled mountains behind. Where else would she be? Nowhere else but where that precious saint of hers had sat.

The creak of leather against wood, the clanging of metal utensils reached the seated Ibrahim from a long way off. Reluctantly, but without rancour, he felt himself slide back into worldly awareness. He listened with his eyes closed. Two camels, no more, and one rider, the tinkling charivari of the plodding camels still half an hour's march away. His earlier premonition returned: Fate mounted on a camel, followed by a camel. If Fate can plumb the Dead Sea and ascend Mount Ararat, there is no place to hide. Suspending further speculation, he composed himself and waited.

When the camels scented the water, they brayed loudly and fought the rider's control. Shouts, curses and the pummelling of a staff echoed off the hills as the maddened beasts thundered past the hillock to come to an abrupt halt at the pool. Ibrahim rose and circled the hillock; standing near the blocked entrance to the cave, he leaned against the embankment and watched the heavy man beating his thirsty camel. It would not kneel and the bulky rider slid awkwardly down the animal's side to come crashing to the ground on hands and knees. With a pained curse, he struggled to his feet. Even before he turned to look about, Ibrahim knew him.

Standing behind the errant camel and shading his eyes, Hassan squinted at the gaunt figure standing in the shade. After a few blinks of his eyes, a scowl of recognition crossed his features.

'So it's you again…the beggar, the holy fool.'

'Beggar and fool are true enough,' Ibrahim conceded with good grace, 'but I am certainly not holy. More important, your sight has been restored. Isn't that a wonder and a blessing!'

'I didn't come all this way to discuss my affairs with the likes of you,' Hassan snarled. 'Where is Maryam?'

Ibrahim folded his arms across his chest and lowered his head. Who else but Anwar could give him back his sight? Who else would? He comes here to ask forgiveness – once again. What will he do now? Ibrahim raised his head; if Hassan saw the depths of sadness etched on the emaciated face, he gave no sign.

'Are you deaf? Didn't you hear me? I want to see Maryam!' Hassan bellowed.

192

'So do I, Hassan, more than anything else in this world.'

'Where is she, damn you?' Hassan crouched, lowering his head threateningly. 'Is she in Bashtahal?'

'Yes...yes she is. In her grave, next to her mother.'

'What? Don't you lie to me, you miserable scum, don't you try to take out your vengeance on me with goading jokes. Tell me the truth!' Hassan threw back the folds of his robe and unsheathed a scimitar.

'Would that it were a joke,' Ibrahim cried. 'You think I would make such a joke? She is dead, Hassan, and I should not have to tell you the cause. She never fully recovered and the last fever carried her away. I shall go there today to place a flower on her grave...will you come with me?'

Hassan took two steps forward, brandishing the scimitar. 'If you don't tell me the truth right now, I'll cut it out of your stinking, lousy hide.'

For one brief instant, Ibrahim's instincts took over. He shifted one foot back, bracing himself and digging his toes into the sand. He sighed and shook his head, admonishing himself. Straightening, he drew his own tattered garment back, exposing his chest.

'I have told you the truth, Hassan. If you think butchering me will change that, then butcher me you must. May God have mercy on you.'

With a scream of rage, Hassan raised the sword and lumbered forward. Looking down, Ibrahim saw his toes still clenched tightly. He drew the foot back and, in lowering it behind him, the heel pressed down on the tail of a small asp that was sticking out from under a rock. The serpent's head whipped about and the fangs sank into the Achilles tendon. Ibrahim lifted the offending heel and winced.

With both hands, Hassan lifted the blade high over his head. As he began the swift downward stroke, a clap of thunder sounded deafeningly from atop the hillock. A blinding bolt of lightening struck the sword and upraised arms, smashing the blade into fragments. Arms numb and paralyzed, Hassan howled in pain as he fell to his knees. Face masked in terror, he looked up. The second bolt crashed down, smashing against his brow. He tried to lift his hands to his stricken eyes, then plunged forward, his face crunching into the sand and stones.

Tearing a strip off his robe as he stepped forward gingerly, Ibrahim looked up when he tied off the tourniquet above his knee.

'I did not call upon you, Musa,' he shouted toward the hilltop. 'Restore his sight.'

'Ibrahim…Ibrahim…help me, I am blind,' the fat man screamed into the ground. 'For the love of God, help me!'

'Don't be a fool, Ibrahim,' Musa called back, 'that disgusting swine nearly killed you. I ask nothing in return, just say Hawwaz owes it to you.'

Ibrahim picked up a shard of the blasted scimitar and cut across the fang marks. Even squatting, the foot drawn up over his other knee, it was not easy to get the tendon in his mouth. He started sucking blood furiously and spitting mouthfuls on the ground.

'What happened?' Ibrahim looked up to see the terrifying demon standing next to him.

'The ironies of Fate, Musa,' Ibrahim answered wryly. 'In drawing back my foot to deny it the right to kick sand in his face to save my life, I stepped on a serpent. Droll, isn't it?'

The demon bent his great height forward. 'Let me help, I can cure you instantly…'

Ibrahim held up his hand. 'You shall do nothing for me. Not you, nor Hawwaz, not even Hassan…none of you owe me anything. Just take away his blindness. Now!'

'Is that a command? Musa growled. 'You think very little of your life…'

'Very little indeed, I assure you. You would hardly strike Hassan down for attempting to kill me, then do the job yourself. Or would you, Musa?'

The demon stepped back as though he was hearing his name spoken for the first time.

'How do you know me, Ibrahim? I have never before appeared to you.' The demon scratched his unruly thatch of bright red hair.

Ibrahim's eyes crinkled as he smiled. So like children, he thought, with their boundless curiosity.

Sand stuck to the sobbing face as Hassan raised his head. 'Ibrahim, where are you? For the love of God, help me. Who else is here...Ibrahimmmmm!' The cry choked itself off and the head sagged down, burying itself in the sand again.

'Do you remember the first time you blinded him?' Ibrahim asked. 'You bound him to a covenant he could not possibly keep, you knew that. You used a vision of Maryam to betray him.' Ibrahim looked fearlessly into the puzzled demon's green eyes. 'I saw it all in your father's scrying stone.'

'You couldn't. You don't have that power, Ibrahim.' Musa stared at the man as he sucked his wounds. 'That is...yes! You must have had a very special medium ...who?'

'That is true, I had the help of a very special woman, one who could see that stone and its pictures in a bowl of coloured sand...'

The demon jumped back and roared with fury. Turning, he pounded his fists on the boulder nearest him, splintering it with the sound of thunder. Hassan screamed and buried his head, drawing it back into the folds of his robe. When Musa regained control of himself, he turned a tear-stained face to Ibrahim.

'Her name was Farah, was it not?' Musa demanded.

'Yes, that is her name...'

'Was!' the demon howled. 'She is dead. I used to bite her nipples till they bled, but she never turned me away. She loved me, she didn't hate me, she never hated me...she loved me. Now, she's gone.'

'Oh, no.' Ibrahim stood, loosened the tourniquet for a moment, then tightened it again. 'I am so sorry...' He stopped speaking, his eyes searching the demon's, searching for some subtle trickery. 'Musa, are you telling me

Farah was your mother?' With quiet grief, the demon nodded. 'Are you saying…Anwar is your great-grandfather?' Again, Musa nodded.

Overwhelmed, Ibrahim limped forward to place a gentle hand on the demon's shoulder. Heat radiated from the green skin with the fierceness of molten metal, but his hand was unscathed.

'Take the curses off him, Musa…please. And promise you will never afflict him again.'

Indifferently, Musa waved a hand and the sand whirled and eddied beneath Hassan's face and arms.

'He is safe…as long as he never breaks his oath about Maryam again,' Musa stated flatly.

'Musa,' Ibrahim choked, 'why do you make light of my loss…when you feel your own so fully?'

'I make light of nothing. You just don't know what a snake lies there…' The demon shrugged the hand off his shoulder and turned as Hassan's face lifted. When he saw the gigantic figure with green skin, red hair and glowering mien, Hassan screamed like a wounded animal and drew back, covering his face with his hands. A great gush of vomit sprayed past the fingers and, at the same moment, he lost control of his sphincter muscles. With a roar of rage, the demon opened his mouth as wide as a pit and dived straight at the cowering, befouled man. Musa disappeared just before his gaping jaws struck Hassan, but the man had already fainted with shock.

XXI

Of all the provisions and equipment Hassan had managed to steal along with the two camels, Ibrahim refused everything but a bag full of dates and a freshly filled waterskin. When the sun dropped behind the mountains, Ibrahim had mounted the saddled camel with great difficulty. His leg was swollen and had turned an unhealthy colour; that it pained him agonizingly, he did not mention. Hassan had begged him to stay - even after offering the camels - saying he would fetch a surgeon from Bashtahal. Ibrahim's delirium cut across his lucid simplicity many times. He had to get to Jerusalem, it was of the utmost importance. Then why was he leaving so much of the necessary gear behind? Ibrahim had pointed to the water and the dates as if to say anything more would be excess baggage.

Ibrahim slumped forward in the saddle as the strangely tractable beasts plodded toward the oasis. Try as he might, he could not prevent the frequent onslaughts of sleep...or, is it simply losing consciousness? he asked himself. The thought that he had underestimated the venom of a small serpent, or overestimated his own strength disturbed him; not that a fear of death had found him, merely that he was so determined to reach Jerusalem before it was too late. He had sensed a force of Fate coming toward him in the guise of Hassan. It was only the materialization of Hassan which had linked that insight to Anwar. Nothing must stop his flight to Jerusalem, he must reach Anwar before it was too late.

A sharp, stabbing pain jerked the lolling head erect. For the last time, he untied the tourniquet; this time he could not feel the rush of blood. With undismayed sadness, he understood that there was no further point in

197

applying the strip of cloth; it was probably now doing more harm than good. As he knew so well the body he had trained to obey him in accepting the greatest privations, the crazed desire he felt for water was abnormal. He looked up at the stars and judged carefully, calculating his arrival at the old oasis an hour or so before dawn. Relenting, he took a long, shuddering drink. If it stays down, he comforted himself, my plight is not at all as bad as it seems.

He was too engrossed in Hassan's plight to spend much time thinking about his own. How the man had whined and cried, begging him not to leave. Pleading with him not to call back that horrible monster who obeyed Ibrahim's commands. No matter what he said, Hassan would not be convinced that Musa was nobody's tame demon. Blubbering and sobbing, he just continued to beg that no more punishment would be visited on him, for he would surely go insane. On and on he went, repeating how sorry he was for what he had done, but what could he do now to make it up? Maryam was no longer there to hear his repentance.

How many hours had they talked? Ibrahim wondered drowsily. Had Hassan understood one word of it? Oh, yes, he promised, he would stay at the hillock and devote himself to prayer and meditation; he would change himself, become a new person. He would spend the rest of his life atoning for his crimes. So easily and glibly he had spoken the words, so readily committing himself to the life of poverty and purity, but had he understood one word of it?

The encroaching numbness fought for his mind, but he resisted it doggedly. There was something else...what words had been so upsetting? Something ominous, something like a riddle he had not found the answer to. Ibrahim forced himself to sit upright, shaking his head to clear it. A riddle that didn't make...yes, Maryam! If Hassan did not break his oath again...but how could that be? Hassan would have to dig up her body...Ibrahim shuddered, driving the macabre thought from his fuzzy mind. Try as he might, the grisly vision persisted. Before his eyes, he saw Hassan digging furiously, throwing great clods of dry earth into the air. Soon, the air was filled with dust and the vision became so misty he could hardly discern bare outlines. From the animal sounds insinuating themselves into his fevered brain, he knew Hassan was committing a sacreligious and unthinkable act upon the corpse. He screamed and plunged forward, nearly pitching from the saddle.

The baggage camel trotted forward until it nearly touched the leading beast. As though arranging itself magically, Ibrahim's body lifted up and came to rest seated properly on the saddle. The reins slid over the neck and head of his camel and the baggage animal moved ahead. If Ibrahim was aware of this extraordinary sight, there was no response from him. The baggage animal, with the trailing reins suspended in mid-air to one side, led the saddled mount toward the oasis at a somewhat less leisurely pace. Ibrahim was aware of something cooling his head and cheeks and the sound of exquisite, unearthly singing tinkling faintly in his ears.

Ibrahim struggled to regain consciousness many times during the rest of the journey; his eyes would open but he could not focus them. If the stars were in their usual places, they looked strange and inconstant as he blinked at them. He tried to recapture his thoughts about Hassan. Learning to be poor, hungry and alone would be so difficult for him…as it was for many. Would he find that essential spark inside himself?…before he could complete the thought, his head sagged again. Then there was water. It dripped on his head and face. His mouth and nose were in it and he began choking.

'Be careful,' a thrilling voice warned, 'just your mouth, not the nose.' He felt his head being lifted and settled in a delightfully soft and fragrant place.

'Who's there?' he croaked, struggling to focus his eyes. He saw nothing but blurs of light and shadow. 'I can't see, my eyes disobey me.'

'Perhaps they will obey me,' the sweet voice answered; it sounded like the singing he had heard on the camel. He felt a hand pass over his lids and could not fathom if it were fiery hot or terribly cold. Whichever, it sent waves of delicious energy passing through him. When he looked up, he saw a radiant and incredible face above his own. It seemed to light up everything around him. His cheek was pressed into a breast with the scent of a rose garden.

'Who are you?' he mumbled, his entire body trembling with some strange sensation he did not understand.

'Think very hard, Ibrahim. Try to think down deeply to another world, another place of knowing. You will find my name. You do know me.'

He felt himself sinking and floating off at the same time. At the very edge of consciousness, he arrested himself by a great effort of will.

'That's right, just the way you taught yourself to control your dreaming,' the wonderful voice directed. 'In that land, try to see clearly.'

The unearthly beauty he had seen before he closed his eyes still shimmered behind his eyelids, the lovely scent still filled his nostrils, but he was no longer there. He was inside a dream that was not his own. If not his, then whose? he asked himself. A sensation of great familiarity and power drew him like a magnet. Then, he knew.

'You're Aysha,' he said in a much stronger and clearer voice. 'You are Anwar's guardian angel.'

A soft laugh answered him; distant, like a camel bell from afar, but more musical, more magical.

'Anwar won't admit that, I assure you,' Aysha told him. 'No matter how hard I try, he spoofs me for assuming so much. You know me, Ibrahim, because he shared his dreaming with you. Are you frightened?'

'Why would I be frightened? Are you not protecting me?' he asked with total innocence.

'Yes, of course. But I am taking you on your final journey…are you ready?'

'If only there had been time to place one more flower…' he began, but his voice vanished.

'We'll stop on the way, dear Ibrahim, we'll stop on the way. We will each place a flower in remembrance.

Maryam is sure to be pleased with that.' He felt her turn his head slightly and the lovely nipple placed itself in his mouth. The last thing he remembered was a glorious feeling flowing through him and the place of dreaming expanded to infinity.

XXII

Anwar sat on the boulder where Ahmad El-Sayed had once sat and looked across to the ledge. He didn't have long, he knew, for soon the perfect moment of twilight would descend. For as long as he could, he wished to beam his love and blessings to Abdullah, Fatima and the tiny Isa. He watched Fatima kindle the fire for their one frugal meal of the day. The baby slept peacefully on a bed of straw, covered with a sheepskin. Poor Abdullah, he is so deeply saddened and Fatima cries almost constantly. Against all his own deepest convictions, for those two he would have extended his life…were that in his power. Yet, what would it prove? Merely to postpone the parting? And were not one hundred and fifty-two years enough…more than enough? Abdullah moved across the ledge and sat near the fire, drawing his knees up and placing his hands on them. He bowed his head and kissed the ring with the Seal of Solomon, his last gift from Anwar. One day, it would pass on to the babe.

Unseen, when the moment arrived, Anwar rose and simultaneously shifted sideways in the fabric of space. There, at last, was the chink between worlds. With a wan smile and a shrug, he placed himself in that immeasurable space and waited. Would it be likened to a moment, a minute or endless days? Did it matter in the infinite scheme?

'Are you pondering the inponderable once more?' a musical voice asked him. He looked up to see a thing of radiant splendour fill the white void before his eyes.

'Aysha, my dear, I am so pleased to see you…but why are you made up in such strange fashion again?'

'It's not the same,' she retorted vehemently. 'This is really how angels look. I may never see you again, can't you just once tell me I look like an angel?'

'My lovely Aysha, you are indeed as splendid as any angel. Now, would you try to look like one of the fabled houris?'

Aysha pouted. 'You're making fun of me, Anwar. I did try so hard...'

'Now, now, don't be upset,' he comforted her, 'but you really must not take these things literally.'

'But in all the great books...'

'Yes, my dear,' he interrupted her tirade, 'every religion gives such descriptions...of course. It is...well, a motivating force. If one is to verbalize the ineffable, one must choose terms that all can understand.' She sobbed and he reached out to pat her hand. 'Come, Aysha, I love you just the way you are. Be that and you will please me.'

The angelic vision disappeared and Aysha's form assumed its natural Djinnhood. Two tiny infants were cradled in one arm, each suckling a nipple. Unlike human infants, they were fully formed replicas of Hawwaz and Hutti on a miniature scale. Each opened one eye and glared warily at the old man.

'I thought it might be sobering and maturing for those two,' Aysha explained with a deep blush. 'Do you think it was wise?'

'Of course,' Anwar agreed readily. 'Have the fathers seen them yet?'

'You never know with males of any kind. Hutti did that silly chuck-under-the-chin thing fathers do...I thought his son would bite his finger off. Hawwaz, of course, is so upset by the loss...'

'I'm stopping on the way...that is, if you don't mind?' He unwrapped the parcel resting on his knees and exposed the brilliant pearl.

'Oh...' Aysha looked distressed...'I am sorry to have arrived so late. I knew you would find your way but...' She cast her eyes down with genuine distress.

'You mean Ibrahim?' he asked gently. She nodded, but did not look up. 'Did he go well, was he happy?'

'Oh, Anwar, I wish you could have seen him. His

203

soul was so like yours, I've never quite seen another like it.'

'Even Maryam's?' he asked with evident surprise.

'Frankly,' she sniffed, her mood changing completely, 'I don't pay that much attention to women.'

'She was a wonderful person, Aysha,' he reminded her, 'she gave selflessly to others everything of herself.'

'Oh, I know that, I didn't mean to detract from any of that. Anwar, she will be remembered by all those people...surely.'

'I hope they will remember the man who tended her so lovingly,' the old man said wistfully. 'He could have been everything a man of God can aspire to, yet he chose that.'

'Anwar,' she leaned forward and sought his eyes, 'is it really worth it...all of the sacrifice? Will it ever bear fruit?'

'Well...' he shrugged meekly and thought for a moment...'surely it must. As we teach our children, three steps forward and two backward...you must believe, lovely Aysha, it is not all in vain.'

'Goodbye, Anwar.'

'Goodbye, my splendid fairy. Please be a guardian angel to those two I left behind...and their infant, will you?'

'Anwar, you have already bequeathed them all you could...but I will do as you ask. What about the villain?'

'Hassan? No one shall interfere with him. Soon, he will reach his own crossroads. The choice will be his. Farewell, my dear.'

The chink between the worlds, which was little enough, parted so that Anwar might pass; he was now little more than nothing. He floated through many lands until he recognized the purplish hue of the one he sought. Drifting on a current of his own making, he passed many gorgeous fountains and endless numbers of trees ladened with exotic gems of endlessly proliferating colours. When he found the specific tree for which he searched, he slowed the current until it became a stationary, benign whirlpool that steadied him in one spot before the tree.

Hawwaz was alone, sleeping deeply. Anwar looked

about, expecting to see Hutti loom up from an indistinct nowhere, but nothing marked the horizons even slightly. Anwar lowered himself until he settled lightly on the purple carpet below. From behind the tree against which Hawwaz's head rested, the detached ranji poked an enquiring head. With paternal affection, the old man crooked an inviting finger. The ranji hesitated, quivering nervously. Anwar held up the glowing pearl. The ranji shook even more tremulously, then slithered forth, yearning overcoming shyness and suspicion.

'It's yours...I merely return it to you...intact. Here, take it,' he coaxed.

The ranji sidled closer, waves of vibrational communication preceding him, aimed at the indistinct wraith poised over the velvet carpeting. Anwar listened sympathetically to the lament of cruel exploitation, the voice of an accomplice used against its will.

'It's all right,' Anwar's spirit assured the ranji, reaching out to attach the pearl to its base. 'You will be pretty much in charge from now on...you see, he will no longer be able to detach you separately. All, or nothing at all. Perhaps this way he will learn a bit of humility...sort of live and let live...don't you agree?'

The ruby tip bounced up and down in gleeful agreement. A moment later, it slithered back behind the tree, already hatching up some agonizing mischief for the unsuspecting Hawwaz.

The unsuspecting Hawwaz slumbered on as Anwar's penetrating gaze probed him to his very depths. Soon, a shadowy semblance of Hawwaz rose to a sitting position, leaving his physical body on the ground behind. Hawwaz blinked his eyes a few times with incredulity, then his hands crept forward stealthily.

'You're here!' the Djinn whispered with gurgling delight. 'It is not the astral projection, you diabolical old conjurer, it is the real thing! Come to Hawwaz, come to Hawwaz.'

'You're wasting your time, dear boy,' the old man interjected. 'Yes, it is the real soul you see, but you are too late. The body has already been interred. Besides, you are still in a rather...ahhh...detached condition? Save your strength, the battle is lost for all time.'

With a dazed look, Hawwaz let the hands fall to his shorn groin.

'What a shame you were not immortal,' he wailed softly. 'At least then, you might have lived up to the rest of your preposterous expectations.'

'Don't be so bitter, Hawwaz,' the old man chided, laughing quietly. 'Unlike you, I never thought myself immortal...albeit, my life did go on to an unseemly length. You, however, will find it much more difficult. You, *think* you're immortal.'

The Djinn's face was so stunned, it might have been struck with a heavy object.

'Yet that too is relative,' the old man continued, gazing patiently into the startled and unbelieving eyes. He described a small fly familiar to the streams and rivers in the mountains far north of Bagdad. It breaks its chrysalis on the river's bed and floats to the surface, dancing there for a brief moment before rising in the air. Before the day is done, it mates on the wing and descends once more to lay its eggs on the surface of the water. Finally spent, the fly dies and sinks beneath the surface. All of this occurs in the space of a single Earth day. In the last moment of its life, were the fly thinking such thoughts, the span of a human's life would seem like immortality. To the man so viewed by the fly, a Djinn's life, by comparison, would be likened to immortality. Quite justifiably so, were the context so limited. However, only the One, the Creator is patently immortal, ever-lasting...without beginning or end. Soon, the day of the Djinn would reach its twilight. All but the One has both beginning and end, all but the One serves in definitive time and thus becomes obsolete, eventually. When that time came, the Djinni too would slip into myth and join that great body of mythos, which in its own way was unending. When man realized his full potential and completed his evolution, the old concept of the human would become obsolete. Djinni were fixed in a matrix with no such potential. Perhaps this was why – at some deep, unconscious level – they were so terribly envious of those poor, powerless creatures who crept about the Earth's surface.

Mouth agape, truly speechless for once, Hawwaz watched the vision of Anwar fade as he continued the longest journey unknown. He tried to cry out, but the projection of himself Anwar had coaxed out of his body slipped back effortlessly and the Djinn was fast asleep.

A short while later, Hutti came striding along, deep in thought. He approached the tree from behind and halted, surprised to see Hawwaz's ranji curled up and sleeping atop the hitherto missing pearl. Cautiously, he tip-toed up to the sleeping member and lifted it as gently as he could. Stealthily, he rounded the tree and placed his burden on the ground between his sleeping friend's sprawled legs. With a few deft twists and turns, he secured the apparatus to Hawwaz's groin. Hutti stepped back a few paces and studied his handiwork admiringly. He gave the sleeper's foot a sharp kick.

'Whufph! What's the matter with you?' Hawwaz sat up angrily, rubbing his eyes.

'Look! You must have had a visitor. Very nice, I must admit, but you know what it means?' Hutti sat down and yawned, stretching his arms.

Hawwaz gazed at his good fortune, dumbfounded. Happy surprise gave way to cunning glee. Then the truth struck.

'He's gone! He's gone forever...'

'That's right, Little Brother,' Hutti agreed with rather malicious relish. He was still angry about Hawwaz's defection at the Fountain of Forgetfulness, despite the advent of the son he wanted. 'And about time, too. One of these days, that obsession would have destroyed you.'

'One of these days...' Hawwaz murmered absently, his brows knitted with concern. 'One of these days...it was something about days and time...'

'What are you talking about!' Hutti snapped.

'Anwar's message, Hutti...I've forgotten...it was so like a dream. Maybe it was a dream...'

'That pearl is no dream,' Hutti vouchsafed positively. 'He was here, all right, there is no other way I can think of.'

'It was so important, you have no idea. Our whole survival is bound up in it...oh, dear, why did he have to go?'

'Oh, stop it, you little fool! Forget him! There are plenty more where he came from.'

'Are there?' Hawwaz whimpered. 'I wonder.'

XXIII

Hᴀssᴀɴ ɪʙɴ ᴍᴏʜᴀᴍᴍᴇᴅ ᴅᴀʀᴛᴇᴅ ᴛʜʀᴏᴜɢʜ a dark, open doorway and pressed himself against the wall; his chest was bursting, but he fought to hold his breath. Shouts and running feet pounded past his hiding place, rounded the next corner, then died out in the distance. He tucked the freshly cooked chicken inside his tattered garments and stepped out of the doorway. Folding his hands piously across his abdomen and the chicken, he kept to the shadows of the alley's buildings until he reached the city's western gates. The guards ignored the beggar as he slipped furtively past them and gained the darkness of the road to Bagdad. He moved as quickly as he could, putting a safe distance between himself and Bashtahal. His hilltop retreat was less than an hour away.

It wasn't his fault he was reduced to stealing chickens, the blame rested squarely with those filthy, rotten beggars in the town...as though they owned it! First they shunned and threatened him because he was fat and well-dressed – that sort of thing could give beggars a bad name, they told him. And now, when he was tattered, worse than many of them, and so skinny his bones stuck through his skin? They shunned him and harrassed him just the same. No matter where he stationed himself, they set upon him...never one at a time, the cowards...oh, no, they weren't brave enough for that.

He stopped to rest for a moment, glaring up at the full moon. He bared his teeth and growled at it. Hunger and thirst...is there nothing else in this stinking world but hunger and thirst? His hands quivered as the desire to wolf down the whole chicken overcame him. He caught himself up, remembering the bitter lessons of indulgence and starvation. Dole the meal out, devour it bit by bit, it lasts longer…and so does the body. The body! Nothing but a manufactory of wastes. The more you feed it, the faster it makes more and more dung. What an accomplishment! We are nothing but mechanical contrivances for making dung.

Striking out along the road again, he reached through the tatters and tore a leg off the chicken. When he opened his mouth, twin jets of saliva spurted out. He growled admonishingly at his teeth. Just let it rest on the tongue, touching the palate lightly. Suck the juices slowly. Do it correctly and the flesh will not fall from the bone till we're home. Then, nibble it gently, speck by speck. Not until dawn will we crack the bone and suck the marrow. And we will grind the bone until it becomes a nourishing and digestible powder. The chicken must last for days, remember, or it's back to raw snakes and lizards…remember how sick that makes us?

Trudging along, the thought of the raw reptiles made his stomach tighten painfully. His mind flashed back along the jumbled days and weeks of his new life. Empty your mind of all thoughts, said our pious Ibrahim, but not one word about our empty belly. How does a man atone, feel contrite when his guts are screaming at him? Answer that, O holy beggar! Surreptitiously, he glanced over his shoulder. He never allowed himself to visualize that terrible demon, but every time he reviled Ibrahim, he felt unduly nervous.

The first week he had been able to sit on the hillock throughout each day. He accepted the first hunger pangs as a proof of his new piety, the bona fides of contrition, leading to redemption. In the end, he skulked into the city, ravaged with hunger. At least he had taught himself patience…and new skills. How cunningly he had studied the habits of the snakes and lizards, knowing just when they would creep out to bask in the sun. One doesn't throw stones, he learned through painful experience, one drops the right size and weight of rock…from the top of the hillock. Only stupid amateurs spoil meat, not the seasoned hunter. Head shots were essential.

He shivered as he remembered once more those first bits of skinned, raw meat. A few tentative chews, the attempt to let the slippery, gory gobbet slide down his throat and then water and bile came gushing up through his nose. His stomach had retched so relentlessly, he had lain helpless on the ground, in his own mess, for hours. Who learns the secrets of fire when there are retainers to take care of that? He had learned...through trial and error. With the eyes closed and the mind held in check, roasted lizard tasted like chicken!

He tried to cloud the thought, but his mind brought pictures of his nights, secreted in the crevisses once used by Najmuddin and his men. Once he had tried to sit on the hillock through the night, at first only mildly alarmed...what about retribution? At night, the snakes could get at *him*. Finally, he had fallen into a fitful sleep, seated rigidly as he had seen fakirs sit at their meditations. What dreams! No use trying to obscure it, there was no doubt about the girl's identity, Maryam's body and face were so startlingly clear, it seemed she was actually there. When the orgasm started, he had cried out in fright, nearly felled by a heart attack of terror. That terrible demon had visited the dream upon him...trying to catch him out. What had he said that day? 'He is safe as long as he does not break his oath again,' ...was that it? Or the first day in Bashtahal, when the beggars had beaten him and left him senseless on the ground. When he recovered, he had stolen dates and bread...also, a flower for her grave. In the night, he had stretched out on that grave weeping, begging forgiveness. How it had started, he never recalled, but before he knew what was happening...with a roar in the night, Hassan cut off the thought. Even now that terrible monster could be reading your thoughts, you fool!

His legs were aching and footsteps dragging when he reached the base of the hillock. He drove his teeth into the leg bone. More glorious juices filled his mouth as he climbed with determination. No more of these distractions. Tonight we keep the vigil with purpose. Empty the mind of all that is extraneous, of all low and lustful things.

No rumbling guts, just mystical accomplishments.

The chicken was consumed before the sun rose. With a scowl of frustration and resentment, Hassan glared at the approaching dawn. What in the name of God was he doing here? Why had he listened to that fool, Ibrahim? He concocts demons to frighten me, they all concoct illusions? How do I know I was really blinded? If a man can be paralyzed by fear, if he can see visions that are mere illusions, can he not imagine himself unable to see? What is it all for, anyway? The woman's dead! All my prayers and lamentations cannot bring her back. Nothing that's done can be undone...even if I lived forever – even if I sat on this stupid hill for all eternity, what would it change? I am a fool, I have been taken in, set up by these religious fanatics. It is nothing more that sweet vengeance. I have suffered enough...if this goes on much longer, I will lose my mind.

Hassan fairly flew down the hill to drink at the shallow pool, now sadly depleted. He stripped off his rags and washed his body. Look at it! Flaps of tired skin sagging over bones and nothing else, yet it goes on manufacturing dung. If I stay here much longer, there will be nothing left. Some caravan is bound to pass soon. This time, instead of hiding like a thief and criminal, step forth boldly and ask to join. There will be work to do, you will earn your keep. What difference if the destination is Baktria or North Africa? Who would know you now in either place? A few months, a year at most, and you will make friends with wealthy merchants...he broke the thought off and wrapped the tatters about his gaunt body. Standing at the side of the road some half mile from the hillock, he looked in both directions. Through the heat of the day, he sat at the roadside, rising about once an hour to gaze up and down again. When evening came, his belly was screaming at him so loudly, his ears began ringing. When the light failed, he grasped the offending stomach and squeezed it viciously. That's what comes of devouring the whole chicken. From now on, it will be better to sit up on that accursed hilltop and listen. Only a caravan of ghosts could move past here soundlessly. If the night proves unlucky, then it is roast snake for the morning.

212

Sitting atop what used to be Hawwaz's favourite pinnacle, Musa watched the scrawny caricature make its way up the side of the hill in the dark, stumbling and cursing. Had Musa been visible and the night brighter, Hassan might have seen a look of utter contempt that would stop his heart. Though demons know more than most men about the cosmos and its ordering, they are totally indifferent, totally without reverence. Lost and soulless, they have nothing to gain by it one way or another. With no hope of redemption, what purpose? Standards and values are other things. Wasted, meaningless cruelty is not appreciated. Even less, the fraud and hypocrite. A demon will respect, albeit reluctantly, sincere faith and unshakable devotion. Hassan affected Musa as raw snake meat disgusted Hassan.

With a final curl of his lip, the demon watched Hassan settle himself for the night's vigil. Then, he looked far up the road, many leagues off, to the approaching riders. A small caravan, he noted, with three merchants and less than a dozen retainers. Twenty camels loaded with merchandise. He shot one last glance in Hassan's direction, then estimated the speed and distance to the caravan. They would arrive an hour before dawn. With no sound, the demon shot through the air and, a moment later, walked along with the caravan, listening to the conversation. Within half an hour, he had gleaned all the information his curiosity-prone mind needed. These were the sons of Ibrahim ben Yussef, Suleiman, Ali and Hammad. This, he grinned, should prove a very interesting encounter...a more mind-shattering one I could not invent. A few seconds later, he was sitting on the pinnacle again. If the fool doesn't hear all that noise, I shall have to invent a rather large snake to awaken him. Musa chuckled and hugged his knees.

Hassan jumped and twisted his body, staring intently into the darkness to his left. It was *not* his imagination, he scolded himself, something did jingle out there. Then, quite distinctly, he heard the faint tinkle of a camel bell. The man held his breath as he trained his ear. Definitely...

213

the creaking of harness…and not just one, many camels were approaching from the direction of Bagdad. Allah, be merciful, let the destination not be Bashtahal. Let it be Mecca, Alexandria…anywhere!

Tatters flying, he sped down the hillock and on toward the road. Traders from Africa, from far-off Tangier…maybe even Cordova…they've been to Bagdad and now return homeward. They will take me and I will work hard. He forced himself to stop muttering, but he was so agitated he had to hop from one foot to the other to calm himself.

The first pale glimmer of light outlined the approaching rider as it silhouetted the distant minarets of Bashtahal. Hassan gulped, sensing a rich and well-fed face and body rising above a fat and healthy camel. Two more riders approached and stared down at the miserable wretch trembling at the side of the road.

'Take me with you, masters,' Hassan implored. 'I will work like a slave, I will do your bidding…'

'Take you with us?' the first man scoffed. 'I can imagine the work you'd do…we've seen the likes of you in every caravanserai from Baktria to Cordova. What do *you* steal?' The other two roared with laughter. One of them urged his camel forward until he could lean down to examine Hassan more closely in the faint light.

'Yes, what is your speciality?' he asked. 'From the looks of you, it wouldn't be anything so grand as gold and silver. Just food, I'd wager.'

Blushing and humiliated, Hassan looked down at his rags and held out his hands in humble submission.

'I know how I look,' he cried, 'but it is all a terrible mistake. I am not a thief or beggar, I was a rich merchant once… just like you, my lords. I am not a thief, I was robbed…'

The words were drowned in peals of laughter. The three richly dressed riders rocked back and forth in their saddles.

'Did you hear the tale he was about to tell, my brothers?' the man nearest Hassan asked the other two. 'This rich and powerful merchant was ambushed and robbed and left to die…only an hour's walk from Bashtahal.'

Panic gripped Hassan when he saw one of the riders rise in his stirrups and signal the caravan on. The other two turned their camels.

'Wait, you must believe me,' he screamed in desperation. 'It is all true. Ask anyone...Hassan ibn Mohammed was a very rich man until...'

'Who?' all three riders shouted back. The one who appeared to be the leader, who had first approached Hassan, slapped his camel's rump and nearly rode Hassan down.

'What was that name?' he threatened, leaning far over the side of his mount. Crouching, Hassan repeated his name. The other two drew nearer to stare down at him.

'You son of a dog, we would have left you food and decent clothing. We are not without charity. Do you think the name Hassan ibn Mohammed is unknown to us, the sons of Ibrahim ben Yussef? It would take three of you to make one Hassan...'

'Yes...yes,' Hassan blubbered, wringing his hands. 'Ibrahim. He is my old friend, my dearest friend. He left only a few days ago, on his way to Jerusalem. I am to meet him there, we are going to start a new venture...'

Hassan did not see the scimitar leave its sheath, but he heard the wind whistle past the descending blade. The flat of the blade struck him so forcibly between the shoulders that he was catapulted to the soft sand at the roadside where he rolled over and over in the sand, fearing another attack.

Tears of fury choked him, his mouth twisted into a grimace of sheer hate, but he stayed where he was, stretched out on his belly as though he were unconscious. Seething, he heard the caravan move away down the road. The vilest of oaths were thundered after the receding riders, curses raining down on the head of Ibrahim and the rogues he had sired. Hassan was snarling and jibbering like a maddened beast, his entire body shaking uncontrollably, his fists pounding impotently on the sand. High above on the pinnacle, Musa spat between his feet and snapped his fingers.

At first, Hassan did not realize that something was moving under him; he was aware only of the spasms of fury in his own body. Then something forced his head back and he looked down, trying to ascertain through his tears what was shifting beneath him. His body rose as he rubbed the back of his hand over his eyes. Air whistled through his windpipe…he was looking down into Maryam's face!

A bright streak of pink crossed the sky, heralding the approaching dawn. Hassan pressed his hands down on the sand to lift his chest. Below the golden head, under his own body, a naked Maryam was rising up from the sand. He gasped and shook his head like a wet dog. No, it was a gold statue…a solid gold statue! How could that be? He lifted his hand and shook the sand free before touching the statue's shoulder. It couldn't be a statue, it was warm, it gave to his touch. It must be Maryam…Maryam resurrected…Maryam come back from the dead and covered in gold. He felt naked limbs open beneath him and as they did, his tattered old rags gave way. Eyes wide and round, spittle dribbling from his mouth, he gurgled deep in his throat, quivering as he wrapped his arms about the form.

His body began to bounce up and down grotesquely as he held the statue-like form tighter and tighter, locking his arms about it for fear that it would disappear as inexplicably as it had appeared. It was his, his, all golden and warm, hot and delicious…as the seed spurted from his body, the statue began sinking back down under the sand, the desperate man unable or unwilling to release it. He screamed and cursed, feeling sand closing in over him, but he still did not let go. A few moments later, the side of the road gave no sign that anything out of the ordinary had occurred.

Musa rose to his feet, then up on his toes to stretch and yawn deeply. He turned his head to squint at the rim of the sun breaking free of the horizon, snapped one look at the quiet sand below and snapped his fingers once more. The pinnacle was deserted.